DONALD E. WESTLAKE

BABY, WOULD I LIE?

THE MYSTERIOUS PRESS

Published by Warner Books

A Time Warner Company

MYSTERIOUS PRESS EDITION

Copyright © 1994 by Donald E. Westlake
All rights reserved.

Cover design by Jackie Merri Meyer
Cover illustration by Wilson McLean .

The Mysterious Press name and logo are registered trademarks of Warner Books, Inc.

 Mysterious Press Books are published by
Warner Books, Inc.
1271 Avenue of the Americas
New York, NY 10020

Ⓦ A Time Warner Company

Printed in the United States of America

Originally published in hardcover by The Mysterious Press.
First Printed in Paperback: October, 1995

10 9 8 7 6 5 4 3 2 1

The best way for me to thank my friends in Branson is not to mention them by name: You know who you are. Thanks for the use of the driveway, the house, the bus, the restaurant, the laughter.

For Chris and Susan Newman, who at the beginning pointed and said, "Look!" (and whispered, "Fried,"), and who at the end pointed out (some of) my errors, they can put my devoted thanks in with their knowledge that without them this book could never have been written; they're just going to have to live with that.

To the country balladeers of yesterday and today, singer-songwriters who perfected the art of describing the rougher road, my unfeigned and uncomplicated admiration; my poor efforts on you turf herein are mere homage.

As to the tabloidoids, thery're as scurrilous as ever.

Alas, 'tis true I have gone here and there,
And made myself a motley to the view,
Gor'd mine own thoughts, sold cheap what is most dear,
Made old offences of affections new.
Most true it is that I have look'd on truth
Askance and strangely; but, by all above,
These blenches gave my heart another youth,
And worse essays prov'd thee my best love.

William Shakespeare, Sonnet 110

Forget not, brother singer, that though Prose
Can never be too truthful or too wise,
Song is not truth, nor Wisdom, but the rose
Upon Truth's lips, the light in Wisdom's eyes.

Sir William Watson

BABY, WOULD I LIE?

Sara drove out of the wilderness. Inside the purring air-conditioned Buick Skylark, a rental from the airport, she rolled southward from Springfield through the tumbled Ozarks, more a furrowed plateau than a mountain range, on toward the new home of country music, forty miles away: Branson, Missouri.

The early-afternoon sun stood high in the hazy sky ahead, beckoning her on. The road at first was wide and flat, two lanes on either side of a broad median, but as she plunged deeper into the scrubby hills it curved and twisted and rose and fell like life itself. Soon it narrowed from four lanes to three, and sometimes two. Often she was stuck behind campers and mobile homes, sometimes behind pickup trucks, occasionally behind larger older American cars; whenever a passing zone appeared, she whipped on by, leaving the American flag decals and NRA decals and half-scratched-off Desert Storm decals and comical bumper stickers—I'M SO TIRED I'M RETIRED"—in her wake, and kept driving south.

All around her, the Ozark hills mounded like hairy bellies, scrub grass clinging tenaciously to the hard, stony ground, as though she were steering the Buick across a mastodon with mange. In clumps on the sunlit tan landscape, there were trees, gnarled and twisted and shallow-rooted and dark of leaf and branch, hunched like covens of malevolent witches, watching her progress, cackling as she sped by.

Deciding to steep herself in local color—she was an investigative reporter, wasn't she?—Sara switched on the radio and immediately heard, ". . . favorite from Ray Jones, one of Branson's own," in a young and twangy voice.

Ray Jones—the reason she was here. Think of that. There's an omen for you.

According to the background material she'd read in the plane—two planes; change at St. Louis—Ray Jones used to be a major country-and-western star, a singer-songwriter with a long string of hits and a large following. But it had been ten years since he'd made the charts with a new record (tape, disc), and, in fact, his career had now reached the point where collections of his greatest successes were offered for sale on late-night TV. Like a number of similar entertainers, men and women with a hit-making past and a residue of loyal fans and continuing name recognition but with no recent or likely new successes to keep the career fueled, Ray Jones had opened his own theater, sensibly enough called the Ray Jones Country Theater, down in the new home of old country music: Branson, Missouri.

This was all a brand-new world to Sara Joslyn, intrepid girl reporter of New York's *Trend* magazine, but that's what investigative reporting is all about, isn't it? New worlds.

"We wish old Ray the best in his current trouble . . ."

Oh sure. His current trouble, old Ray, was that he was on trial for a particularly gruesome sex murder; it would take a good old boy to wish him the best, wouldn't it? I should be taping this, Sara thought, but it was already too late. The disc jockey was introducing the song: "Here's one of Ray's biggest hits—'Baby, Would I Lie?'"

"You're kidding," Sara told the radio. A bouncy country intro began, the up-front drums and electric guitars elaborated by a subtle background of trombone-saxophone riffs.

"Turn that fucking thing off."

"But it's you, Ray."

"I've heard me," Ray Jones said, and shuffled the cards.

It was a gravelly voice, smoky, whiskey-flavored. It was a barroom-brawling voice, a woman-cheating voice, a drunk-tank voice:

I know you've heard I've got a wife and family,
Waiting for me down in old Tehachapie,
But I am telling you that there's no strings on me.
Baby,
Baby,
Baby, would I lie?

"Yes," Sara said.

I know you've heard I drink and toke and gamble some,
I've got enemies will say that I am just a bum.

"Count on it," Sara said.

But with you by my side, I know I'll overcome.
Baby,
Baby,
Baby, would I lie?

* * *

It's a put-on, Sara thought, but then she thought, I bet it isn't.

> *When we met at the Poker Bar,*
> *You admired my guitar;*
> *I admired your new car.*
> *You were heaven-sent.*
> *Sometimes I might've done wrong,*
> *Been in places I didn't belong,*
> *But if your love for me is strong,*
> *You know I will repent.*

It's too blatant to be a put-on, Sara thought. With that voice, that honky-tonk music thudding along in the background, it's supposed to be taken seriously. Do the fans take it seriously? What do they think it's about? Is this irony, or is it real? Does Ray Jones know?

> *I know you've heard I did some time in Yuma jail,*
> *And when I left, some girl got stuck to pay my bail;*
> *But with you, babe, I know I'm never gonna fail.*
> *Baby,*
> *Baby,*
> *Baby, would I lie?*

"My God," Sara said, and the sign by the road said Branson in seven miles.

2

Ray Jones looked at his hole cards. "Not my day," he said, and folded the seven of spades. Then he got to his feet and crossed his living room to look out the glass doors and beyond the wooden-railed terrace to the golf course. Thirteenth tee. Makes sense.

It hadn't been Ray's day for quite a while, all things considered. First the cock-ups in building the theater on the Strip, then the breach-of-contract suit from those bastards in Nashville, then the IRS, and now this murder trial. Some parlay.

Ray still wasn't sure it was right to let his songs play on the radio during the trial; seemed disrespectful somehow. Seemed as if he wasn't taking that poor bitch's death seriously. But every one of his advisers—and Ray Jones, it seemed to Ray Jones, had more advisers than a horse has flies—every last one of them had told him to let the songs play on, trial be damned. Each one for his own separate reasons.

Warren Thurbridge, for instance, his trial lawyer, criminal attorney with all that silver hair, said, "You're going to have a sequestered jury, Ray, since it's a capital case. For the length of the trial, those people will not have radio, TV, newspapers, nothing from the outside world to confuse their judgment. And what you want is for those jurors to enter into that cloistered situation with your songs circling in their minds."

" 'Baby, Would I Lie?' 'The Dog Come Back?' Are you sure?"

"You just keep twinkling at them, Ray," Warren Thurbridge advised.

Jolie Grubbe, his regular lawyer, the hardest fat woman alive, the one who did his contracts and divorces and was handling this current problem with the IRS, had her own reason. "You pull your songs," she said, "it looks like embarrassment and remorse, and that translates as guilt. If you aren't guilty, don't act guilty."

Well, that was part of the problem. The situation wasn't quite as simple as Jolie thought, but he couldn't very well go into a song and dance on the subject, could he? Not even with Jolie Grubbe.

Chuck Wagner, his manager, took a different tack: "There's twenty-six theaters in Branson, Ray, and half of them got a superstar on the inside: Willie Nelson, Mel Tillis, Loretta Lynn, Moe Bandy, Andy Williams. Doin' two shows a day. Plus all those Baldknobbers and Presley families and Foggy River Boys that was here before you headliners ever showed up. You got to let the people know you're in town, Ray."

"The trial will tell them."

But Chuck shook his head, pointed at the surrounding hills, and said, "That's over in Forsyth, in the county seat. These tourists here don't know a thing except Branson and the lakes." He pointed in another direction. "Stuck in traffic out there on the Strip, taking forty minutes to go half a mile, they got their *radios* on. You want them to hear *you*, Ray, and say to one another, 'Let's go see that boy.' "

"If they ever get out of the traffic."

"Right."

Cal Denny, Ray's oldest friend and closest crony, the nearest thing in the world to somebody he'd trust, had a typically Cal reaction: "You got to *sing*, Ray," Cal said, bony face all wide-eyed with astonishment. "What you got there's a God-given talent; you got to give it to the people. It don't matter what happens anywheres else."

With a twisted smile, Ray said, "The show gotta go on, right?"

But one of the great things about Cal was that he was so honest, so straight, so simple, so dumb. That's how he'd survived all the years, all the hassles, all the storms that had raged through Ray Jones's life, so that today he was Ray's oldest friend, they having met forty-two years ago in fourth grade in Central District School 6, Troutman, Georgia. And that simple honesty made Cal take Ray's showbiz question at face value. "*Yeah*, you gotta go on!" he said. "And you gotta let the radio say you're here. You can't disappoint your fans. You got people there, you got families, drove hundreds of miles to see you, Ray; they been plannin' this trip all year."

Which was probably true, too.

Milt Lieberson, Ray Jones's agent, a fat fellow who was somehow stuck halfway between frog and prince, had flown down from L.A. to offer still another argument: "Airtime translates into record sales," he pointed out, "which translates into royalties. And you have never in your life needed money more than you do right now."

Well, that was true enough. And the thought of money led inevitably to thoughts of the prick from the IRS, Leon Caccatorro, the nerd in gray wool, weighing in with the official point of view: "The government wouldn't want you, at this point, Mr. Jones, to do anything that might interfere with future earnings."

"I bet the government wouldn't."

"The government would prefer you to carry on your career as usual," said Leon "The Prick" Caccatorro, "regardless of any other legal problems you may face."

Other legal problems. Charged with murder one, kidnapping, aggravated assault, rape, sodomy, and a few other little indictments placed like scalloped potatoes around the edge of the plate. Here in a death-penalty state: poison gas in Missouri, the pellet under your chair. Some legal problems. It took a prick like Leon Caccatorro to phrase it in just precisely that bloodless way.

Well, despite this mountain of problems, Ray Jones's music would, it seemed, continue to be pumped out over the airwaves; wise, down-home, cynical, sentimental, playful, good-ole-boy: whatever the customer will take. Will take to his or her gnarly little heart, no matter *what* the outside world—the world outside 'country, that is—says that bad boy did this time.

Here's what the outside world said Ray Jones had done, this time. According to the indictment, on July 12 of this year, at approximately two in the morning, Ray Jones had driven his Acura SNX sports car out of Branson on Route 165, south past the turnoff to Porte Regal, the home/condo/golf course complex in which Ray owned this nice three-bedroom two-story wood-brick-stone place right off the thirteenth tee, had continued on south, and just before the bridge over Table Rock Dam, he had turned off onto the small road leading down to the Shepherd of the Hills Fish Hatchery, parking near the edge of Lake Taneycomo, with the imposing hydroelectric dam just up to his right. Accompanying him had been one

Belle Hardwick, a spinster of this parish, thirty-one years of age, a cashier at the Ray Jones Country Theater on the Strip. As the indictment would have it, a disagreement had occurred within the automobile, causing Ray Jones to strike out, breaking the nose, cheekbone, and two fingers of the left hand of Belle Hardwick. Whether Ms. Hardwick had then attempted to leave the vehicle by her own volition or had been pulled from it by Ray Jones was a matter not decided upon in the indictment; in any case, with her on the ground beside the car, states the indictment, Ray Jones proceeded variously to rape and sodomize Belle Hardwick, in the course of which he broke two of her ribs and one large bone in her upper right arm. Then or shortly thereafter, Ray Jones also attempted to strangle the woman, who remained alive, though probably comatose, despite his efforts. He therefore then dragged her down through the brush and weeds to the bank of Lake Taney-como, thrust her into the water, and held her down until she drowned. After an ineffectual effort to keep the body submerged by entangling it in roots and wedging it with branches, Ray Jones had returned to his car and driven on home to Porte Regal, where he had disposed of his muddied and bloodied clothing in some fashion, then gone to bed.

Here's what Ray Jones had to say in response to all that: He said it was bullshit. He said anybody in the world could screw Belle Hardwick for a kind word and a drink, and the kind word was optional. He said he was home alone in bed asleep at two that morning. He said his Acura SNX sports car was kept out in the driveway with the key in the ignition, and a dozen of his cronies and pals knew that's where he kept it, and sometimes one or another of them even borrowed the car. He said he had trouble enough without this bullshit.

Here's what the state of Missouri and the county of Taney

claimed to have in terms of evidence: the woman's body; a statement from the guard at the entrance to Porte Regal that at approximately 2:30 that morning he had waved to a person he had assumed to be Ray Jones (but couldn't be absolutely sure) entering the complex behind the wheel of the Acura SNX he knew damn well was Ray Jones's or he wouldn't have let it in; blood on the seat and mud on the floor of the car in question, and the blood matched that still inside Belle Hardwick; tire prints at the murder scene that matched the tires on Ray Jones's Acura SNX. Additionally, there was the evidence of an insomniac neighbor of Ray Jones who, while warming milk at her kitchen stove at 2:40 that morning (by the clock on the stove itself), had noticed lights on downstairs and upstairs in the Ray Jones house, had heard guitar music, and had further smelled smoke, maybe from a fireplace, although it was a particularly hot and muggy night, even for Branson in mid-July, weather conditions that had created the insomnia in the first place. (The burning of the incriminating clothing was implied.) Also, there were witnesses who had seen Ray Jones and Belle Hardwick speaking together earlier that evening at the Ray Jones Country Theater. (Unfortunately, whatever additional evidence of a liquid or viscous nature there might have been to place Ray Jones at the scene and in the victim had been dissipated by the actions of Lake Taneycomo in the five hours the late Belle Hardwick had floated in its attractive waters before being found by three elderly fishermen shortly after seven the next morning.)

Here's what Ray Jones had responded to all *that*: that the dim-witted old broad next door couldn't find her ass with both hands. Her banker son in St. Louis owned the house and came down to play golf on weekends, and he'd parked his senile old mother there because it was cheaper than both an alarm system and a nursing home. She had the wrong night, that's all, if she actually had gone spying at almost three in the morning and seen lights over at his place. As to the sound of guitar playing, when he *did* make music at night, it was to try out new material or new arrangements and he *always* videotaped himself in his living room and dated the tapes, and the tapes were right there in that closet under the stairs and the cops had seen them all and there were none for the night of July 11 to 12. As for the fireplace, he'd used it a total of two times, both of them the first week he'd owned the house, only to discover it had been built without regard for the niceties of fireplace construction, such as where you put the throat and the smoke shelf, and the correct balance of height and width and depth of opening, so that the damn thing smoked enough to cure a turkey. If somebody had taken his car and misbehaved in it, he was sorry, but glad anyway they'd at least brought the car back. As to talking with Belle Hardwick at the Ray Jones Country Theater, she was an employee of his; he talked to his employees all the time. So what?

So the indictment. Starting day after tomorrow, jury selection.

In the meantime, life, if that's the word he was looking for, went on. The feds, principally in the person of Leon "T P" Caccatorro, had groused and fidgeted about the $2 million bail but grudgingly admitted it was better for all concerned, including the government of, by, and for the people, that Ray Jones remain outside earning rather than inside tarnishing his reputation with the wrong kind of jail time. (Drunkenness, brawling, wife beating, drug taking but not drug dealing, hitting a cop after a speeding stop—all could produce the right kind of reputation-enhancing jail time.)

Not since Jerry Lee Lewis had the people been serenaded by a potential killer; the Ray Jones Country Theater was absolutely sold out, 827 seats, two shows a day, 3:00 and 8:00 P.M. In the meantime, between shows, waiting for the trial, he went on doing what he'd always done, May to November, the last four years, ever since joining the country gold rush to Branson. He hung out with his pals; he played golf on this nice easy course outside his door; late at night, he tried to write songs or rework old material in front of the fixed video camera over there mounted next to the VCR above the TV beside the stereo equipment, in the mahogany built-in with the Mexican doors.

Fewer pals now; mostly just the people who still had business dealings with him. The four guys seated at the round table in his living room at this moment, continuing the stud hand without him, were his manager, Chuck Wagner; his froglike L.A. agent, Milt Lieberson; his scrawny-bearded musical director, Lennie Elmore; and his best friend, Cal Denny, the only one who was there even though he didn't have to be. The nation's press—hell, the *world's* press—was beginning to camp out at the entrance to Porte Regal, the closest they could get to this house, and a lot of Ray's fair-weather friends had decided this just wasn't the right moment to stand up and be counted in his corner. Well, we'll remember, boys, we'll remember.

Out this window, beyond the terrace and the wood railing, the lawn sloped gently down to a little skinny artificial stream along his property line, a trickle of water thin enough to step over. Beyond it, the land sloped gradually upward, immediately crossed by a narrow blacktop ribbon of road, just wide enough for the little two-person, two-bag golf carts. And beyond the blacktop was the tee for the thirteenth hole, so there were usually three or four carts parked down there. Five carts now, ten people up by the tee. Interesting how not a one of them looked in this direction; Ray Jones was an embarrassment, just at the moment, in this land of peaceful retirement and Christian privilege.

Or maybe it was the K-9 deputy they weren't looking at. Once again, a deputy and a sniffer dog prowled this way and that across Ray's lawn, searching hard, and he knew for what. The messed-up clothes, that's what. Even the prosecuting attorney over there in Forsyth was having trouble with that 3:00 A.M. fire story. The ashes from Ray's useless fireplace had been *examined*, bagged, taken away, and studied by *scientists*, and they knew the "burned the clothing in the fireplace" story was a crock. They were still hoping, with their sniffer dogs, to find someplace he might have buried the stuff.

Well, good luck, Ray silently told the deputy and his dog, but you got all you're ever gonna get on me. The question is, Is it enough?

"Hey, Ray," Chuck called from over at the table. "You in or out?"

"Always in. You know me," Ray said, turning his back on the golf course and the deputy and the beautiful weather here in Afterlife Village. "Just give me a hand I can play, will ya?"

3

"There isn't any there there," opined Harry Razza, standing at the intersection of routes 76 and 165, where, beneath a nonfunctioning traffic light, a brown-uniformed deputy sheriff pinwheeled and pirouetted, directing endless lines of slow and patient pachydermic traffic on and off and along the Branson Strip, where all the theaters and restaurants and family attractions baked in the summer sun.

"That was Winston Churchill, I believe," Louis B. Urbiton suggested, trying to locate the source of Harry's quote.

But Harry would have none of it. "Not a bit, old man," he said. "Lord Mountbatten it was, in re Africa."

Bob Sangster, the third member of the group, who had been watching the hyperactive deputy out there under the traffic light as though waiting to see him explode, said, "Dorothy Parker. Los Angeles."

"Nonsense," Louis B. Urbiton decided, and that was that.

The three men had apparently somehow annoyed their driver, the chap who'd been paid quite handsomely to deliver them from the airport up at Springfield to the Palace Inn in Branson. However it was they'd managed to put his nose out of joint, his revenge had been terrible. Instead of at any hotel at all, he had deposited them here at this intersection, had dumped their luggage from the trunk of his vehicle to the sidewalk, and had departed. And now, without transportation, without a native guide, left alone and friendless at this godforsaken intersection in the middle of the untamed wilds of America, what was to become of the Down Under Trio?

The Down Under Trio, as they were known to their coworkers, were all originally from Australia and had kept their slithery accents to prove it. All had once upon a time been journalists but now were employed by a scurrilous rag called the *Weekly Galaxy*, headquartered in a section of central Florida that looked—and was—even more godforsaken than this spot here, were that possible. The trio consisted first of Harry Razza, an aging matinee idol with thickly sculptured—and no doubt dyed—auburn hair, a remarkably untrustworthy narrow mustache, and the roguish smile of one who sees himself, despite all the evidence to the contrary, to be quite the ladies' man. Second, there was Bob Sangster, a rangy, laconic, workmanlike fellow with a large nose and the unruffled manner of a paid-up union member. And finally, there was Louis B. Urbiton, oldest and usually drunkest of the trio, an indefatigable reveler and cutup with a deceptively mature and even bankerish mien.

Though not at the moment, in emergency conditions here at this *intersection*. "Something must be done," announced Louis B. as he sensed the bourbon growing warm in the flask in his hip pocket, subjected to all these harmful rays of the sun.

"Ah, yes," Harry agreed. "But what?"

"That fellow never gets tired," Bob pointed out, nodding at the metronomic deputy.

The deputy had halted eastbound traffic on 76 to permit a lot of left turns here and there. "Let me see what I can do," Harry offered, and approached a pickup truck in the stopped line of traffic, its cabin containing a man and a dog—the man driving—its bed empty. The dog's window was open. Speaking politely to both man and dog, Harry said, "B'pardon. Do you know the Palace?"

Man and dog both glowered, reacting to Harry's accent. The dog kept his opinion to himself, but the man said, "You a faggot?"

Harry recoiled, his mustache wrinkling. "Are you," he demanded, "asking me for a *date*? The *cheek*!"

The man blinked. "What?"

"Next, you'll want the *dog* in with us! What sort of place is this?" Without waiting for an answer, Harry turned about and made his way back to the sidewalk and his two compatriots, saying, "Perverts, would you believe it? In small-town America."

The deputy had to wave at the man and the dog in the pickup a *lot* before they got their wits about themselves enough to drive away through the intersection. Meantime, Louis B. said, "Let me try next."

"Be prepared for a shock," Harry advised him.

The deputy had now stopped the northbound traffic on 165. Louis B. threaded through the turning southbounders over to a station wagon containing one woman and an indeterminate number of children—somewhere between four and seven. Producing from his clothing one of the many bits of false identification he kept on and about his person, he said, "Madame, I am, as you see, a journalist with the *Washington Post*, on an important assignment with my confreres over there, to—"

"Police!" screamed the woman.

"We are legitimate journalists, Madame, and—"

"Rape! Assault! Police!"

"Madame, intercourse with you of any kind is the furthest—"

"Children! Help!"

The children rolled down their window and gleefully threw a lot of candy at Louis B., most of it covered with lint. Some stuck to his clothing—for days—but most simply made stains, then rolled to the ground.

"Good day, Madame," Louis B. said, lifted a nonexistent hat, took a jujube in the eye, and marched with dignity back to the sidewalk. "Not a friendly place," he informed his team.

"Well, I'll give it a try," Bob said. Taking from his pocket a twenty-dollar bill, he stepped off the curb and raised both arms high above his head, the twenty stretched between his hands.

Immediately, a six-room mobile home driven by a gent of 127, with his 124-year-old wife in the copilot's seat, slammed to a halt right next to them. The driver took his teeth from his pocket, popped them into his head, turned a white smile on Bob, and said, "Where you headed?"

"Palace Inn."

"Climb aboard. You and your pals take the living room. Martha, give the boys some ice water."

"Hospitality," Bob murmured, turning over the twenty to the sweet-faced Martha. "It makes the world go round."

4

And what fresh hell is this?

It wasn't Sara's own life that was passing before her eyes with horrid slowness as she edged infinitesimally forward with the rest of the traffic; it was somebody else's life, someone Sara automatically both pitied and loathed. Nevertheless, Sara felt as though she were the one drowning.

Texans Bob-O-Links. Foggy River Boys. Ride the Ducks? What the hell is Ride the Ducks? Baldknobbers? Presleys? Isn't he dead? All these signs, all these billboards, all these flashing lights, moving by her car on both sides in slooooooww mo.

The highway from Springfield had emptied Sara here at last, without warning, into the worst traffic jam she'd ever experienced in her life. Campers, pickups, huge tour buses, station wagons, every kind of motorized vehicle known to man—all crept both ways along this narrow, winding ridge road, two traffic lanes and an empty center lane for immediate left turns *only*, flanked by any number of country-music the-

aters intermixed with the most appalling examples of family
fun: water rides, roller coasters, parachute jumps. Bungee
jumping inside a tower. Family restaurants; all you can eat
at our buffet. Family motels. Family shows. Family shopping
malls. And all of it perched like colorful scavenger birds along
the teetery rim of this ridgeline, so narrow that beyond the
gauntlet of fun on both sides of the road, the stony land could
be seen to fall precipitously away into semidesert, as though
God had blasted everything else in the whole world and had
left just this one meandering highland line of neon glitz as a
reminder of what it was that had teed Him off in the first
place.

Sara snailed westward. This endless traffic was like a punishment in a fairy tale; you have to push this vehicle forever
with your nose while crows peck at your eyes. No, not crows;
there's nothing black in Branson.

And there's no such thing as entertainment for the whole
family, either.

A traffic light. (The pinwheeling deputy had left an hour
ago, the light functioning less entertainingly in his place.) No
one, faced with this light, seemed to know what to do next
or which way to turn. (That's why the deputy.) Get *on* with
it, will you?

Through the light. Roy Clark; well, at least it's a name a
person has heard of. And just beyond Roy's lil ole Celebrity
Theatre is the Lodge of the Ozarks, which *Trend*'s travel
person had assured Sara was the only possible place to stay
in Branson.

Yes? Modest, discreet, dark wood, no flashing lights, a nice
absence of the word *family*. Encouraging.

In the nice lobby, Sara used her *Trend* Optima card on the
extremely nice lady behind the counter and was just writing

her name when an Australian voice behind her said, "Would that be the delectable Sara?"

She turned and, by golly, it was Harry Razza, a coworker of hers from the old days, back when she had been employed by the *Weekly Galaxy*, the nation's—probably the world's—most despicable supermarket tabloid. "Harry!" she said, honestly happy to see the Razzer again. "Of *course* you'd be here."

Harry basked in her good fellowship, and they smiled at one another in honest pleasure. He might have an undimmable belief in his winning ways with the fair sex—as he himself would no doubt have phrased it—but he and Sara had gotten all that nonsense out of the way at the very beginning of her time with the *Galaxy*, and now the sight of him merely brought back those old days of heady irresponsibility, when sneaking a microphone into a television star's bathroom was the height of journalistic achievement. She could look herself in the mirror these days, an honest and worthwhile human being, a decent citizen, a true investigative reporter for a serious and respectable magazine; but she had to admit, those old days had been fun. The sight of Harry Razza brought it all back.

As did Harry's next remark: "A terrible place, this, Sara. You must have done something astonishingly wrong in your new employment to be exiled out to these pastures."

"Come on, Harry," she said, "we're both here for Ray Jones, and you know it."

"Some sort of minstrel, I understand," Harry said, waving away Ray Jones with a dismissive hand. "Became a bit too enthusiastic in the hayloft; the bint din't survive." Casually, he added, "She's a cousin of Princess Di, you know."

Sara laughed out loud and accepted her key from the extremely nice lady, who was at this moment sprouting extra ears all over her clean forehead and concrete-permed hair. "Harry, you guys are still the same," Sara said, picking up her bag. "I'll see you."

"Not one place to drink in this hamlet," Harry informed her. "That's how horrid it is. We've set up a little hospitality suite, you know, just for our friends, over at the Palace. You go out here," he said, pointing at the door, "turn left, go just one mile through this horror, and you'll find a cottage inaccurately called the Palace. We're in Two-two-two. Easy to remember, yes?"

"Very easy," Sara agreed.

Harry stepped closer, lowering his voice, looking serious and concerned. "I'll tell you how bad this place is," he murmured. "They have an Australian restaurant. Could you believe it? With oysters."

"That doesn't sound bad."

"Look about you, Sara," Harry advised. "Do you see an ocean?"

"You may be right," Sara said. "See you later, Harry."

"Don't forget. Two-two-two."

"I'll remember," Sara assured him, then went up to her standard-issue motel room, neat and inert. Having unpacked, she phoned Jack Ingersoll, her editor back in New York, to say, "While checking in, I ran into Harry Razza."

"Oh, good old Harry," Jack's voice said in her ear. Jack, too, had worked for the *Galaxy* at one time, where he'd been both Sara's and Harry's editor. "Did he try to get you drunk?"

"Apparently that's difficult in this town. No major hotel

with a bar, no airport with a bar, nothing central and useful. So the *Galaxy*'s set up a hospitality suite at one of the other motels. The Down Under Trio's out rounding up the nation's press."

"Go over there," Jack said.

Surprised, Sara said, "What? Why? You know what they're up to; it's the same stuff they used to do for you."

Which was to *eliminate the competition*. Given a story like the upcoming Ray Jones trial, the *Galaxy* would undoubtedly flood the area with anywhere from fifty to a hundred reporters and photographers and sneak thieves, and the task of the Down Under Trio was to distract, befuddle, and snooker the rest of the press, thus hobbling the world of journalism with booze and disinformation like the Princess Di gambit, while keeping all actual scoops and sidebars and juicy tidbits in the story for themselves; that is, for their team at the *Galaxy*. Sara might once have been a coworker of Harry Razza's, but today she was a rival, so why would Jack want her to fly into the *Galaxy*'s web?

"Because," Jack explained, "they need stuff for this week's paper, and you don't. You are there to study the whole scene, to do a think piece and a summing-up after it's all over. And what's going to be a big part of that scene, all along the way? The *Weekly Galaxy*."

"Ah," Sara said, following the idea. One concept that Jack had retained from his days on the *Galaxy* was that the story is never really the story. The story is just the doorway that lets you get inside and find and cover the real story, the story you *want* to cover. So Jack had just nosed out one possible story, which was not, in fact, the upcoming murder trial of country singer Ray Jones but was—surprise, surprise—the

Weekly Galaxy. In the past, *Trend* had tried and failed to do a *Weekly Galaxy* exposé; maybe this was the time.

This could be fun, Sara thought, and said, "Two-two-two."

"Right you are," Jack said, misunderstanding.

5

After a late lunch with some state legislators over in Branson, Warren Thurbridge drove back to the defense team's offices in Forsyth, the county seat, and when he walked in, Jim Chancellor was standing there, a lot of computer printout in his hands. He had good news, and he had bad news. "We've got our first jury lists. We can go over them now," he said. "The phone company's at work in your office, so maybe we should use the conference room."

"Phone company?" Warren didn't like that; everything was supposed to be done and ready to go. "What for?"

"Beats me," Jim said. He was a local attorney, under forty, amiable, chunky, with a good sport's thick black mustache. "They just said there was a little glitch."

Warren, frowning massively, strode to his office, stood in the doorway, and there they were, a man and woman, both in plaid shirts and jeans and work boots, both wearing white hard hats with the word CONTEL on the side, both lumbered with big heavy tool belts jangling and dangling with equipment. They had Warren's desk shoved out of the way and were doing something to the spaghetti of phone wires at the baseboard along the back wall. While the man went on working with a small screwdriver, the woman, apparently sensing the weight of Warren's glare on her back, turned, smiled brightly, and said, "Just a couple more minutes."

Jim stood behind Warren, outside the room. "We can use the conference room, Warren," he said. He was new at saying "Warren," and it came out a trifle lumpy.

But Warren pointed to the papers in Jim's hands and said, "That stuff's *our* secret. We'll wait."

"You're the boss," Jim said.

That's right. Warren Thurbridge was not Ray Jones's criminal lawyer. He was much more than that; he was the chief attorney of Ray Jones's defense team. As such, he was a cross between a battlefield commander and a movie producer, and he looked the part: distinguished, handsome, confident, heavyset, a very well preserved sixty-one, with silvery hair and piercing eyes and a booming laugh that could as readily turn into a roar of rage or a silken snakelike hiss of contempt.

What Warren Thurbridge was good at was deploying large forces to powerful effect. He wouldn't be a damn bit of use one-on-one, walking into court as a lone counselor arguing the case of one small defendant. But that didn't matter; no one would ever think to offer him such a job. Nor would he accept it. What he would accept, and happily, was the Ray Jones kind of case. Lots of publicity, lots of money, and maybe even a shot at getting the son of a bitch off. Perfect.

Headquarters of the Ray Jones defense team was a recently defunct furniture showroom, a broad one-story glass-fronted structure across the street from the courthouse. Inside, the building had been a hollow shell, with offices at the rear that had once held the shop's owner and credit manager, two people with a penchant for making wrong decisions. Gray industrial carpeting had covered the main showroom floor, with indentations in it where the unsold furniture had once stood, and old phone lines had jutted like hairy moles from the walls.

Now the place was transformed. Beige draperies covered the front showroom windows. Office furniture and equipment and cubicle partitions made a bustling atmosphere within. Phone and fax lines were in place, plus copiers and a darkroom and a water cooler everyone was too busy to gossip around. Twelve car parking had been obtained at the rear of a nearby restaurant. Warren himself was installed in the former owner's office, with furniture that looked too good to be rented but was, and the onetime credit manager's office was now the conference room, with bulletin boards, TV, VCR, and a polygraph.

The staff in this building numbered seventeen, beginning with Warren himself, and Pat Kelly, his secretary of the last twenty-one years, plus five young attorneys and two legal secretaries from Warren's home office in Dallas, plus Jim Chancellor, who had once himself been the Taney County prosecutor, plus *his* secretary, plus six various researchers and clerks, all of them very busy.

What they were mostly busy with at the moment was the list of potential jurors. What with one thing and another, fewer than 9,000 of Taney County's 22,000 residents were eligible jurors, and Warren wanted to have at least the beginning of a handle on every one of them before Wednesday—day after tomorrow.

Normally, in a particularly gruesome murder like this one, well covered in the local press, it would be almost automatic to ask for a change of venue to some county beyond the reach of regional papers and TV, but Ray Jones was already a famous person, famous everywhere. The national press would definitely cover this trial, so there was no way to get out from under the glare of publicity.

Still, fame could cut both ways. In the four years since Ray Jones had built his theater and bought his house out at Porte Regal, he'd done a number of things to ingratiate himself with the community, lending his name to hospital fund drives, putting on a charity performance for the local Boy Scouts, things like that, things any sensible celeb would do when trying to establish roots in a community. Some portion of that pool of potential jurors would harbor warm feelings toward Ray Jones as a result of his good deeds in Branson, and it was part of the job of Warren Thurbridge and his team to find those people and get them on the jury. Swallow the bad publicity, hope the good publicity does some good. Stay at home in Taney County.

This is where Jim Chancellor came in. A local boy, former prosecutor, he could tell you *something* about half the people on the jury list—but not till the phone people left.

In the meantime, Warren busied himself at Pat Kelly's desk, going through his message slips. Nothing important; he'd spent part of the drive from Branson on his car phone to the Dallas office, getting brought up to date on the firm's other affairs. In fact, most of these messages were from the media; the usual press feeding frenzy was about to begin. Later on, Warren would be more than happy to wage his Ray Jones battle in public, a kind of warfare at which he excelled, but at the moment journalists were useless to him, and so he'd have nothing to do with them. "Have Julie take care of these," he told Pat, Julie being the file clerk who would also double as media spokesperson.

"Right," Pat said as the phone workers came out of his

office, both grinning happily but apologetically, saying, "All fixed. Sorry for the inconvenience."

"No trouble," Warren assured them, now that the trouble was over, and he and Jim went at last into his office and shut the door, while the two phone workers left the building and walked down the block to the Contel repair truck they'd obtained the same way they'd gotten the IDs and the tools and the hard hats: bribery.

Stashing their hard hats and tool belts in the back of the truck, the ex–phone repairers drove sedately away, circling one extra block to go past a small RV park. Half a dozen RVs, big, ungainly traveling hotel rooms on wheels, faced the street in a row across the front of the park, and in the driver's seat of one of these an old geezer sat reading the latest *Modern Maturity*. When the Contel truck went by, he looked up, grinned, and gave an everything's fine O sign with thumb and first finger. The former phone people waved and drove on, and the geezer went back to reading about how retirees could avoid paying their fair share of the cost of society. Behind him, two technicians from the *Weekly Galaxy* hunkered over recording equipment, and the sound of Warren Thurbridge's voice was heard, saying, "Now, Jim, don't hold anything back. Say what you want about these people. Not a word of this will ever leave this office."

6

The *Weekly Galaxy* hospitality suite was jumping when Sara arrived a little after five o'clock. Three connecting rooms of sofas and easy chairs and big-screen satellite TVs. A bar in each room, with a generous gent in a black bow tie behind each one. White cloth–covered tables offered the kind of airy snacks that stave off hunger without protecting from inebriation. And present for the largesse were many representatives of the fourth estate.

The first thing for Sara to do was get a full glass, for protective coloration. A few customers were ahead of her at the bar she chose, giving her an opportunity to see just how lavish a hand these bartenders had, so when her turn came, she asked for a white wine spritzer with lots of ice, and then, as she moved among the three rooms, she didn't drink it. Nor did she stop to chat with anyone; at first, all she wanted here was a general feel of the occasion.

The occasion was unbuttoned, is what it was. Mostly, these were the entertainment reporters of our news-hungry nation, more of them from television than print, and more from cable than network, which meant the room wasn't exactly awash in high-flown rhetoric about the nobility of the journalistic profession. These were mostly wannabes, people who'd started covering showbiz only after they'd given up their own showbiz dreams. Many garage bands, many regional theater productions, many department-store modeling jobs, many public access-channel shows, all shimmered in the past around these people, giving them that weird edge, that manner of caring passionately about something they don't care anything about at all. It can pass for sophistication, in the dark, with the light behind it.

While she wandered around, getting a sense of the scene, of the people here, the kind of journalist assembled for this story—okay, the competition, if you insist—familiar faces from the bad old *Galaxy* days, familiarly ravaged, passed by from time to time. She made no effort to establish contact. Principal among these faces and among the most ravaged were the Down Under Trio, those practiced enticers, hard at work sabotaging American journalism. Sara saw them one at a time, sheepdogging their victims to the party.

Harry Razza she saw first, the matinee idol who'd told her about this cheery reporter trap. He came in with a pair of girls all in dark leather, who had perfected the ability to giggle and sneer at the same time, so they were definitely from either a teenage magazine or MTV. Harry gave them to some boys and left.

A little later, Sara saw another of the Down Unders, Bob Sangster, the one with the big nose and an easy working-class manner, who had reeled in an older gent smoking a pipe and wearing leather elbow patches, a former reporter retired to *People*, probably. And sometime after that, in came Louis B. Urbiton with a pair of scruffy thirtyish proles under his wing, urban cowboys who'd dressed themselves down at the mall exclusively in imitations—polyester and vinyl. These must be reporters from one of the *Galaxy*'s direct imitators, the *Star* or the *National Enquirer* or one of those. True competitors, in other words, toward whom no mercy would be shown.

Louis delivered his latest bag to the tender mercies of the nearest bartender, clapped them on the back, and departed, staggering only slightly, eyes only a bit redder and wetter than usual. It was a tough dirty job, but somebody had to do it. And none better than the Down Under Trio.

"Sara!"

That had sounded more like a cry for help than a greeting, and when Sara looked around, she saw why. It was Binx Radwell who had called to her, a fog of free-floating angst in the shape of a man. A blond guy in his mid-thirties, Binx Radwell had a more or less normal head and body, except that it was all covered by a quivering padded layer of baby fat. Then equal parts of panic and perspiration had been larded on top of it all, as though he were about to be put on a spit for several hours over an open fire. Given the usual expression in Binx's eyes, that's exactly what he expected to happen, any minute.

Sara's invariable reaction to Binx was helpless pity combined with helpless impatience. Why didn't he just pull his socks up, for heaven's sake? Why was he always so *afraid* all the time?

Well, she knew why. He worked for the *Galaxy*, that's why, and he lived with his wife Marcie and their children at the very outer edge of his income; disaster was never more than one false step away. A couple of years ago, in fact, Binx had actually been fired, not because he'd been doing anything worse than usual but merely as an example to the troops. Having been an editor, and *very* well paid, he'd floundered and wept and semidrowned for a little while, and then the *Galaxy* had hired him back . . . as a reporter, at half the salary.

So Binx had every right to look the way he did, which was like an abused child. Giving her pity free rein, reining in her impatience, she said, "Binx, how are you? You look great," she lied.

"So do you, Sara." He tried a smile, Binx did, which looked very much like an expression you might see in the display case at the fish market. "Marcie and I are thinking about a separation," he said, lying right back at her.

"Oh, you and Marcie were born for each other," Sara assured him.

Binx looked more stricken than ever. "You really think so?"

Looking around, Sara said, "Whose team is this? Not Boy Cartwright, I hope," she said, naming her least-favorite *Galaxy* editor.

Within his terror, Binx looked almost pleased, proud of himself. "*My* team," he said with simple modesty.

Delighted, Sara said, "Binx! You're an editor again!"

"After Massa died—"

"What? Massa died?"

Deadpan, he said, "Massa's in de cold, cold ground."

Bewildered, not getting it, Sara said, "You're kidding me."

"You hadn't heard? Come over here," Binx said, taking her elbow, fondling it, leading her to the quietest corner of the room, saying, "It's true. It happened at the morning editorial meeting. He was yelling at the editors, you know, yelling there weren't any good stories anymore, pounding on the table and waving that beer bottle around, and all of a sudden he made the most kind of a *jungle* sound, all deep and loud and rattly—we could hear it way over at the reporter tables—and *flop*. Right on his desk, in the elevator."

Massa, actual name Bruno DeMassi, was the creator and owner and publisher of the *Weekly Galaxy*, a man of many appetites, most of them gross. "That's hard to believe," Sara said. "The *Galaxy* without Massa."

"It was so weird, Sara," Binx told her. "He just lay there facedown, arms stretched out, spilling his beer, and he twitched a couple times, and nobody wanted to go near him, and finally Boy went over. You know how he simpers and does that English accent."

"Oh, don't remind me."

"Oh, good, you remember," Binx said. "Boy said, 'Chief? Chief?' And he touched Massa, and then he turned around, and he was very solemn and he put his hand over his heart like Napoleon, and he said, 'The Chief is with us no more. The Chief is dead.' And somebody—nobody knows who, just somebody—somebody said, 'And we have a new Pope.' And everybody started to laugh." Binx blinked in remembered amazement. "Nobody could stop," he said. "It got everybody. There's Massa lying dead on his desk, and hundreds and hundreds of people laughing. It went all through the building, upstairs, downstairs, people holding their sides, people falling down on the floor, they were laughing so hard. And even when Jacob Harsch came down from the top floor to find out what was going on, nobody could stop. It just went on and on." Binx slowly shook his head, his sweaty round face pinkly incandescent with the leftover glow of the awe of that transcendent moment.

"Is Harsch running the *Galaxy* now?" Sara asked. Jacob Harsch had been Massa's assistant, as cold as Massa had been hot.

But Binx said, "Oh no. He's out. They brought some people up from hell to run things."

"Hell? What do you mean?"

"It turned out," Binx said, "there was some sort of corporation deal, and when Massa died, all this money went to his widow, and a corporation owns us. They're a Florida real estate development company, so you can imagine."

"Barely," Sara said.

"They took their most evil executives," Binx said, "the ones that snap at sticks you put through the bars of the cage, and they put them in charge of *us*. Oh, Sara," Binx said, and fondled her forearm this time, "you got out when the getting was good."

"I guess so," Sara said, and they were interrupted at that point by the arrival of Don Grove, the world's most pessimistic reporter, another former coworker of Sara's, who this time ignored Sara and turned his doleful countenance on Binx, saying, "I don't suppose you could use—"

"You remember Sara, Don," Binx said.

Don considered Sara, considered his answer. "Yes," he decided, and turned back to Binx. "I don't suppose you could use the dead woman's grandmother, got proof the family's related to Princess Di."

"*We're* spreading that story, Don," Binx said.

"Oh." Don nodded at Sara. "Nice to see you again," he said without enthusiasm, and went away.

Binx looked fondly after his retreating reporter. "Good old Don," he said. "He's one of the few things in life that keeps me cheerful."

"Oh, you," Sara said. "You're just sunny by nature."

7

A little after seven, best friend Cal Denny drove Ray Jones from his home in the Porte Regal enclave out onto 165 north, headed up to the Strip, and turned left. They weren't in the Acura SNX sports car, since the Sheriff's Department still had that impounded as evidence in the murder case, but Ray had three other cars at the house, so it was the maroon Jaguar town car they rode in, Cal at the right-hand-drive wheel, Ray in the front passenger seat on the left.

Traffic was its usual mess on the Strip, the tourist families inching along, grubby little faces pressed to grubby safety-glass windows, looking for tonight's thrill. In this direction, they could choose from theaters housing Roy Clark, Mickey Gilley, Jim Stafford, Ray Jones, Boxcar Willie, Christy Lane, Willie Nelson/Merle Haggard, and Ray Stevens, plus wowzer-dowzer attractions like Waltzing Waters (exactly what it sounds like, plus colored lights), White Water (exactly what it sounds like, plus you in an inadequate rubber raft), Mutton Hollow (CRAFTS, CRAFTS, CRAFTS), and a variety of foods much faster but not much more interesting than the traffic.

With a seating capacity of 827, the Ray Jones Country Theater was about standard for the neighborhood, on a par with Roy Clark's Celebrity Theatre on one side of him and Mickey Gilley's Family Theatre on the other side and the Jim Stafford Theatre across the way. (You say *theatre;* I say *theater*.) Other theaters were bigger. Down the road, Christy Lane filled two thousand seats twice a day in season, as did Andy Williams back the other way. And every one of those seats was occupied by someone who'd gotten there by *car*, along the Strip.

And this wasn't even the worst. Summer family time was pretty bad, but wait till after Labor Day, when all the families have gone home to stick their sticky kids back in school, and the retirees in their RVs show up. The retirees hate kids, so they wait till September. Then they come to Branson, get out on the Strip, forget where they were going, and slllloooooowwwwww dooooowwwwwwnnnnn.

It wasn't too bad this evening, though. The maroon Jag bopped along at speeds up to a mile an hour, inching by Roy Clark, and as Cal drove, his bony serious face as intent as though he were completing one of the trickier parts of Le Mans, they discussed the situation: "Reporters are starting to show up," Ray said.

"Yeah, I heard," Cal agreed, nodding his head while intently watching the overloaded station wagon from Mississippi in front of him. "You want me to pick one, huh?"

"But the right one," Ray told him. "We got all these entertainment-beat people, calling in markers all over the place, agents and bookers. I'm getting calls from L.A. and New York and Nashville and every fucking place. Everybody wants an interview, and I'm not gonna *give* an interview."

"Right," Cal said.

"I'm keeping a tight asshole on this," Ray said, "and you know why."

"Uh-huh," Cal said.

"You, and only you."

"Right," Cal said. It was part of the strength and the solidity (and the stupidity, too, if truth be told) of the man that it didn't even occur to him to say, "You can trust me, Ray." Of *course* Ray could trust him. Otherwise, Cal wouldn't have been permitted this little task.

"I don't want any of those entertainment people," Ray went on. "They're no damn use to me on this thing."

"Right," Cal said. He kept watching that station wagon.

"And the tabloids, too," Ray said. He'd thought long and hard about this, once the opportunity had come along. "The *National Enquirer*, the *Weekly Galaxy*, the *Star*—they can't print a thing to do me any good."

"They're fun, though," Cal said as the station wagon ahead turned off into the Roy Clark parking lot. Now they were behind a camper from Wisconsin. *Intruder*, the camper claimed was its brand name, and who could doubt it?

"Not this time," Ray said. "Not even fun. And TV won't do anything for me, either. I need *print*. The *New York Times*, maybe the *Washington Post*. Not *USA Today*."

"Uh-uh."

"A magazine'd be even better," Ray said. "A serious one. *Newsweek* or *Time*. Not a monthly; they'd have me strapped in the death seat before the damn thing came out."

"Weekly," Cal said. He knew that much.

"Take your time," Ray told him.

Looking surprised, Cal said, "Ray? I *am* takin my time, pokin along behind this camper here."

"Finding the reporter," Ray explained, with what only

looked like patience. "We got a couple of weeks; we can wait and get just the right one."

"Oh, sure," Cal said. "I know what to do."

Ray grinned at the earnest lumpy profile of his oldest friend. "I don't know what I'd a done without you, Cal, over the years," he said.

"Well, you didn't have to, did you?" Cal said, making the right turn onto the precipitous parking lot around and behind the Ray Jones Country Theater.

This steeply sloped blacktop parking lot, not uncommon along this narrow ridge, gave the fast-fooded families and the sedentary retirees a little more heart exercise than they'd bargained for, but so far there was no objective evidence that the parking lot had actually killed anybody. And if there were any such evidence, Ray didn't want to hear about it; he had trouble enough already.

Not including theater business. Forty-five minutes before showtime, and already his parking lot was half-full. All those polyester-wrapped tons of tourist lugged themselves upward toward the entrance at the front of the building, and those who recognized Ray Jones in what should have been the driver's seat of the Jag, but was not, grinned and waved at him, offering him their silent solidarity—silent because his windows were firmly shut and the AC fully on. He grinned and waved back, friendly old Ray, showing them both hands and no steering wheel, and a lot of them peered more closely, realized it must be some kinda expensive foreign car with the steering wheel way over *there*, and grinned even bigger, happier than ever.

Country-music fans don't envy or begrudge the material success of the performers, and that's because they don't see the country stars as being brilliant or innovative or otherwise exceptional people (which they are), but firmly believe the Willie Nelsons and Roy Clarks are shitkickers just like themselves, who happened to hit it lucky, and more power to them. It meant *anybody* could hit it lucky, including their own poor sorry selves, so these people, most of whom could lean down and rest their Coke cans on the poverty line, took sweet vicarious pleasure in the overt manifestations of their heroes' lush rewards.

A reserved spot down at the back of the theater, a full eighteen feet below ground level at the front of the theater, was kept open for whichever car Ray chose to come to work in. (One of the great attractions of Branson for the country performers, who used to spend two to three hundred days a year on the road, is that they can now commute every day from *home*.) An exterior flight of stairs led from here up to the outside door to Ray's dressing room; maybe not exactly the only dressing room in his career with a window but certainly the only one with a view: miles of Ozark mountains.

One of the other nice things about Branson for the country stars is how *clean* it is—no mobsters, no scuzzy high rollers from Detroit or Kuwait, no hard-eyed hookers. You didn't have to go through life watching your back every damn minute. Mel Tillis once said Branson was a cross between Mayberry and Vegas, and that's what he meant. When Andy Williams opened his Moon River Theater, his special guest was Henry Mancini, who happened to have written "Moon River," and when Henry Mancini said onstage that Andy Williams had worked his ass off to get the theater ready on time, Andy Williams said to him, "We don't use words like that in Branson." To make the story better, he wasn't kidding. To make the story better than that, he wasn't wrong.

Waiting for Ray in his clean, well-lighted dressing room

were musical director Lennie Elmore, already in his tux, plus Ray's private secretary, Honey Franzen, a blonde in her mid-thirties who was still just as good-looking and almost as slender as she'd been a dozen years ago when she'd sung with the Jones Girls, the backup trio Ray used to have, which he'd given up when he'd moved to Branson. Branson doesn't go for t&a, and why else have a girl trio backup? In any case, Honey Franzen, who was as smart as she was good-looking, had by then long switched from singing backup and waving it all around onstage behind Ray to being his private secretary and steady private comfort, the place where, when he had to go there, she had to let him in. She had, in fact, hired her Jones Girl replacement, and a few years later had fired the girl again, along with the other two final Jones Girls. That was just part of the sort of thing Honey took care of for Ray.

Tonight, though, it was Elmore who wanted a word with Ray first, saying, "The new reed guy's come up with something."

"Oh yeah?" Bob Golker, the former reed man—clarinet, some flute, various saxophones—a sideman with Ray for years, just as good drunk as sober, had taken a job in L.A., and his replacement was not accomplished in exactly the same ways; better flute, not quite so good sax, a jazzier sense of rhythm.

Elmore said, "He's gonna do flute instead of clarinet behind Henny on 'Orange Blossom.'"

"Is it okay?"

"They both like it. You listen tonight, see what you think."

Ray shrugged acceptance. "Orange Blossom Special" was done solo on violin on virtually every stage in Branson, night after night; anybody who could enliven the damn thing had Ray Jones's support.

Ray walked around the counter to the kitchenette part of the dressing room, opened a cupboard door, reached in, stopped, looked, and said, "There's no Snickers in here. Goddamn, I took the last one yesterday. I meant to get some more; I forgot."

Cal said, "I'll get you some."

"Thanks, Cal."

Ray came around the counter again as Cal left the room via its interior door, to go upstairs through the theater to the concession stand out by the box office. Honey was over at the desk, looking at the computer, where the theater layout on the screen showed every seat sold. "Honey," Ray said, "come on in back with me; I got a headache."

"Sure, baby," Honey said, and led the way back into the changing room while Lennie Elmore left to tell the new reed man the change was okay.

8

The map of Branson in Sara's hotel room indicated all the attractions—that's what they called them—along the Strip, and when Sara picked out the Ray Jones Theater, it looked as though it must be very close to the Lodge of the Ozarks, separated from it only by Mickey Gilley's theater. Wouldn't it be faster to go there by foot than by internal-combustion engine?

It would. Sara, the only walker in sight, reached the theater at ten minutes to eight, to find the parking lot blocked by a sawhorse bearing the sign PERFORMANCE SOLD OUT. She walked by it anyway and went inside to the lobby filled with theatergo ers to see what her press card could do.

Nothing. The twangy little girl in the box office assured her that sold out actually meant sold out—no more seats available. The term *house seats* did not appear to be part of her vocabulary. Not only that, the girl informed her this evening's performance had been sold out yesterday and that both of tomorrow's were already sold out as of now. A seat was offered for the matinee day after tomorrow. "Maybe later," Sara said.

"Be gone later," the girl said complacently.

Maybe so. Still, Sara didn't feel like planning her life that far ahead. Also, there had to be some way her press connection could be made to work for her. It was true she wanted to see Ray Jones at work, but it was also true that she wanted him to become aware of her presence in his peripheral vision, without her joining that hopeless line of media people who were trying and failing to get interviews. Long ago, she'd learned that the best way to approach celebrities was obliquely.

So she thanked the twangy girl for her advice, declined the matinee two days off, and turned away to leave. A man held the door open for her and she stepped outside and looked around, trying to decide what to do next.

"Miss?"

She turned, and it was the man who'd held the door for her. Fiftyish, he was baggily dressed and blockily built, with a worried-looking bony face. In one hand, he carried three candy bars. He said, "Excuse me, did I hear you say you were with some magazine?"

"I am, yes," Sara said, wondering what this was about. Surely he wasn't trying to pick her up.

He said, "I didn't catch the name of it."

"Trend," Sara said, really doubting this fellow was one of *Trend*'s readers. Around them, other non-*Trend* readers straggled up the slope and into the theater.

He seemed to chew on the name for a few seconds, then said, "Weekly or monthly?"

"Weekly," she said. Feeling obscurely compelled to explain further, she added, "We're a New York-based service and cultural magazine. I'm here to cover the Ray Jones trial."

"For your magazine. *Trend.*"

"Sure. I'm sorry, I don't see what . . ." And she gestured, inviting him to do some explaining of his own.

Which he promptly did. "Oh yeah," he said, "I oughta tell you who I am. I'm Cal Denny. I'm a friend of Ray's. I'm kind of connected, uh, with, uh . . ." And he waggled the candy bars at the building beside them.

"Oh."

"I heard you trying to get in."

"Apparently, full is full."

"We're doin' real good business," he allowed.

Sara grinned. "God bless Belle Hardwick, eh?"

He looked startled, then abruptly grinned back, as though they now shared a dirty secret. "I guess you're right," he said. "You want to see the show?"

"In return for what?"

"Huh?" He wasn't very quick, Cal Denny, but sooner or later he got there: "Oh!" he said, and blushed, actually blushed. "No, I just thought you'd . . . I heard you in there . . ."

"Thanks, then," Sara said. "There's room after all, huh?"

"Well, not really," Cal Denny told her. "But there's a seat in the back that's only used two different times, by somebody in the show. You'd have to go stand by the lighting guy just those two times, and the rest you could sit down."

"It's a deal," Sara said. Sticking out her hand, she said, "Sara Joslyn."

"Hi, there," he answered, and awkwardly shook her hand, as though not used to physical contact with a woman. Soon he let go of her hand and led her back into the theater, where they joined the shuffling throng crossing the lobby to the two interior entrances. Cal Denny led them to the doorway on the left, where what looked to be a high school boy, in a thin pink blazer too big for him, stood collecting tickets. Denny murmured a word to the boy, pointing his thumb over his shoulder at Sara, and the boy nodded and waved her on in.

Inside was a theater like any other; longer than wide, the floor sloping down toward the front, rows of red plush seating parted by two carpeted aisles, a dark red curtain closed over the stage. At the rear, a platform displaced most of the last two rows of the center section, and on it, inside a simple two-by-four railing, hulked a fairly complex-looking light board in the care of a fat man in a Yosemite Sam T-shirt and Yosemite Sam beard. This was the lighting guy.

Denny in a half whisper introduced Sara—"This lady's a reporter. She'll be in the Elvis seat; let her know when she has to get out of it"—and Yosemite Sam nodded hello and agreement. Then Denny showed her the Elvis seat, on the aisle next to the lighting platform, and bent down to murmur, "I gotta bring Ray his Snickers now," showing her the candy bars.

"Oh. Right."

He went away, and Sara watched the people come in: families, many many families; children of all ages, most of them not overweight; adults of all ages, most of them overweight— rural people, small-town people, working-class people. These are the faces in the crowd when a farm is auctioned off for back taxes. They filed in, well-behaved, cheerful, carrying soft drinks and popcorn and candy as though they were going to the movies. They found their seats and organized themselves and faced the curtain, and it opened.

Houselights down. The six people on the simple stage, formally dressed and armed with musical instruments, began to play and sing country music, none of which Sara had ever heard before. Two of them were women, slender and pretty, with important hair, both dressed in glittery tight black gowns that covered them from neck to toe and enclosed their arms to below the elbow. They played guitars. The four men wore slightly odd tuxedos; one of them played piano, one drums, one an electric bass, and one a bewildering variety of wind instruments, all lined up on a chrome rack beside him.

Which of these was Ray Jones? Sara had expected more of an impressive introduction. Was it Ray Jones's conceit to present himself as no more than a simple sideman who'd made good?

No. None of these people was Ray Jones, which became clear at the end of the first number, when the male guitarist introduced his co-musicians and himself and then engaged in some simple comedy routines with the others before dropping into another song, this one showcasing the talents of the pianist and the singing quality of one of the girl guitarists.

So this was the warm-up act. The audience seemed content with it, laughing at the old jokes and applauding the displays of musicianship. Sara sat and waited for Ray Jones.

Tap tap, on her shoulder. It was Yosemite Sam, beckoning her to join him on his platform. She did, and he gestured for her to squeeze herself flat against the rear wall. She did that, too, while onstage another musical number loped along like horses on a bridle path, and into the seat she'd just vacated slipped Elvis Presley, complete with all the black hair and a glittery shiny white suit with gold and glass beads all over it. Onstage, the song came to an end, the audience applauded, and the lighting man swung a big spotlight hard around and switched it on just as Elvis erupted out of his seat, shouting and hollering and waving his arms over his head. Sara, against the wall, was just out of the harsh beam of white light.

The audience laughed and called out with surprise, and with the spotlight tracking him, Elvis went tearing down the aisle and up onstage, still hollering gibberish, until the male guitarist, who doubled as MC, calmed him down, and then they did the joke, which was that Elvis wanted to announce he'd just seen Glenn Miller alive in a nearby supermarket.

Glenn Miller? Did these people know who Glenn Miller was?

Apparently. They laughed and applauded this small joke and then the MC asked Elvis to sing a song as long as he was there, but Elvis said he had to rush back to the supermarket to see if Glenn Miller was still there. He ran offstage and the audience laughed and applauded some more. Yosemite Sam gestured that Sara could resume her seat, which she did, and the show went on.

A little later, the warm-up act finished, the curtain closed, and a loudspeaker voice announced, "Ladies and gentlemen—Ray Jones!"

A somewhat bulky fiftyish man in a dark blue tux, under what might be his own mussy black hair but was probably a really good rug, and carrying an acoustic guitar so adorned with bright colors and wild designs that it looked like somebody's favorite motorcycle, came out through the center split in the red curtain and stepped over to the microphone left there by the MC. A spotlight shone on him, and the applause was long and loud and truly enthusiastic. When it died down, the man sang, in his gravelly, well-traveled voice, a sappy air called "It's Time to Write Another Love Song (This Time, the Song's for You)."

More applause at the end of this song and then the curtain reopened, and there were the musicians again, with more instruments than before. Ray Jones said a few words of welcome to the audience, thanking them for coming, asking them if they didn't think this was a really terrific bunch of musicians up here (they did), making a couple of small jokes about Branson traffic and the well-known desire of all fathers everywhere to go fishing instead of to the theater, and generally making himself accommodating to the crowd. He said nothing about murder trials or tax problems or anything troublesome.

Then he strummed a chord on his guitar and said, "Now, folks, I'd like some help on this one, if you feel up to it. I think you know the words I mean, where I want you to come right in and join me. If you could do that, we could really get something going here, I'm pretty sure. *And—*"

The musicians started a lively, fast-paced introduction, which the audience clearly recognized; there was laughter and applause and a stirring in the seats. Then Ray Jones leaned in to the microphone and sang:

> *A lot of stuff I tried, that people said was good,*
> *But, dang, you know, they lied, or I misunderstood;*
> *I may be countrified, but here's my attitude . . .*

Ray Jones lifted his head and shouted over the music, "That's your cue!"

And, on the beat, the audience en masse gave him the line:

> *If it ain't fried, it ain't food!*

Astounded, Sara turned to look at Yosemite Sam, who was grinning inside his beard as though remembering with pleasure every greasy meal he'd ever faced. And all through the theater, happiness was loud and palpable as Ray Jones went on:

> *Oh, I've been stupefied, by stuff that's steeped and*
> *   stewed,*
> *And I've been mystified, by things that I have chewed,*
> *If you want me satisfied, just watch as I conclude . . .*

The audience didn't need any priming from Ray Jones this time as they roared him the line:

If it ain't fried, it ain't food!

It's an affirmation, Sara thought; it's a declaration of class solidarity; it's a tribal anthem; it's a credo; it's a social statement at the bedrock of self-image and belonging, and I have to remember this for the piece for *Trend*. This is who we are; that's what these people are singing, and we're all here together, and there's no strangers to laugh at us or look down their noses. This is who we are.

Meantime, Ray Jones had gone on into the bridge, and Sara's foot was tapping along with the beat:

They got snails, and frogs' legs, and lobster on a leash,
With chocolate-covered ants they do get pushy;
They got squid in its ink, they got tofu and quiche,
And when the oven breaks down, they got sushi.

Half the audience was clapping along with the song now, and Sara had to resist the impulse to do the same. Ray Jones, grinning, nodding, pounding his own left foot on the stage floor, drove them all into the peroration:

You know I got my pride, it isn't that I'm rude,
But I just won't be denied, even if it starts a feud.
Only one thing's qualified, when I am in the mood . . .

Everybody bellowed it out:

If it ain't fried—

Grinning, winking, Ray Jones side-talked the mike:

You know this is true—

Everybody:

If it ain't fried—

Ray Jones:

There ain't nothin else to do—

Everybody, including (to her utter astonishment) Sara:

IF IT AIN'T FRIED, IT AIN'T FOOD!

Cheering, rousing, standing ovation. Openmouthed, amazed, Sara turned to stare at Yosemite Sam, and he grinned at her and winked.

9

FACSIMILE TRANSMISSION SHEET

TO _Jack Ingersoll, Special Projects Editor_
Trend Magazine

FROM _Sara Joslyn_

NUMBER OF PAGES INCLUDING THIS PAGE_2_

If all pages are not received, contact 417 333-5599

Facsimile transmittal number 417 333-5555

Dear Jack,

Herewith, a preliminary report and a suggested approach:

The exhilaration of finding oneself in the very heart of the American ethos is hard to describe. Despite the complications and sophistication of 200 years of history, Americans are still essen-

tially the same rugged, simple people who first
braved the unknown to carve a civilization
from this new continent's wilderness. The process
of taming that wild and beautiful land continues, here
in Branson, Missouri, among these rugged rocks
and sandy scrubs, where the eternal verities of
family, honesty, and valor now unexpectedly find
themselves confronted by many of our post-
modern ills: murder, rape, dark passions, and a
complex, cynical, uncaring legal system.

Branson is country-western star Ray Jones's
spiritual home, as exciting as Atlantic City, as
clean as Disneyland, as fresh and new as wet
paint. And these people are Ray Jones's people,
honest, simple, slow to anger or judgment. In this
confrontation between Ray Jones and the citizens of his soul, the presence of the world's press,
eager for a kind of meaning they can understand, seems almost irrelevant.

Sara Joslyn

Jack Ingersoll showed the fax to his boss, Hiram Farley.
"I think I'd better go down there," he said.

"Go now," Farley said.

10

Upon sending her initial fax to New York, the morning after attending the Ray Jones show—she'd actually written it last night but still thought it a good, evocative first draft this morning, and so sent it—Sara decided to do some legwork, which actually meant carwork, which meant that awful traffic outside. But there was no way to avoid it; Sara joined the hordes searching for the world's cheapest pancakes, struggled through them at last, and pointed the nose of the trusty rental east.

Forsyth seemed weird at first, until Sara realized that what made it so odd, after Branson, was its normality. This is what small towns actually look like—sleepy, quiet, a bit dusty. Low buildings flanking wide empty streets. Lots of cars and pickup trucks parked at the curbs, but little traffic moving.

The county courthouse was a neat two-story building, modern, beige, with unnecessary horizontal gray stripes to show an architect had been around, the whole surrounded by trim lawn and plantings. The rear facade featured a tall oval-topped two-story window surmounted by a functioning clock, and the front facade consisted of some sort of Mayan arched entrance, plus a bit of grammatic confusion: TANEY COUNTY COURTHOUSE it said over the door, but in larger letters above that were the words TANEY COUNTY COURT HOUSE. So apparently, there were two factions in Taney County: those who thought *courthouse* was one word and those who thought *court house* were two words, and both factions, this being a democracy, had been satisfied.

Sara wandered for a while in the neat fluorescent interior of the building, unchallenged. It was almost empty, particularly upstairs, where the courtroom waited, untenanted and unlocked. Sara took a few pictures of the simple bare space with its fuzzy blue-seated wooden armchairs, long dark brown attorneys' table, Missouri state seal like a huge bronze Roman coin over the judge's bench, gaudier Taney County seal on the side wall, four rows of spectators' pews in dark wood, and the drooped flags of both nation and state standing upright to flank the banc like a pair of colorful lances.

Downstairs again, Sara opened doors and asked questions of the few but friendly clerks she encountered until she reached the office suite of prosecutor Buford Delray, whose friendly secretary smiled with real regret as she said, "I'm sorry, but Mr. Delray's awfully busy right now."

"I realize, with the trial coming up," Sara agreed, "but surely he can spare just a few minutes for the press."

"As a matter of fact," the secretary said, her smile now bubbling with excited pride, "Mr. Delray's meeting right at this moment with a reporter from *The Economist.* That's an English magazine, you know."

"I know," Sara said. It surprised her that *The Economist* would be here in Taney County this soon. What would be their angle on a story like this? "I could wait," she offered.

"You could, I suppose," the secretary said, sounding doubtful. "With jury selection tomorrow, you know, there are many demands on Mr. Delray's time."

"I'm sure there are."

"It all depends, I suppose, how long the other gentleman is in there."

How long could *The Economist* legman talk to a rural Missouri prosecutor? "I'll wait," Sara decided, and sat in the only available chair.

"Up to you," the secretary said. She showed Sara one last smile, then turned back to her typing, of which she had an unending supply.

Sara waited. She waited for thirty-five minutes, with increasing impatience and disbelief, and then at last the inner door opened and out walked Louis B. Urbiton.

Louis B. Urbiton! The oldest and drunkest of the Down Under Trio!

The Economist! Louis B. Urbiton of *The Economist*! Why, that snake in the grass! Waiting thirty-five minutes for Louis B. Urbiton and some *Weekly Galaxy* scheme! Steam curled from Sara's ears. Her split ends resplit.

Behind Louis came a hearty butterball in his mid-forties, a round-bodied, round-headed, well-packed man with a politician's smile and big open politician gestures and shiny beads of politician perspiration on his gleaming high forehead. "Nice to meet you, Mr. Fernit-Branca," he was saying to Louis, patting the horrid man on his horrid shoulder. "Dew drop in anytime."

"Than kew," Louis responded, with a dignified nod. He gave the secretary an equally dignified but somehow more chummy nod, then laid upon Sara a blank, bland stare and departed.

Blow his cover? Blow that pompous ass—*both* of these pompous asses—right out of the water? "How would you like to know, Mr. Prosecuting Attorney, that you just spent the last hour with a famously drunken *Australian*—not even English, Mr. Prosecuting Attorney, as anyone with the slightest sophistication would have realized at once—famously false reporter for the *Weekly Galaxy*?"

He wouldn't like to know it. It would be bad for Louis B., of course, but it would also be bad for Buford Delray's self-esteem, and *that* would be bad for the person who'd blown the whistle/cover/them out of the water. One of the first things every professional reporter learns is that killing the messenger is the rule in this life, not the exception.

So there was nothing to be done about Louis, at least not now and not directly. There would be nothing gained, unfortunately, were she to stand as tall as one can possibly stand in flats, point the forefinger admonitory, and cry out, "J'accuse!" No; to admit even *knowing* a *Weekly Galaxy* reporter would open a whole nother can of worms, wouldn't it? It would.

Meanwhile, as Sara was confirming her impotence to herself, the faithless Urbiton had departed and the gulled Delray was giving Sara a politician's appreciative leer, until the secretary said, "Buford, this is a lady from some New York magazine."

Talk about the kiss of death. Buford Delray's face closed up like a Parker House roll. The first name of all New Yorkers, as the whole world knows, is Smartass, as in, "Some Smartass New Yorker tried to put something over on me today, but us country boys ain't as dumb as they think." And meantime, an Australian from Florida was even now waltzing out of town with Buford Delray's jock.

Frantic beneath, calm on the surface, Sara said, "I'm from *Trend* magazine, Mr. Delray, and I—"

She'd been moving forward, intending just naturally to ease on by him into his office, but he rolled like a beach ball into her path, a cold little pursy smile on the front of his Parker House roll. "I'm sorry, Miss, but I—"

"Sara Joslyn," Sara said, and stuck her right hand out.

Which he did not take: "—have very little time for the press at this juncture, as I'm sure you can understand. Perhaps after the verdict."

He was rolling slowly backward into his office, hand on the doorknob. Sara pursued, trying to look as though she weren't in pursuit. "Sir," she said, desperation getting the best of her, "*The Economist* won't print anything about the case, certainly not in this country, but *Trend*—"

"I'm looking forward to the *series* of stories *The Economist* plans to run, Miss," Delray interrupted, with his smug smile. "And to *The Economist*'s photographer, as well. If you'll excuse me." And he shut his office door in Sara's face.

Louis was long gone, of course. Sara circled the courthouse like a cat girdling a chipmunk hole, but Louis B. Urbiton was nowhere to be found.

A *photographer*! That's what the scam was all about. If it were possible to put out a newspaper for the illiterate, the *Weekly Galaxy* would be it; nowhere on earth do pictures so literally take the place of thousands of words as in the supermarket tabloids, and none more so than in the *Galaxy*. While Louis B. Urbiton would spend the next week or so listening attentively, admiringly, even slavishly, at the feet of the dimwitted Delray, *Weekly Galaxy* photographers would be the *only* photographers permitted unlimited access to the courthouse (or court house), the murder scene, the witnesses, and anything else that struck their magpie interest, because,

of course, the main point in Buford Delray's tiny mind would
be the appearance of Buford Delray's words, not his fat face,
in the pages of one of the world's most distinguished news
journals.

I'm gonna get em, Sara promised herself as she marched
to her car for the angry ride back to Branson. I'm gonna nail
'em to the barn door, and Buford Delray *is* the barn door.

And that's a promise.

11

Jack Ingersoll stood on the sidewalk outside Sara's hotel and watched the families ooze by in their station wagons, campers, vans, pickup trucks. I'm going to get the *Weekly Galaxy*, he thought as he watched his onetime readers seep past. This time, I'm gonna get em.

Jack Ingersoll at thirty-three had already lived too many lives. A counterculture journalist to begin with, he'd gone straight from college to the *St. Louis Massacre,* an antiestablishment weekly newspaper fawningly modeled on New York City's *Village Voice.* Though it was great fun at first, the fact had eventually become clear, even to the dewiest-eyed among the Massacrees, that they were accomplishing nothing. They were preaching to the (very few) converted, and it didn't matter what wonderful exposés their industrious digging produced. Human beings know only what they want to know, and if they don't want to know the facts, the data, the *truth,* this wonderful truth you have just unearthed for them at great risk and with uncommon brilliance, they just won't listen. Won't listen.

Jack's contemporaries didn't sell out, exactly. They just

moved on to better-paying jobs (after all, they had families now) with more careful publications. Jack stayed longer, until in fact the *Massacre* was shot out from under him; that is, bought by a conglomerate that turned it into a youth-oriented music and movie paper. Before the *Massacre*'s massacre was complete, Jack underwent a sea change, a total conversion of all the atoms of his body and brain into their opposites. He didn't sell out a little; he sold out a *lot*. The biggest salary bucks in the world of journalism were to be collected at the *Weekly Galaxy* and its supermarket sisters, and that was because, of pride and prestige and self-esteem and the knowledge of a good job well done there was fuck-all at the *Galaxy*. They made up for the lack, quite handsomely, with money.

This second Jack was as skeptical and faithless as the first had been engagé. While his co-Galaxians squandered their lavish incomes as fast as the bucks rolled in, Jack spent as little as possible, hoarding it all away in expectation of the winter ahead. "Sooner or later," he would say in those days, "they fire everybody."

And it is true that they would have fired Jack as well, eventually, if it hadn't been for the arrival at the *Galaxy* of Sara Joslyn, girl reporter. Not cynical and burnt-out like himself, she was still fresh from journalism school, with just a touch of employment on an old-fashioned New England local paper to give her a false sense of professionalism.

There's something seductive about life at the *Galaxy*; it's *The Front Page* without redeeming social significance. Always nosing after a scoop, always a fire engine to chase. Sara had taken to it like a buzzard to entrails. Though Jack had been unable to drag himself out of his mire of unbelief, he had nevertheless staggered at last into action to save Sara. In the nick of time, they'd managed their escape from that particular Pleasure Island, before the donkey ears became too noticeable.

And now *Trend*: "The Magazine For The Way We Live This Instant." It's true the magazine devoted too much of its space and attention to listing the fourteen best real estate agents in Manhattan and the seven best shortcuts to the Hamptons, but in with the service slop for the trendoids and wannabes there was also good investigative journalism, of politics both local and national, of crime both financial and melodramatic, and of chicanery both public and private.

All of which made *Trend* the perfect place for a *Weekly Galaxy* exposé, if Jack—and Sara, bless her, wherever she was at the moment while Jack paced the sidewalk out here in front of the hotel—if the two of them could nail down the particulars. The new owners, the old scams. The old felonies: bribery, theft, false representation. Oh, get them.

Not get them for those people out there in the slower-than-molasses traffic. Those were the *Galaxy* readers, and they would not want to know the truth about their favorite reading matter, and therefore would not listen.

No, the better way to put it to the Galaxians was to make them figures of scorn and obloquy in the eyes of the movers and shakers of their own world, the communications business, combiz: press people, TV people, ad agency people, music biz people, all that vast ebb and flow of ideasmiths who among them create the zeitgeist, the view of reality in which we all swim. Most of them live at least some of the time in New York, and most of them read *Trend*.

A car came slashing along the verboten center lane, flashing its lights and blasting its horn at those tremulous souls who might be thinking of making a left turn in *any* direction. This car and this driver stood out like a panther among sheep; who could it be but the awaited Sara?

No one. The rental radiated so much menace that a camper full of kiddies actually *backed up* to let the bandit slice *rightward* back across its own lane of traffic and slew to a juddering halt at the Lodge. Already smiling, already knowing the identity of that driver, Jack crossed the sloping asphalt as Sara sprang from the car, slammed its door, spun around, and said, "What the hell are *you* doing here?"

Still driving. Jack grinned at her. "I love you, too."

"Fax it to me," she suggested, and started around him toward the building, then stopped, turned back, gave him a look of deep mistrust, and said, "You are *not* taking over this assignment."

"Of course not," Jack said.

"You are an editor; I am a reporter."

"Exactly."

Skepticism still darkened her features. She said, "So what are you here for?"

"Your body."

"Oh, that's all right, then," she said. "Come on."

As they walked toward the hotel, he said, "I couldn't get connecting rooms."

"That's okay," she said. "We'll connect."

In the afterglow, she said, "It was my fax, wasn't it?"

"Yeah," he admitted, and nuzzled her throat. "Your throat smells wonderful after sex," he murmured. "Has anyone ever told you that?"

She laughed, hugging him, twining their legs together, wrinkling and roiling the damp sheet even more. "Once an investigative reporter," she said, "always an investigative reporter."

Reluctantly, he removed his nose from the side of her neck and the butterfly of her pulse. Leaning up on one elbow, he said, "I wasn't going to ask *who*."

"Not this conversation," she agreed. "Next conversation."

With her hair messily around her smiling face, spreading over the pillow beneath her head, she was so beautiful, he couldn't stand it. "I don't want there to be anything in the universe," he said, "except you and me and this room, floating through space and time. Eternity, right here."

She gave him a look of amused disbelief. "What did they feed you on that plane?"

"Except," he went on, looking around the room, "one electrician, to put a dimmer on the lights."

"I think the phrase is 'to put the lights on a dimmer.' "

"I believe I'll shower now," Jack said, crawling backward off her and off the bed.

"Some editor," she commented, and pulled up the top sheet. Curling shrimplike beneath it, she said, "Wake me when you're done."

"Maybe."

They sat in the little chairs by the small table under the hanging lamp in front of the view of Mickey Gilley's parking lot, and Sara said, "Okay, the approach was wrong."

"Agreed," Jack said.

"I shouldn't have just sent that one page of fax."

Jack cocked an eyebrow at her. "*That's* what was wrong with the approach?"

"Now listen," she said. "I'm not turning my back on the *Galaxy*."

"Good. No one should ever turn his back on the *Galaxy*."

"I'm just saying," she just said, "there's something in this singer, too, what he represents."

"The proles," Jack told her. "The mouth-breathers. The underclass." He pointed. "Those people in those used cars out there."

"Don't be so condescending," she said.

"Why not? I'm smarter than they are, faster, funnier, richer and probably better-looking."

She reared back, the better to study him withal. "Are you being provocative?"

"That, too," he agreed. "I'm more provocative than they are. Sara, honeybun, our readers don't care—"

"I hate it when you call me honeybun."

"That's the first time I ever did."

"And I hated it."

Casually, he said, "Who else called you honeybun?"

She gave him a look. "All those guys that nuzzled my neck," she said.

"Oh, those guys."

"You were saying something about our readers."

"I was. I was saying they don't care about the shitkickers, is what I was saying. Our readers care about wealth and prestige. They care about power and fame. They care about success and excess. Bottom-feeders are not a matter of deep interest to the readers of *Trend*. That is why I am going from here to the *center* of journalistic misuse of money and power, the *Galaxy* hospitality suite."

"Two-two-two."

"And very very."

"Will you do me a favor?" she asked.

"Anything."

"After the *Galaxy*, go to the show. The Ray Jones show."

"Oh, for Christ's sake, honeybun—"

"That's twice."

Heavily, he shrugged and nodded his acceptance of the inevitable. "All right," he said, "all right, all right, I'll go—"

The phone rang.

"—see the Ray Jones show," he finished, as Sara got up and went over to the bedside phone. "And *you* concentrate on the *Galaxy*."

"Sure. Hello? Oh, hi, Cal." Sara listened, then smiled all over her face. "That's great! Cal, I really appreciate this. I'll be there. Absolutely. Oh, Cal? Listen, my editor's in town . . . from the magazine? Could you put him in the Elvis seat tonight? Thanks, Cal. I'll tell him. His name is Jack Ingersoll. Right. See you tomorrow, nine A.M. Bye."

Sara hung up and smiled at Jack. "You are looking at a genius," she announced.

"The Elvis seat?"

"Don't worry about it. You just present yourself at the Ray Jones Theater a little before eight tonight. Go to the guy at the door and tell him who you are. He'll explain all about the Elvis seat. The thing is," she went on, "Ray Jones sells out, every show, over eight hundred seats. And there're no house comp seats."

"I'm looking forward to this," Jack said insincerely. "What was he calling about? Cal, was it?"

"He wanted to tell me how my neck smelled after sex."

"Sara, you are beginning to annoy."

"I don't really care," she told him, flashing her sunniest smile. "His name is Cal Denny; he's rather sweet—"

"Unlike some."

"He's Ray Jones's best friend, and they're all going over

to Forsyth tomorrow for jury selection. Ray Jones and his whole band and Cal Denny and everybody, showing solidarity."

"And?"

"And I," Sara said, "have been invited along." She pirouetted in front of him, arms and hands at a graceful angle. "Just call me supergroupie," she suggested. "I'm going on the team bus."

12

Ray wasn't giving any interviews these days because of the upcoming trial, but back before this latest truckload of wet manure had hit the fan, he used to give interviews all the time. The entertainment press, which lives on a modification of the Will Rogers motto—they never met a star they didn't like—is *access*. Access to the public eye, the public ear, and the public brain, if there is such a thing. Access was vital, was the lifeblood of the star's career, because, as Ray well knew—as every headliner well knew—the public brain, if there is such a thing, has an extremely short attention span. They'll forget you in a New York minute if you give them the chance. So the stars and the wannabes and the usedtabeens all crowd the entertainment media, the magazines and the TV shows and even (if nothing else is happening) the radio. They all smile and look relaxed and easy, they meet the interviewer's eye with a confident and friendly gaze, and they blandly ignore the interviewer while they talk right through him or her and directly into the public brain, if there is such a thing.

After a while, every headliner develops a patter, a routine, a whole arsenal of set paragraphs and stock answers to all those expected, unoriginal, unthreatening questions. Press *this* button, *that* answer pops out. Here's what you got when you pressed Ray Jones's various autobiographical buttons:

"Well, I was born a bunch of years ago in a little town in Georgia you've never heard of, Lynn—I can pretty well guarantee you that. Oh, try you? [Chuckle] Sure, Lynn. It's called Troutman, not that far from Hazlehurst, on the road toward Albany. Oh, it's a *little* town, Lynn, a bump in the road. I believe a travelin' preacher got a flat tire there once and that's how the place got started. No, I mean it. By the time the poor man raised enough money for a new tire, he had a congregation. They were as dirt-poor as he was, of course, as I was, as we all were.

"I grew up there in Troutman, fishin', goin' to school when I remembered, runnin' with my pals. My daddy worked for the electric company, when there was work to do—outside, stringin' lines mostly. Anytime a big storm come up from the Gulf, there'd be Daddy, puttin' on those big boots and that yellow slicker and yellow rain hat, in the pickup, on the way to the trouble. When I was just a little one, I wished I could go along with him, nights like that, and I thought that's what I'd do when I grew up. If it hadn't been for the music, I suppose that's where I'd be right now, up some power-company pole in south-central Georgia, whistlin' along with the birds.

"The music? Well, Lynn, this may sound weird, but it's the Lord's honest truth. I first started to sing on hayrides, 'cause I was afraid of girls. No, that's true, Lynn, in those growin'-up years, I was truly afraid of girls. [Chuckle] I don't suppose I ever entirely got over it.

"But that was the singin' side. On the musical *instrument* side, that came earlier. I was introduced to the guitar when I was, I dunno, six or seven, over to school. Nobody in my family was musical, unless you count beatin' time along with the jukebox on the bar, but when I started goin' to school, there was this guitar. We were in a real poor school district, and that guitar was the entire music department, some beat-up old box hadn't been in tune since the rebs come home. Well, I fell on it; I took to it; I wrestled with that guitar from when it was bigger than I was. I figured out how to tune it, too, and that's how I found out I had this natural ear. By the time I finished grammar school, I was pretty good at that old guitar. Didn't know anything *else*, but I sure did know the guitar.

"And you know, Lynn, I was so grateful to that school for lettin' me at that musical instrument and for givin' me time to learn it and get to know it that I was really proud, some years back, to be able to repay those people just a little bit. I give them some musical instruments, a piano and such, and some money to help keep them up. So maybe some other little fella like me, dirt-poor and ignorant, might go in there the first day of school and find out music is *his* life, too. I purely wouldn't have wanted to miss it, Lynn. Music has been very good to me.

"I admit I dropped out of high school, which I *don't* recommend to any kids out there that might see this, but my excuse is, I didn't do it until I had a place to go. Me and my best friend, Cal Denny, and I'm proud to say he's still my best friend to this day, we put together a tape—you know, the old reel-to-reel tape; I'm talkin' years ago here—we put together a tape of me on guitar and Cal on drums, except we didn't have drums, just had Cal with some sticks, hittin' everything in sight, and the two of us singin', and we did our own versions of Eddy Arnold songs and Hank Williams songs and sent the tape off to a record company in Florida, and they wrote us and said if we'd come down sometime they'd audition us, no promises. So we quit school right then and there, the both of us, and hitchhiked on down to Tallahassee, and that was how it all got started.

"Of course, I still got kin in and around Troutman, and I get back there as often as I can, which isn't often enough, but when I can. Because, you know, Lynn, the one thing for sure for all of us in this business, in this show business, is, you got to remember where you come from. You got to remember who you are, or you'll go nuts. You got to keep in touch with your roots."

A lot of that bushwah was true, more or less, but it wasn't anywhere near what you could call the *whole* truth. What it left out, mostly, was Ray Jones himself and how he learned to deal with the world.

Ray started as the runt of the litter, fourth of nine kids, not late enough to be the baby, not cute enough to be the pet, not big enough or strong enough to fight his own battles. A scrawny, undernourished little weed, he learned early on that his choice in life was a simple one: Be smart or be tromped. He was *never* going to get what he wanted just by reaching for it, like the big guys, so he had to find some other way to satisfy himself. Or else stop wanting things.

Never. Born hungry, Ray was hungry his entire life, but he'd never let the hunger show. He was hungry for food, for love, for success, for ease, for safety, for money, for women. He was born hungry for *everything*. Fortunately, he'd also been born smart.

Indirection. Guile. Use your brains. Use the other guy's strength. Get what you want without anybody noticing you wanted it, or they'll take it away from you.

He perfected his survival techniques in that grammar school with the famous old guitar, which really did exist, in a janitor's closet, though nobody connected with the school gave a damn about it or him or ever encouraged him toward music or any other damn thing except to show up every day and keep his mouth shut unless asked a direct question. He'd borrow that guitar when nobody was looking, practice where nobody could hear, and slip it back when nobody was around. He was his *own* encouragement.

The main thing Ray learned in school was how to use his brains as an asset rather than a liability. If he did homework for the big dumb guys, they'd be on his side in case of trouble. At the same time, his own homework was sloppy and uncaring, and usually got a lower mark than the same assignment he'd done for somebody else. That way, he never got a reputation as a *brain*, which in a poor hick school is the worst thing that can happen. Only the big dumb guys he was helping could have known he was actually sharp as a winter wind; but the whole point about them was that they couldn't put two and two together, wasn't it?

Later, in the consolidated central high school, there was always somebody else he could convince to lead the way, whenever there was a chance somebody might get burnt. Most people like to lead, or to think they're leading, and Ray was happy to encourage this leadership belief in those he was putting into danger. Sometimes it was Cal Denny who opened the door or stole the bottle or whatever it might be, but usually somebody else; from early on, Ray had a warm spot for Cal, who was big and dumb without being mean, and so Ray wouldn't use him as a foil or a battering ram unless there just wasn't anybody else available.

Ray's leaving school and hitching to Florida in search of a music career did have some truth in it, though not much. He and Cal actually did make the tape he talked about, on a tape recorder Cal had stolen—while Ray stood watch from a safe distance—from the high school music department, a section of the school devoted exclusively to the marching band. (Ray wasn't a member of the marching band, they having no use for a guitar and he having no use for them.)

But music wasn't the main reason Ray left town all of a sudden in the middle of his sixteenth year, dragging Cal along for protection. The main reason was a girl, the first great love of his life. He doesn't mention her now, partly because it ended badly but also because he can no longer remember her name; not that he tries hard.

This girl had a regular boyfriend, one of the few rich kids in town, son of the drugstore owner. It was he who took her to the movies, bought her sodas, necked with her in his father's car. But it was Ray who got her pregnant.

Whoops. It wouldn't have happened if she hadn't lied to him, another lesson he carried with him from his high school years. She'd lied because she wanted to get away from her home, and the only way she could think of to do that was get married. She wanted to marry Ray because she thought he'd be more fun than the drugstore boy, so she lied, and then she pretended she was surprised and scared and helpless.

At that time, Ray'd had the letter from the record company for about four months but hadn't done anything about it because he found their manner tepid, not even offering him bus fare for the audition. But now he pulled out this letter, showed it to the girl while holding his thumb over the date, and said, "I'm not gonna marry you. See this letter? These music people want me. I'm goin' to Florida and I'm not comin' back. My advice is, get into the backseat of that drugstore car and get yourself knocked up all over again."

Which is what she did, being smarter than he'd thought. And that's why Ray went off to Florida to find the life that was waiting for him, originally as a sideman on extremely minor-league session dates, playing other people's music in other people's groups, but learning, every single day.

The following year—they were in Nashville by then— somebody told Cal the baby'd been born, so Ray's got a kid out there someplace, grown up now—boy or girl, he never did ask. Be funny if the kid was in the audience some night, neither of them knowing. A song in that? Nah.

Actually, the birth of the baby had led to Ray's first set of original lyrics. Some impulse had driven him to buy one of those comic Nashville postcards and send it to the girl c/o the drugstore, writing on it: "I'll remember you, always, and think of you real often with a smile. I hope you'll be forever happy and learn to live without me after a while."

13

Binx Radwell sat hunched on the folding chair in the rental house, elbows on the folding rental table, frightened eyes blinking at the maps taped and stapled and nailed to the paneled wall, and tried to ignore the cold sweat pouring from his body like condensation on a porcelain toilet, tried to ignore the volcanolike rumblings in his intestine, and listened to the words buzzing up along the phone lines from *Galaxy* headquarters in Florida. This was the voice of one of Binx's many lords and masters, new lords and masters since the change of ownership of the newspaper had bared Binx's vulnerable flesh to colder winds than even he had heretofore known possible.

It was at field headquarters that Binx was undergoing this latest episode in the perpetual slow flaying that was the story of his life. Whenever the *Weekly Galaxy* went out into the world on a major story—celebrity scandal, child in well, celebrity death, religious fruitcake sex *or* religious fruitcake violence scandal—the first thing it did was rent a house in the local area, rent a lot of office furniture and office machinery to fill that house, bung in a bunch of phone lines, staff the place with reporters and photographers and editors from the main headquarters down in Florida, plus whatever local stringers they might have available, and start boppin. In long-con terms—and the *Weekly Galaxy* is nothing if it's not a long con—this is the store, and its purpose is the same as it was for Yellow Kid Weil and the other long-con experts of yore: to pretend to be what it isn't.

For instance: Let us say you are Cherry Chisolm of the *Weekly Galaxy* and you wish to interview Ray Jones's ex-wife, who is being paid handsomely by Ray Jones to keep her flappin' trap shut. If you call Ray Jones' ex-wife—also named Cherry, interestingly—and say, "Hi, I'm Cherry Chisolm of the *Weekly Galaxy* and I'd—" that's as far as you'll get before she hangs up. But if you call and say, "Good afternoon, I am Laura Carrington, calling on behalf of the Countess Sylvia Bonofrio. *Mademoiselle* has asked the countess if she will chat with you for publication. Now, as you know, Countess Sylvia rarely gives interviews *herself*, but feeling the empathy toward you that she does, and I'm sure you remember the absolute *hell* the countess went through seven years ago when Alfredo—Well, I'm sure she'd rather I didn't go over all *that* again." And so on.

At some point in this flapdoodle, the ex-wife will ask to call back, won't she? She listened this long, but she's doubtful; she wants to talk it over with her lawyer and her boyfriend and her best girlfriend, so she'll ask if she can call back. Now, you don't want to give her a hotel telephone number, do you? You don't want your calls to go through a hotel operator who might very well have already been suborned by some other scurrilous paper, do you? You don't want a hotel maid to wander into the room during the *next* call, do you, while you're talking with an Italian accent and *being* Countess Sylvia?

Of course not. If you wish to use a phone, if you wish to set up a darkroom (in the bathroom), if you wish to interview a witness, a relative, a venal police officer, if you want a private conversation with anybody at all in which both information and money may change hands, you don't want that happening in a hotel, do you? Or anywhere out in the world, right? What you want is your own house. Every time there occurs in the world what the *Galaxy* thinks of as a major story, therefore, the *Galaxy* begins by renting a house.

This particular story's house, at 1023 Cherokee, was in the old original part of Branson, the part that existed when the only strangers who'd ever heard of the place were bass fishermen. (Of course, once the Army Corps of Engineers put in those flood-control and hydroelectric dams, converting the flood-prone White River into a lot of weird-shaped lakes, there wasn't any bass fishing anymore because of the severe temperature change of the water, but not to worry. They put in the fish hatchery, near which Belle Hardwick would eventually expire, and stocked their fake lakes with trout. From a real river with real bass to imitation lakes with interjected trout, the fishing equivalent of a carnival game. But, hey, fish are fish, right?)

Anyway, 1023 Cherokee was owned by a nice widow lady who lived mostly in a nearby nursing home these days. Her house was so thoroughly low-maintenance, it, too, could have been put together by the Army Corps of Engineers; beige paneled walls, beige wall-to-wall carpeting, Formica and Scotchgarded beige furniture. (All the furniture was now out in the carport, under tarps.)

It was in this place, surrounded by photographers caring for their equipment as endlessly and lovingly as any infantryman cares for his rifle, plus reporters on the phone, reporters on the manual portable typewriters given out by the *Galaxy* to any of its staffers forced to face the rigors of the road, reporters studying the road maps and topographical maps and real estate maps and all the other maps defacing the nice widow's walls, reporters sleeping on the floor under tables, reporters arguing with other reporters, photographers taking photos of minia- tures set up on shaky tables, which just *might* be made with extensive retouching to look like aerial photos of Ray Jones's house out at Porte Regal, or the murder scene, or photos of the courtroom or Ray Jones himself behind some sort of bars, it was in this restful setting that Binx Radwell, editor, boss of this madhouse, sat and listened to the voice from Florida.

The owner of this particular voice, this nasty voice like a cross between a moped and a dentist's drill, was a demidemon named Scarpnafe. He was not an editor, not a fact checker, not an evaluator, nor any of the other normal horrors of the editorial department; he was some sort of "manager," possibly an "assistant flow manager," or a "deputy product manager." This was an added layer of harassment, inserted by the new ownership, who had sent to the *Galaxy* building from their corporate headquarters down in Homestead a number of their minor devils to form a new level of control. These days, every employee of the *Galaxy* had one of these demidemons perched on his or her shoulder, second-guessing, haranguing, nitpick- ing, prodding, never satisfied. Narrow pasty people, young and skinny, in dark blue suits and narrow ties, with the pinched faces of creatures taken off the breast too early. *Way* too early.

This one, Scarpnafe, had just called to say do more, get on with it, faster, deliver or die. "Thursday," said this rasp of doom, "we go to press."

This had been true for many, many years, going back much longer than Binx's employment, since the paper came out

every Friday to catch the weekend shopper, but Binx perforce
had to receive the fact as though it were a startling and
inspiring piece of fresh news. "Ah, right!" he cried, and turned
his head aside from the phone to burp, a bad-tasting burp.

The voice in his ear whined on: "Jury selection is tomorrow,
in the trial."

Oh, that jury selection. "That's right. That's right," Binx
agreed, nodding spastically as sweat droplets sprayed from
his head.

"Tomorrow is Wednesday."

"Yes, it is! It is!"

"We will want those jurors."

"Yes, of course," Binx agreed, having no idea what
Scarpnafe meant. *Want* those jurors? Scarpnafe made it sound
as though he wanted those jurors lightly sautéed on a bed of
lettuce, but that couldn't be right, could it? Oh God, what
now?

"Their names," Scarpnafe explained.

"Naturally." Binx sighed, afraid to feel relief—not yet.

"Bios."

"Absolutely."

"Interviews."

The volcano sent a little lava into Binx's throat, just a little.
"Interviews? But, but—"

"Not afterward," Scarpnafe elaborated. "Now, before deliberation."

"The thing is, uh, the only thing is, little, uh, thing. Is,"
Binx said, swallowing like mad, rubbing his belly with his
free hand as though to soothe a dangerous cat, "the thing is,
the jury's going to be, uh, sequestered."

"Sequest?"

"Ered."

"What's that?"

"Well, uh, locked up. It's a death-penalty thing they do, serious cases; they put the jury in motel rooms, lock them up; they can't read the papers, watch television—"

"This is America!" Scarpnafe cried, outraged.

"Well, uh," Binx explained, hating to be the bearer of such tidings, "apparently that's the way they do it . . . in America."

"Bribe a relative," Scarpnafe ordered, rolling very well with the punch.

"They don't get to talk to their relatives," Binx said. "Not without a bailiff there."

"What are they, in prison?"

"Just about."

"Bug the motel!"

"Uh," Binx said as rivers of sweat foamed and whitecapped the rapids of his body. He could think of nothing else to say. He sat there, the phone at his damp ear, mouth open like a gargoyle on a French cathedral.

"Well? What's the problem?"

Binx knew the answer to that one. "Nothing!" he cried brightly, and then inspiration—or perhaps desperation—struck. "Just as soon as you fax me the order, sir, I'll put my team on it."

"Fax?" The nasty voice was suddenly wary. "What do you mean fax?"

"Oh, don't you have our fax number? It's four-one—"

"I know the fax number! Wait a minute, Radwell. Are you saying you want this order in writing?"

"Yes, sir."

"With my signature, I suppose."

"Yes, sir."

"In other words," Scarpnafe said, "you think this particular use of journalistic technique might go one small step further than First Amendment protection would cover, is that it?"

"Well, sir, Mr. Scarpnafe, uh, you know, the courts, the judicial system, they get a little antsy if they think you don't take them seriously."

"Radwell," Scarpnafe said, on solid ground again, "how many judges and prosecutors do you suppose read the *Weekly Galaxy* on a regular basis?"

"Outside Florida, sir? Probably not very many."

"We take our *readers* seriously, Radwell. No one else in the world. Do you understand that?"

Of course he did. It was what made life at the *Galaxy* so challenging. "But, sir, Mr. Scarpnafe, uh, state courts, you know. It isn't like some movie star gets mad at us, sues for a couple years, gets tired. State government, uh, outside Florida, they could probably do more to us than we could do to them."

"Hmmmmm," Scarpnafe said. As with any satrap, he found it discomfiting to be reminded of the limits of his power.

Grasping the moment, lowering his voice in an attempt to sound both supportive and self-assured—two lies in one inflection—Binx said, "Mr. Scarpnafe, sir, I have some experience with situations of this sort. My team and me." (Might as well spread the responsibility in case something went wrong.) "We'll get you great stuff, guaranteed, everything within the range of possibility. More than anybody else on any other paper, I can promise you that."

"What *about* the other papers, Radwell?" Scarpnafe demanded, leaping away from that uncomfortable area where he had no control. "And magazines. And television people, too. MTV, isn't that what they call it?"

"One of it, yes, sir." Now here was something to feel pleased about, proud of. Permitting just a trace of self-satisfaction to creep into his usual obsequious manner, Binx said, "We have many of them in our charge already, sir. Unless the *Christian Science Monitor* shows up, I think we'll have the media pretty much under control. That's print and broadcast both, sir."

"Good."

End with the devil saying *good*; segue out of this. "And speaking of that, sir," Binx quickly said, "I probably should go back over there now, make an appearance, keep them all happy."

"Remember what I said, Radwell."

Had to get that in there, didn't you? "Oh, I will, sir," Binx said. "It's engraved on my . . . brain." (He was going to say *heart* but decided to be less accurate.) "Well, I'm off to the open house."

Well, yes; but if he didn't want to empty that suite over at the Palace, he should shower first. So he did.

The shower was good; the vodka and Sprite was better. Binx bopped around the party, cheery and eager, too cheery and overeager, sweating again already but not even caring anymore, greeting old friends and new, dismayed at how many of these goddamn friends were new and just how horribly new they were, not letting it get him down, managing to touch this female rump, that female waist, the curve of some other female breast, most of them younger than they used to be. You know, your young firm female flesh is very nice, but this is ridiculous. Here are these girls, six feet tall, weighing less than a hundred pounds, encased in leather and rubber, and perched on top of each is the face of a twelve-year-old. Granted, a twelve-year-old on uppers, but still.

Jack Ingersoll, over there, across the room. *There's* an old friend, goddamn his eyes, Jack Ingersoll, compact, clean, self-contained, like a lumberjack on his day off, moving through the party like a census taker.

We used to work together, Binx reminded himself, squinting across the crowded room at this recent arrival, this guy clutching a bottle of beer and moving slowly, inexorably through the room, dropping a word here, a word there, counting the house, clearly counting the house.

He's doing what *I've* been trying to do, Binx thought. He paused in gnashing his teeth to knock back a little more vodka and Sprite. He's doing what I've been trying to do, and he's so much *better* at it.

There was a complicated hate-hate relationship between Binx Radwell and Jack Ingersoll, at least from Binx to Jack, dating from when Jack was also a *Weekly Galaxy* editor. In fact, once Binx had clawed his way back up to his own second posting as editor, he'd inherited Jack's team—the Down Under Trio and Mary Kate Scudder and Chauncey Chapperrel and the rest. All except the ones who'd left—Sara Joslyn and Jack himself, gone off to a happy life of nonmarital sex and legitimate journalism up in New York; and, of course, Ida Gavin.

Jack Ingersoll was everything Binx wanted to be; Binx admired Jack with a hopeless, helpless infatuation. Jack was self-assured, straightforward, stoic, and single, everything Binx was not. What could Binx do, poor man, but clothe that envy and admiration in the thickest, heaviest cloak of hatred and then overcoat the whole package with a fawning smile of false camaraderie? Nothing; so that's what he did.

But not just yet. First, another vodka and Sprite. Standing on line at the handiest bar, Binx brooded on the meaning of Jack's presence here. *Trend* had sent Sara down to cover the

Ray Jones trial. *Trend* was not topical in the way the *Galaxy* was and would not actually cover the trial until it was all over. So why would Sara's editor follow her? And why, knowing the *Galaxy* as well as Jack Ingersoll did, would Sara's editor, having for no comprehensible reason followed her to Branson, Missouri, then come *here*?

I must be clever, Binx told himself hopelessly, as he ordered his fresh drink. I must be cleverer than Jack and find out what he's up to. Because, damn his eyes, he's up to *something*. And Binx, with the instinct of the field mouse when the shadow of the hawk passes by, knew without question that whatever Jack was up to, it bode no good for Binx Radwell. No good at all.

Slinking forward like a minor footpad in Dickens, Binx actually washed his hands together as he at last stood in front of Jack Ingersoll, amid the milling throng; or, that is, the free hand washed the hand holding the vodka and Sprite. "Jack! Long time no see!"

"Well, Binx," Jack said, saluting with his beer bottle, "*you* look like shit. Sara tells me you're an editor again."

"You can't keep a bad man down," Binx suggested.

"Very true." Looking around, Jack said, "Do I see some of my former unindicted coconspirators here?"

"It's mostly your team," Binx said, feeling proud and humble and furious at the humility and embarrassed by the pride and defensive over all. "The Aussies and Don Grove and everybody."

"Gee, Binx, it sure brings it all back," Jack told him. "And I don't miss it for a second."

"Oh sure you do. The fun, the camaraderie, the thrill of the chase."

"The terror, the pressure, the Valium, the heart attacks, the failures. And now I understand you have an even more vicious management than before."

"Oh shoot," Binx said, "if you want to talk *reality*." Then he cleared his throat. He liked it so much, he did it twice more. Then he said, "Uhhhhhhhhh, *how* come, uh, how *come*, uh, how, uh, come, you're *here*? Here."

Grinning, Jack took a folded sheet of fax paper from an inner pocket and extended it, saying, "Don't tell Sara I showed you this."

Binx had no idea what this paper was going to be. He hated unexpected things, and so many things in life came under that category. With vague memories of nightclub hypnotists who put people under merely by handing them a card to read, Binx opened the slimy curly fax paper and, with increasing astonishment, read Sara's projected lead. "Good golly, Miss Molly," he said.

"That," Jack said, "was after Sara experienced the Ray Jones show at the Ray Jones Theater once, in person."

"There must be something in the water," Binx suggested.

"I'll be finding out," Jack said. "I promised to go there tonight myself. They're saving me the Elvis seat."

Assuming that to be some sort of joke he wasn't catching—so much of life, it seemed to Binx, was a joke he wasn't catching—Binx said a neutral "Uh huh" and returned the fax to Jack, who returned it to his pocket. "So that's why you skyed M-O-ward."

"Well, also," Jack said, "Sara *is* my girlfriend. I like to see her from time to time."

So would I, Binx thought, and many images crossed the mildew-stained movie screen of his mind. His wife, Marcie, appeared in one of the images, and he dispatched her with a bazooka. "You know, Jack," he said, musingly, thoughtfully, maturely, "I've been thinking for some time about making some changes in my life. Get out of Florida, maybe move on to—"

"Full up," Jack said.

"Oh, I wasn't thinking about *Trend* in particular," Binx lied, "just any opening you might know of up in the Apple that—"

"Nobody there calls it the Apple," Jack said.

"Big Apple?"

"No."

"New York, New York?"

"Only when drunk."

"Well, what *do* you call it?"

"The city."

Binx said, "How do you know which one you're talking about?"

"What other one is there?"

"You used to be more down-to-earth, Jack," Binx reproached him, and was interrupted by Bob Sangster, the most working-class looking of the Down Under Trio, whose manner was so laconic that passing doctors sometimes took his pulse just to be sure. "Say," he said. Actually, being Australian, he said, "Sigh."

"*Hel*-lo, Bob," Binx said, as though heartily.

"Right," Bob said obscurely. "Ever heard of a shadow jury?"

"It has dogged my footsteps," Binx said, "my entire life. You remember Jack Ingersoll, your former lord and master."

"Oh, right," Bob said, giving Jack the double O. "You went away to America or somewhere, didn't you?"

"No, the city," Jack said.

"Ah, New York, New York," said Bob, who in fact *was*

drunk. Turning back to Binx, he said, "About this shadow jury, the way it seems, what they do——"

"Uh, Bob," Binx said. "Jack isn't with us anymore."

Smiling comfortably, Jack said, "I'm the enemy now."

Binx said to Bob, "So we'll talk later, won't we?"

"What do I know?" Bob asked. "I'm a simple Aussie." And he wandered away, into the milling, drinking, thronging scrum.

Looking after him, smiling faintly, Jack said, "You know, the Down Under Trio I almost *do* miss."

"You were right, though, to make your move when you did." Binx licked his lips. "I've been thinking——"

Jack shook his head. "Binx," he said, "we've always leveled with one another."

Alarmed, Binx said, "We have?"

"When necessary."

"Oh. Okay."

"So I'm going to level with you now," Jack threatened.

"Jesus, Jack, I really wish you wouldn't."

"It's for your own good," Jack assured him, making things worse. Then he said it: "Marcie is your wife. The *Galaxy* is your job. You're never gonna get away from either. Once you accept that, you'll be happy."

"Oh, Jack," Binx said, also leveling with his old palsy-walsy, if that's what we're doing now, leveling now, "no, I won't, Jack. No. I won't."

14

The song that got to Jack Ingersoll, perched on the Elvis seat for the 8:00 P.M. show in the Ray Jones Country Theater, was called "New York Sure Is a Great Big City," and it went something like this:

New York sure is a great big city,
Blow it up, blow it up;
Los Angeles is kinda pretty,
Blow it up, blow it up.

Oh, I don't go to Washington, D.C.,
Those marble halls are not the place for me;
They tell me San Francisco's kinda gay,
I'm telling you that I will stay away.

Chicago is a toddlin town,
Knock it down, knock it down;
And Boston has got great renown,
Knock it down, knock it down.

Oh, the country is the only place to be,
A silo's the tallest thing I want to see;
I'm a country boy, my heart is in the land,
I'm a country boy, I think this country's grand.

"I kind of took it personally," Jack told Sara afterward as they ate a late dinner—late for Branson—in the Copper Penny, one of the few joints in town that served stuff recognizable as food. Only a few local hipsters and musicians were scattered around the dimly lit place, so they had their corner booth and its neighborhood completely to themselves.

"It's that solidarity thing again, you see?" said Sara. "They set up a tribe; they define who's in and who's out."

"*I'm* out," Jack said.

"Sure you are. So am I. And they know it."

Slicing steak, Jack said, "Sara, so what? Where's the news in all this? Where's *our* news in all this?"

"Ray Jones," Sara said, "and his audience."

Jack glumly chewed, hating to have to be a teacher again, knowing it brought out the worst and the snottiest in him. Swallowing, knocking back a bit of the not bad red wine, he said, "Sara, do you really think there's a point to be made that the great unwashed are bad judges of character, that they've got a shitty record when it comes to picking their heroes? Elvis was a drugged-out porker with more sexual hang-ups than a nine hundred number. The televangelists are too despicable to describe, J. Edgar Hoover was a fag-bashing faggot, and Ronald Reagan was brain-dead—they operated him from a Japanese microchip implanted after the fake assassination attempt." Then he perked up, hearing his own words. "Say, that isn't bad," he admitted, and reached for pen and notepad.

Sara grinned at him. "I see. You can take the boy out of the *Galaxy*, but you can't take the *Galaxy* out of the boy." She watched him jot notes. "The microchip?"

"You bet."

"That isn't for *Trend*, Jack; that's even less for *Trend* than Ray Jones's fan club."

"Not for *Trend*," Jack agreed, putting pen and paper away. "For later, after *Trend* fires me."

Sara stared at him. "They're going to fire you?"

"Of course. They fire everybody, sooner or later."

"No, Jack," she said, "not your usual cynicism. Have you heard something, that you're gonna be fired?"

"I don't have to hear anything," Jack said. "What most people don't understand is, *all* jobs are temporary. You get fired, or the company folds, or the technology changes, or the customers move away, or there's an earthquake and they don't rebuild."

"So people who unpack are stupid, is that it?"

"I don't say that," Jack objected. "I don't even believe it. But I do believe I have the jump on them."

Sara shook her head. She hadn't finished her food, but she clearly wasn't eating any more. She sipped wine, sighed, frowned, and said, "Okay, I can see what's wrong with *you*, but what's wrong with *me*?"

"Nothing," he said, wanting to make nice. After all, they had to share a bed tonight.

But she wouldn't accept it. "There must be something," she said, "or I'd find some normal guy, some regular member of *my* tribe to hang out with. But here I am with the Cheshire cat. Why?"

"You want an answer?"

"Yes, please."

She seemed serious, so he was, too. Reaching across the table, taking the fork out of her hand and putting it on her plate, then taking her hand in his, he said, "Then I'll tell you. I'm sorry, but the diagnosis is not good. After a close look at the X rays and the test results, I'm afraid I have to tell you the reason you're staying with me is because you love me. Sorry."

"Hell," she said, squeezing his hand in hers. "I was afraid it might be something like that."

15

Ray approved of Cal's choice; the *Trend* girl was going to be exactly right.

The whole bunch of them were headed over to Forsyth together in the bus, Ray and his assistant Honey Franzen and his musical director Lennie Elmore and the musicians and Ray's manager Chuck Wagner and his regular lawyer Jolie Grubbe, who couldn't understand why he wanted a reporter aboard. "I need a sympathetic press," Ray explained as they were boarding the bus in front of his house out at Porte Regal, the bus already half full of his people, none of them— happily—seeming to be drunk yet, at seven-thirty in the morning.

Jolie Grubbe, a tough lawyer of forty-something, a great big fat woman with no softness to her at *all*, said, "Sympathetic press? Are you crazy?"

"Probably. Get aboard the bus, Jolie."

"There's no such thing as a sympathetic press, Ray, *you* know that."

"Bus."

"Okay, okay."

That big thick body heaved itsel
Ray following. Jolie thudded into the
the right and Ray sat beside her. Across
to his prearranged plan, Lennie Elmore occup
seat behind the driver, with Honey Franzen nex
rest of the guys were distributed in the seats be
taking up two-thirds of the bus's interior, with the rea
holding a john and a galley kitchen. (This, when they tou
was the band's bus. Ray would be in the other bus, with the
bedroom and the shower and the other kitchen and the closets
for costumes: his dressing room on wheels.)

Settled in her seat, recovered from the effort of climbing
up into the bus, Jolie took up the theme again: "*Trend* isn't
gonna give you sympathetic press, Ray," she said. "*Trend* is
a lot of smartass New Yorkers; they blow their noses on
shitkickers like you."

"I have my reasons, Jolie," Ray told her in the deadpan
tone of voice that meant it was time to change the subject.
He eyeballed her. "Okay?"

"Whatever you say," Jolie said, miffed. As though he gave
a shit.

Now they were all aboard except the girl reporter. The big
silver bus with RAY JONES ON THE ROAD in bright red letters
on its sides rolled slowly along the winding roads from Ray's
house through the golf course and the condos and the spread-
out ranch-style houses to the main gate of Porte Regal and
through, then pulled in at the parking lot of Jjeepers!, the
family restaurant just beyond the guard shack, where Cal
had arranged that the girl reporter—Ray couldn't seem to
remember her name—would meet them.

And there she was, bright-eyed and bushy-tailed, coming
out of the air-conditioned restaurant with her big brown leather

...t the heavy bus,
...o the parking lot.
...wanted somebody
...k as though she'd
...er cross the black-
...and the eagerness
...veneer, and knew

...pposed to, and was
...for the girl reporter
to climb aboar... ...nging lithely up the steps. "Thanks again."

"Oh, sure," Cal said, and gestured at Ray, saying, "This here's Ray Jones. Ray, this's Sara Joslyn, from that New York magazine."

"H'are ya," Ray said, and stuck his hand out, and hers was cool and dry and bony. They exchanged strong grips and she said, "I appreciate this, Mr. Jones. I know this is a tough time for you."

"Our seats are back here," Cal said, taking her arm, nipping that interview in the bud, and away they went.

That was the point, or part of it. Whatsername—Sara?— was to be permitted to hang around but not to get chummy. Not real *access*, not to the extent she would ever get the idea she was being set up, since in fact she was being set up. So, for today, she had just this minute been as close to Ray Jones as she was going to get.

The bus coughed and groaned and got itself rolling again, turning left onto 165 south, heading down toward Table Rock Dam to avoid all that traffic mess back up in Branson. Jolie wanted to spend their bus time talking about her latest dealings with Leon "The Prick" Caccatorro, the IRS guy; she was the one negotiating with the son of a bitch. The negotiations were necessary because, as it turned out, Ray had taken some wrong advice here and there, and he'd tuned out once or twice when he really should have been listening, and the way it wound up, all of a sudden he owed the feds so many millions of dollars, they could probably afford another senator or two if they got it all out of him.

Which, naturally, wasn't going to happen, mostly because he didn't *have* that kind of money. Maybe it had passed through his fingers at one time or another, but it was *gone*. So what was happening now was, like any other mob operation, the government was making itself Ray Jones's partner. From now on, any dollar he earned, some of it would to go to his agent and some to his manager and some to his lawyer and some to his ex-wife *and* some would go to the IRS. What was being negotiated now was just what percentage of his income was going to be the feds' blood money and how long this unwelcome partnership was going to last.

There was a certain amount of pressure on Ray to get these negotiations done and over with, because until they were behind him, he didn't know what he could afford or even whether or not it would be worthwhile to go on working. But there was also a certain amount of pressure on the IRS, which helped to even things out. The pressure on the IRS was caused by the well-known uncertainties of both life and fame. If Ray Jones were to die, or if the fans were to turn against him (it had happened to others), the government just might find itself reaching for a slice of pie in an empty pie tin; better for them to make their deal while he was still riding relatively high, make their projections from this year's earnings, not knowing what next year's earnings might be.

And now, as if all of that weren't complicated enough, they

had this damn murder trial to put up with. For all the IRS knew, they were negotiating with a guy who'd be sniffing the state's cyanide a year from now, which made Leon "The Prick" Caccatorro quite visibly nervous. Good.

The negotiations were stalled right now, mostly because of the murder trial, but that didn't keep Jolie from going over every nuance of every word said by every participant at every meeting. Ray himself was staying out of those meetings, so he supposed he should be grateful to Jolie for taking the heat and just giving him the bits and pieces of the thing later, but *Jesus*! No matter how vitally important this IRS case might be in his life, in truth it was goddamn boring to listen to, and whenever Ray got bored, he eventually got irritated as well, no matter how hard he tried to be good and mature and adult.

This time, he lasted about fifteen minutes, to and through Hollister, the village across Lake Taneycomo from Branson. "Enough, Jolie," he suddenly said, rising from his seat, stepping forward into the well next to the bus driver, grabbing the microphone from the built-in sound system under the big windshield. Out front, a Ride the Ducks amphibian vehicle full of tourists rolled along amid the campers and station wagons like something in a Road Runner cartoon. Ray gave it a look, waved back at the kids in the rear row of the open-topped amphibian, then turned to face the bus interior, thumbed on the mike, and said, "Everybody awake?"

Moans and groans.

"Good," Ray said. "Let's rehearse the new one."

More moans and groans. Ray leaned back, half-seated on the shelf under the windshield, while the troops unlimbered their instruments. He could see the girl reporter back there next to Cal—damn! lost her name again—all wide-eyed and eager. Sure, let's give her something to write home about.

Speaking into the mike, Ray called to the new reed man, Jerry, the guy who was taking Bob Golker's place: "Jerry, you know the IRS song?"

"I been studying it," Jerry called back. He was a skinny roundheaded guy with glasses, very cerebral; not as much fun as the drunken Bob Golker, but a better musician.

In the front row, next to Honey Franzen, Lennie Elmore leaned over to say, "He's got it, Ray; he's a quick study."

"Okay." Ray grinned at his people, in his world. "For the benefit of the reporter among us," he said, wishing he could remember the damn woman's name, "let me explain the background on this song. I've been having a little income-tax trouble lately—"

Jolie snorted.

"—and we're still talking it over with the government people. Now, sometimes I get my songs out of my own life, and this is one of them. We're not gonna do this song in public until we've cut our deal with the feds, so, little lady, you're getting a preview here."

She didn't like "little lady," he could see that. Well hell, maybe he was gonna have to write her name down somewhere. Meantime, screw her. "All set, boys?" he asked.

They were all set. This had to be an acoustic version, of course, with no bass and the drummer doing his part on the practice pad on his lap, but they could still all work at familiarizing themselves with the idea of the arrangement. Ray gave the beat, they did the intro, and in he came, sailing on top of the music, belting it to the bus as though the bus were Yankee Stadium:

I'm singin for the IRS.
I got myself in a real mess.

It's all my own fault, I guess;
Now I'm singing for the IRS.

I'm workin out here for the feds.
If I don't, I'll be tatters and shreds;
They own these great-lookin threads.
I'm bein' dressed for you by the feds.

If you think your money's yours, take my advice.
Before you spend a dime, sit down, think twice.
The revenooer's auditors, they ain't so nice;
Where we folks got a heart, they got a piece of ice.

I'm workin' for the government man.
I'm doin' the best that I can,
Goin along with his plan,
Workin' for the government man.

They went through the song three times, the second time
trying an idea of Lennie's, in which the girls came in and
sang counterpoint against him in the bridge, going:

He's singin in the rain.
Won't you let him explain?
He's lost all his money, so
He's broke again.

But Ray didn't like it. It didn't do anything for him, or the
song, or the emotion, or the relationship with the audience.
So the third time, they did it without the girls, and that was
better. Then Ray borrowed Peewee's guitar and walked down

the aisle to the girl reporter and said, "You don't want to hear the same damn song over and over."

"I'm enjoying it," she said, grinning at him. "I can see why you won't take it public until after you make your deal."

He laughed, having a good time with her. "This one's also autobiographical," he lied, and strummed the guitar and went into it:

It's time to write another love song;
This time, the song's for you.
It's hard to write another love song,
Unless that song is true.

The heart that goes into a love song,
That heart just must be real.
The words that go into that love song
Must tell you how I feel.

I've written songs about most everything.
I've written happy songs and blue;
I've written songs I want the world to sing,
But none of them were you.

It's time to write another love song,
An easy thing to do.
Every word I say will be my love song,
Because the song is you.

Finishing, he grinned at her, and she said, "Do you remember *her* name?"

"Ouch," he said. "You got me, damn it. Tell me, and I'll never forget it again."

"Sara."

"With or without the *H*?"

"Without."

"Lean and mean, huh, Sara?" With another good ole boy grin, Ray tapped his forehead. "I got you now," he said, "right here in the old computer."

"I like the IRS song," Sara Whatsit said. "And I liked the fried-food song, too."

"Maybe we'll share some fried food together sometime," Ray said, and bent to look past her out the window at the beginnings of Forsyth. "Looks like we're here," he announced. "Catch you later."

"You, too."

Feeling he'd done well enough for day one, Ray went back to his seat, returning Peewee's guitar along the way, and looked out the big windshield at the mob clustered around the courthouse, dead ahead. TV camera crews, cops, tourists, reporters, all kinds of people. He said, "I never knew old Belle had so many friends."

"You give them what they want," Jolie said, "they'll come out for it."

"I guess."

By prearrangement, a space had been held open for the bus, where Ray would have the shortest and quickest route across the clear space to the building. A brown-uniformed trooper waved them into this slot, with so many hand gestures and body movements, you'd think they were landing a 747. The bus bunked the curb at last, stopped, and the driver opened the door, letting in the roar of the crowd.

Standing, yawning, stretching, Ray said, "Showtime."

"Kill, tiger," Jolie suggested.

Ray was the first one off the bus. Cops were holding the

gawkers back, but their noise was terrific. Another uniformed trooper, this one older and with spaghetti on his hat to show he was of more importance around here, stepped forward, very formal, and said, "Raymond Vernon Jones?"

"I'll say yes to that," Ray told him, and started on by, but the trooper held up a hand to stop him, saying, "Raymond Vernon Jones, I have a warrant for your arrest. You have the right—"

"I already *been* arrested, pal," Ray told him. "We went through this part of the act a long time ago."

"This is a new warrant," the trooper said.

Jolie was out of the bus now and standing beside Ray like a tough blimp. She said, "What's it a warrant for, Officer?"

"Murder," said the trooper.

Ray wanted this shit *over* with. "You're on the wrong page, my friend," he said. "All this is done and over. We're here for the trial."

"I have a warrant for your arrest, Raymond Vernon Jones," the goddamn trooper said, refusing to be sidetracked, "for the murder of one Robert Wayne Golker. You have the right to remain silent . . ."

Ray did.

16

The worst possible situation for a reporter is to be at the back of the bus when the interesting event is happening at the front of the bus. "Excuse me, excuse me, excuse me," Sara mantra'd as she pushed her way down the aisle, making good use of elbows and knees and her heavy shoulder bag, caroming musicians and their instruments back into their seats along the way, single-mindedly plowing her furrow forward.

Still, by the time she got to the bus door, whatever had been happening was already over with and done. While tourists and journalists went nova with excitement all around the periphery, Ray Jones was being escorted in the middle of a swarm of brown-uniformed policemen toward the courthouse, and Ray Jones *was in handcuffs*.

Sara didn't want to leave the bus. To leave the bus would be to lose her advantage, her insiderness, to be dropped at once into that maelstrom of shouting, camera-waving former humans beyond the pale and below the salt. Standing on the bottom step, clutching to the vertical chrome rail as an earnest of her determination not to be cast into the outer sunshine, Sara looked around desperately for an explanation, an ally, *something*, and her eye fell on the fat woman who'd been seated beside Ray Jones on the trip and who now stood down there in sunlight just outside the bus. Who was she? Not his wife, though one never knew. A secretary, maybe, or his sister. Whoever she might be, at this moment she was standing with arms akimbo, fists pressed to where her waist would be if she had one, glaring all around herself like an enraged mother bear. Catching the woman's eye, Sara said, "What happened?"

"An outrage!" the woman declared. She had the kind of rich contralto that goes with such a barrel shape, plus the gravelly hoarseness of someone who's spent too much time shouting for more beer in smoke-filled rooms. "It's a public-relations outrage!" she tromboned on. "A cheap publicity stunt!"

Meantime, Ray Jones and his escort had squeezed themselves through the double doorway into the courthouse, and the mob had become a tidal wave, breaking against the front of the building. And the brassy blonde who'd been seated behind the driver now came pushing past Sara (who clutched harder to the chrome pipe), saying to the fat woman, "I'll get Warren." Having done her homework, Sara knew that Warren would be Warren Thurbridge, Ray Jones's attorney.

The fat woman eyed the mob. "If you can get through."

The blonde was lighting a cigarette, puffing on it madly without inhaling, then taking it out of her mouth to give a critical eye to the large burning red coal at its end. "I'll get through," she said, and hopped off the bus to wade into the crowd, branding those who were too sluggish in getting out of her way.

Sara watched, admiring the technique, filing it for future reference, and then Cal Denny appeared at her elbow, saying, "Jolie, what's goin' on there?"

Jolie was the fat woman. She said, "They arrested him. On the courthouse steps," which was more dramatic than accurate. "They came up and arrested him."

"What for?"

Jolie shook her big head. "The goddamnedest thing I ever heard," she said. "They say he killed Bob Golker."

A gasp, a quick intake of breath so harsh that it was almost like a death rattle, made Sara turn her head and study Cal Denny's profile, right next to her. He was ashen; his lined face looking like tracks on a snowy field, his eyes wide with astonishment and shock. "Bob's *dead*? That's . . ." He faltered, and swallowed noisily, Adam's apple bobbing. "That's *crazy!*"

"I know that, and so do you," Jolie said, and glared again at the courthouse. "And so do they, the bastards."

Cal became aware of Sara staring at him and gave her an anxious look and a scared smile. "A little more excitement than we thought," he said.

"I guess," Sara said, and risked a question: "Who's Bob Golker?"

"He went to California," Cal said. He seemed utterly bewildered. "He told everybody he got a studio job out there."

Jolie, her deep raspy voice full of warning, said, "Cal, we don't have to talk to the press just this minute." She looked at Sara, probably the first time their eyes had met directly, and Sara was astonished at how cold and intelligent the eyes were in that fat face. "The bus ride's over," she said.

I'm gonna get thrown out, Sara thought, scrambling for some way to stay inside, stay aboard. But who was this woman Jolie? What authority did she have? "I'm not with a newspaper," Sara said, talking fast. "I won't be printing anything until the trial's all over, and anyway, I agree with you, the way they handled this, it *was* an outrage, and maybe, from my perspective, I could—"

Cal said, "It's okay, Jolie. I talked with Ray about this lady; it's okay with him."

In the middle of Jolie's large round face, the large round nose wrinkled. "*What* Ray thinks he's doing, I'll never know," she said, and made shooing motions for Sara to back up into the bus. Cal went first, on up the aisle toward his seat, then Sara stepped backward but stayed near the front of the bus, and Jolie followed, grunting and wheezing as she laboriously pulled her cotton-bale body up the steps, clutching to the vertical chrome poles, which Sara half-expected to bend in the middle.

But they didn't, and Jolie, once successfully aboard, said to the driver, "Take us around to the law office."

"Yes, ma'am." He shut the door, and Sara said hesitantly, "Okay if I take Mr. Jones's seat?"

Jolie glowered at her, repelled. "God, you're pushy. A New York reporter, all right." She waggled her fat hand at the vacant window seat. "Get in, then." The bus jerked backward, almost knocking them both off their feet, and Jolie said, "And be quick."

Sara was quick, darting to the seat, Jolie turning and dropping into place next to her as the bus moved slowly backward, the courthouse receding beyond the big windshield, the driver looking in every direction at once in his efforts not to drive over any curious onlookers, of whom there seemed to be several million, including a few in front of the bus, walking forward as it backed up, staring in through the windshield at Sara and Jolie, some of them mouthing questions or statements, some of them jumping up and down to try to see deeper into the bus.

See *what* deeper in the bus? Putting these goofs out of her mind, Sara said, "I'm Sara Joslyn. I'm with *Trend*. I'm sorry, I'm not sure who you are."

Reluctantly, grudgingly, the fat woman said, "Jolie Grubbe. I'm Ray's attorney, not as though he pays any attention to me."

The bus having backed far enough away from the curb, the driver now tried to move it forward, blaring his horn at the people in front, who seemed to think this was television rather than life and that they could just stay in one spot and watch the world swirl around them without actually being dragged beneath the giant wheels of a great big bus. Through this cacophony, Sara said, "His attorney? I thought Warren Thurbridge was Mr. Jones's attorney."

Jolie gave her a sour look. "Are you calling him Mr. Jones so you won't seem like the impudent boorish pushy New Yorker you really are?"

"Yes," said Sara. "I thought his attorney was Warren Thurbridge."

"*And* single-minded." Jolie sneered slightly. "Warren is Ray's *trial* lawyer, the one who gets all the publicity and most of the money. I'm his attorney for everything else, including why we shouldn't have press on this bus."

"Are you handling his income-tax problem?"

Jolie reared back, as much as her poundage would permit. "I may throw you off the bus myself!"

Sara garbed herself in the attributes of offended innocence. "Ms. Grubbe," she said, "it's Ms. Grubbe, is it? Ms. Grubbe, he was *singing* about it on this very bus; it's hardly a *secret*."

The bus was now rolling down the block, trailed by only a few of the goofs, the majority still believing the main action would be at the courthouse. Jolie Grubbe said, "The *first* thing you're gonna do when we get to the office is sign a release."

Sara laughed. "Even before I turn water into wine?"

"You are not here as a friend," Jolie insisted. "You are here as a journalist, and everything you hear and see is privileged. It's *our* decision what and whether you can publish."

"You're speaking in the plural," Sara said. "Who besides Ray Jones makes the decisions?"

Looking very mulish, Jolie said, "Don't get tough with *me*, girl, that's my advice."

"I'm not your enemy," Sara said. "The people who decided to make a publicity stunt out of a second arrest, *they're* your enemy. Why would anybody think Mr. Jones would kill John Golker? He was a musician, was he?"

"His name was *Bob* Golker," Jolie said, which Sara had well known (get them into the habit of giving you information, that's the idea), "and there's no reason at all."

"He was a backup musician in the show?"

"And a drunk. And a skirt-chaser. And I didn't say any of that."

The bus stopped and Jolie struggled to her feet, giving Sara a grim smile. "You can't use anything," she said. "Not without *our* permission."

Nevertheless, Sara got off the bus with the group and walked among them into the former furniture store that was now Warren Thurbridge's headquarters and where a whole lot of people were noisily going *out* of their minds. As Sara stared around at everything, recording and remembering every detail, Jolie grabbed a handy clerk. "Where's Warren?"

"With the judge!" the clerk cried. "That's *all* we know!"

Jolie released the clerk, who scurried off like the white rabbit. Giving Sara her most sour look, Jolie said, "Now we'll see if Warren is worth all the money he gets."

17

"This is *so* prejudicial, Your Honor," Warren Thurbridge said, the strong vibrato of his rich voice barely under control, "I'm going to ask for a mistrial right now."

Judge Berenice Quigley looked both irritated and baffled. "Counselor, the trial hasn't *begun*. You can't have a mistrial before the trial."

"The police action this morning," Warren said, "has poisoned the entire jury pool."

Buford Delray snorted. "I would think, sir," he said, his fat-boy envy of Warren Thurbridge's accomplishments rising around him like heat waves, "I would think your own client's activities have done all the poisoning around here. Though poison does seem one of the few methods he does not favor." And Delray beamed fatuously upon his hanger-on, the British reporter, who beamed fatuously back.

They were in judge's chambers, all seated, though Warren managed to sit in such a fashion as to *look* as though he were pacing, probably waving his arms, even possibly pushing distracted fingers through his hair. Across from this kinetic Warren, Judge Berenice Quigley, a heavyset, stern-looking woman in her mid-forties who was well known to have guber-natorial cravings in her future, sat at attention behind her large polished desk, trying to look evenhanded, though she was possibly the most prosecution-favoring occupant of the entire Missouri bench.

To Warren's right sat prosecutor Buford Delray, looking like a butterball turkey that has just been basted, and beyond Delray, on a sofa off to the side, sat the British reporter, whose presence here Warren didn't understand and certainly didn't approve. He switched to that sore point, letting the original sore point rest a moment, saying, "Your Honor, I don't see how we can have this conversation with a reporter in the room."

"Mr. Fernit-Branca is not a *reporter*," Delray said, voice dripping with condescension. "He's a writer with *The Economist*, a respected London publication."

"I know *The Economist*," Warren growled, and glared at the Englishman. "Fernit-Branca," he mused. "I know that name."

"I suppose you've seen my byline," the fellow said, and smiled fondly at Warren.

Judge Quigley said, "Mr. Delray asked that this one repre-sentative of the press be present. As he's not a daily journalist, not an American, not taking notes, and not intending to print anything until the trial is completed, I saw no reason to refuse the request. There are precedents for such things."

"In those precedents," Warren pointed out, "the defense has been consulted in advance and has agreed."

Judge Quigley's face could become very cold. "I didn't feel that was necessary," she said.

"Evidently."

"Now," she went on, "as to this new charge."

"Another thing I don't understand," Warren told her.

"It's very simple," Delray said, so smug you just wanted to slap his face. "Last night, a body was found in a car in Lake Taneycomo. It had been driven off a cliff on the south side of the river, east of Hollister. The body was identified as one Robert Wayne Golker, who had disappeared just after the murder of Belle Hardwick. Golker was a musician in your client's employ. After his disappearance, Jones put it about that Golker had left to take a job in California."

"Golker himself told people that," Warren objected, "for weeks before he went."

"If you have witnesses to substantiate that," Delray said, smiling in mock pity, "I'm sure you'll bring them forward. In any event, Golker had been drinking heavily, or perhaps had had a great quantity of alcohol forced on him. He was then hit on the head, placed in the car, and the car pushed off the cliff into the lake."

"Drunk, he drove over the cliff," Warren said, "and hit his head when the car hit the water."

"If you have forensic witnesses to offer that theory," Delray said, "I'm sure you'll *hire* them to testify. In any event, Golker died within twenty-four hours of the death of Miss Hardwick. Golker and Miss Hardwick knew one another."

"They worked in the same theater," Warren said.

"Of course. And both knew Mr. Jones. It is the state's contention that Mr. Golker learned of Mr. Jones's murder of Miss Hardwick, either through something Mr. Jones said or some error he made, and that Mr. Jones then murdered Mr. Golker to protect his secret, attempting to make it look like a drunken accident."

"It *was* a drunken accident."

"If you have witnesses you can pay to suggest that possibility, I'm sure you'll parade them before the court."

Judge Quigley tapped her palm on her desk blotter, in lieu of a gavel. "All of that will be decided at trial," she said. "There's no need to discuss it here."

"The discussion," Warren said, "should be about the state's methods this morning. A public arrest, grandstanding—"

Delray interrupted to say, "We take murder seriously in Taney County, Mr. Thurbridge."

"They take grandstanding seriously in the Bar Association," Warren told him.

Judge Quigley said, "Mr. Thurbridge, it was not Mr. Delray's decision to arrest Mr. Jones; that was a police decision. If you have a complaint regarding the state police of Missouri, this is not the forum for that complaint."

Warren looked thoughtful. "Will the Missouri Bar Association believe the state police would take such an action without prior consultation with the public prosecutor? Be interesting to see."

"The *point*, Mr. Thurbridge," Judge Quigley insisted, "is the current matter before the court, which is the capital case against Mr. Jones in the death of Miss Hardwick."

"I don't see how we can proceed," Warren said, "not after this morning's circus."

"We can, of course, postpone, if you wish," Judge Quigley told him. "You may request a change of venue, if you wish. If we postpone, and if the state requests that the matter of Mr. Golker's death be added to the matter of Miss Hardwick's death, I would probably be in favor."

"Never!" Warren snapped. "If the Golker situation is so much as *mentioned* in front of the jury during the trial, you may count on it, I will be before the appellate court that day."

"You will have your say, of course," the judge agreed. "On another matter, if we decide to postpone, I'm sure the state will request that we revoke the bail under which Mr. Jones is currently free, and I would—"

Warren almost did leap to his feet at that point. "You wouldn't revoke bail!"

"Given the fact that there are now two serious and savage murder accusations against Mr. Jones, were we to have a delay of several weeks during which he could decide to flee the country—I believe Mr. Jones is a fairly wealthy man— I would be very much inclined to revoke bail, yes."

Warren considered, keeping himself calm. "You want to go forward, as though nothing had happened."

"That might be best," the judge told him. "I'll let you decide."

"Perform a little circus in front of the potential jurors and then go on as before. If I agree with that, Ray's bail continues."

"Of course."

"If I refuse, you'll lock him up until the trial."

"To assure his appearance, yes."

Warren said, "Your Honor, you don't appear to be interested in even the appearance of evenhandedness here."

"Be careful, Mr. Thurbridge," she warned him. "Whatever treatment you may be used to in other states, we in Missouri can be quite severe in the face of wild accusations. Take care."

Warren gave her a level look. "In a well-publicized and important case like this," he said, "I think we'll all be careful, don't you?"

She shrugged that off. "What's your decision, Mr. Thurbridge?"

Warren brooded. Judge Quigley looked stern and unmoving. Buford Delray looked like the cat that raped the canary. In the little silence preceding Warren's capitulation, the Englishman, Fernit-Branca, said, "Fascinating, American justice, all in all."

18

Afterward, Ray understood that the little interrogation they'd run him through was just bullshit, a stalling session while Warren was being nailed to the wall by the prosecutor and the judge, but at the time it was going on, he didn't get it, and for a few minutes there he got truly rattled. The troopers arrested him in front of the bus, they put handcuffs on him for the brief walk into the courthouse, they took him upstairs and through a hall full of local citizens waiting to be called as jurors—all of whom gawked at the celebrity in handcuffs, a dream come true—they took him into a small underfurnished room, and there they removed the cuffs, read him his rights, took his fingerprints, sat him down at a little metal table, and clumsily questioned him for about half an hour. Clumsily, because in fact they told him a lot more than he told them. There were half a dozen of them, in uniforms and plainclothes, led by a craggy-faced chief interrogator, and from their questions, Ray put together the story: Bob Golker's body had been found in a car at the bottom of Lake Taneycomo, blood full of alcohol and lungs full of water. He'd died no more than twenty-four hours after Belle. And what did Ray Jones have to say to all that?

That was Ray's first real moment of doubt. He almost broke down at that point and told the truth; but one look at those closed dumb official faces all around him and he realized the truth would be utterly wasted if used here. So, while they were stalling him, he stalled right back.

Jury selection had been supposed to start at 9:30, so it had been just a little before that time when Ray and the bus had arrived, and it was just a little after ten when the chief interrogator was called out of the room for a minute. The others halfheartedly went on with their bullshit, but everybody looked relieved when the interrogator came back a few minutes later and said, "Okay, Ray, that's all for now. The deputy will escort you to the courtroom."

"For what?" Ray asked.

The interrogator looked surprised. "For what? You came here for jury selection, didn't you?"

"That's goin' ahead?"

"The deputy will escort you."

The deputy, a blond gelding in tan, gestured with a hand that didn't quite grasp Ray's elbow. "Come along."

Ray looked at his fingers, still black with ink from the printing. "Got to wash my hands," he said.

"No time," the deputy said.

Ray looked at him, looked around at the rest of these assholes, and grinned. "I may be a country boy," he said, "but I know better than to walk into that courtroom and those folks on the jury with ink on my fingers. You've had your fun jerkin' me around, but it's over."

The chief interrogator looked like a fella eating a bad clam. "The deputy will escort you to the washroom."

"That's more like it," Ray said, getting to his feet. "And tell him, while we're in there, keep his hands to himself."

That shocked the dumbos into silence. Ray and the deputy went around the corner to the men's room and Ray washed the black off his fingertips. Then the two of them walked together down the hall full of people waiting to be called for jury duty—Ray now grinning left and right, waving, demonstrating unfettered hands—and into the courtroom, crowded with press in the public seats and lawyers up front.

The judge looked like the orphanage operator in *Annie*; not a good sign. She glowered at Ray for his whole walk between the rear door and the defendant's table. Ray ignored her as best he could, took the empty chair beside Warren Thurbridge, and leaned over to half-whisper, "We havin' fun yet?"

Warren gave him a bleak smile. "When the going gets tough," he said.

Ray looked interested. "Yeah? What happens then?"

"Wait and see."

So Ray waited and saw, for the next two hours until lunchtime, and there wasn't much fun in it. Most of the time, he didn't know what the hell was going on, and when he *did* know what was going on, he didn't like it.

One by one, the prospective jurors were put on the witness stand and asked questions. Sometimes the questions were asked by the judge; sometimes by the prosecutor, Buford Delray; sometimes by the state prosecutor, Fred Heffner; sometimes by Warren; and sometimes by Warren's local legal beagle, Jim Chancellor. The questions had to do with what the people knew about the case and what they knew about

Ray and what attitude they had toward capital punishment. (Those who didn't like capital punishment were automatically excluded, which meant the very first cull was in favor of the bloody-minded. Great.)

There were a lot of other reasons as well for excusing a possible juror: if they said they'd already formed an opinion about the case, for instance, or if they claimed to have somebody dependent at home that needed them every day, or if they thought a woman like Belle Hardwick probably deserved what she got no matter who it was did it to her—there were a bunch of those.

Then every once in a while, there'd be a peremptory challenge, which would mean either Warren or one of the prosecutors just didn't like that juror's face and wanted him or her out of there. It seemed to Ray that every time a potential juror gave Ray even the slightest smile of encouragement or nod of recognition or even admitted to ever having bought one of his records or tapes or CDs, there would be old Buford Delray on his feet again, chanting the old mantra: "For cause!"

What made it even worse, he didn't have his backup group with him like he'd expected. Everybody from the bus was supposed to be here in court, in the seats just behind Ray and Warren, so at least from time to time at one of the more unbelievably boring or stupid parts he'd be able to turn around and make eye contact with a friend, but the mess out front when they'd arrived had thrown everybody off. According to Warren, some of the bunch were over at his offices now and the rest were just wandering around Forsyth, a one-horse town if ever there was one. Leaving Ray, except for his high-priced legal talent, all alone. And the talent was busy.

Time crawled, and most jurors were excused for one reason or another, but nevertheless by lunchtime five people had been accepted and led away through the side door to become jurors. Ray hadn't thought about food at all, and, in fact, wasn't entirely certain he'd ever eat again, the way his stomach was all knotted up, so it was a surprise to him when the judge suddenly said they'd stand at recess for lunch until two o'clock, banged her gavel, and left.

Everybody was suddenly up and moving. Ray said to Warren, "So what do you think?"

"They don't have you yet," Warren said. "Let's go eat. I don't know about you, but I'm starved."

19

While Sara was off having fun in Forsyth, fooling around with murder trials, Jack devoted himself to the real subject: the *Weekly Galaxy*. He was hampered by the fact that most of the Galaxians knew him from the old days and would have no reason to trust him, having no reason to trust anyone, since every man's hand would quite naturally be raised against them, along with the hands of most women and all the more perspicacious children. Still, there was work that could be done. And the first thing was to find their nest, the private home the *Galaxy* would have rented and turned into headquarters for this operation.

To do that, Jack in his anonymous rental car hung around the parking lot of Jjeepers!—the family restaurant just outside the guarded entrance to Porte Regal, the golf course Ray Jones called home—and waited for a Galaxian to try to get in. Surely they'd be bugging the Jones manse and photographing its bedrooms, or at least trying to get onto the property for such purposes, so all Jack had to do was sit here, listen to a fishing program on the car radio, and wait for a Galaxian to go in.

Except that the one he saw, about 10:30 in the morning, was coming *out*. Gloomy Don Grove it was whom Jack recognized, one of the reporters from his own team in the old days, now attached like a bad cold to Binx. Don was at this moment at the wheel of a diaper-service truck.

Really? Jack had heard that cloth diapers and therefore diaper services were coming back, for ecological reasons, but at Porte Regal? It seemed unlikely, almost impossible.

But then he looked more closely and saw the company name printed in flowing logo on its side was Empower Adult Diaper Service, and all became clear. And when Don Grove, at the wheel of the truck, and the guard in his guard shack gave one another surreptitious nods and waves, even more became clear. Suborning employees—the *Galaxy*'s prime business, really.

Jack snapped a picture of the guard, to remember him later, and followed the diaper truck out onto the highway and to the right toward town. The truck stopped a quarter of a mile later, at a convenience store and gas station on the right, where Don pulled up beside the building and stopped. Himself halting a discreet distance away, Jack watched as Don climbed out. He was shucking out of his blue jacket with EMPOWER on the back when a worried-looking guy in a white shirt and blue trousers approached him. While Jack took many photos of the occurrence, the guy clearly asked Don if everything had gone well, and Don assured him that it had. Then Don gave the guy the jacket and the guy put it on, and it fit him just as badly as it had fit Don. Then Don took off his blue Empower cap and handed it to the guy, who put it on, pulling it low over his eyes. Then Don took money from his pocket and gave it to the guy, who looked all around with the most guilty expression you've ever *seen* and then, establishing his criminal intent, put the money in *his* pocket. All of which was memorialized in virtually continuous photos in Jack's two cameras.

At last, the guy got into his diaper truck and drove it away, and Don got into a rental as anonymous as Jack's and headed down a secondary road that skirted the chaos of central Branson. Jack, making himself tiny in Don's rearview mirror, followed.

And jackpot. Don drove straight to a side street called Cherokee, in the old residential part of town, and parked in front of a low brown ranch house that had exactly the appearance of a place that later turns out to have been the terrorists' bomb factory. It was the only house in the neighborhood, for instance, with butcher paper over the windows; and several cars parked in the driveway and on the lawn; and a lot of furniture partially under a tarp in the carport; and enough new phone lines going in for the Joint Chiefs of Staff. This, Jack told himself, watching Don Grove trudge up from his rental to the front door and on in, must be the place.

How to proceed. Frontally; why not? Having reloaded his smaller camera, Jack got out of the rental, took a few preliminary shots from a distance, then walked boldly across the lawn and directly to the front door, which he knew would be unlocked. (Too many people would be going in and out for everybody to have a key.) He turned the knob, pushed the door open, and went in with a big smile on his face. "Hi! How's everybody doing? Pumping out those sidebars?"

Startled faces turned his way. He kept moving forward into the nest, still talking, waving his right hand prominently at everybody and anybody, while his left hand held the camera low, snapping, snapping, snapping. To be able to take useful pictures at hip level, without direct visual aim, is a skill well worth the learning for any investigative reporter, and Jack had learned it thoroughly.

Everything here would be on his film: the maps on the walls, the people at the banks of phones, the photographers with their cameras and many bags, the rented office furniture piled every which way, the wastebasket in the fireplace—a nice touch—even the people posed in front of the blown-up life-size color photo of the courtroom at Forsyth that had been nailed to one wall. (These people, "realies" hired for the occasion because they looked so horribly like the actual readership of the *Galaxy*, had been practicing expressions of nausea and horror when Jack walked in, so that the photo being taken of them would seem to show spectators in the courtroom appalled by the gruesome details of the murder. Kid stuff.)

These realies switched their attention from their photographer to this noisy newcomer but went on looking nauseated. Meanwhile, the regular staff was getting its wits about it. The fact that Jack looked so familiar had given him some lovely extra time. People lifted their heads and saw a face they'd very often seen in the past in circumstances like this, and it was only a few seconds later they remembered *that* was Jack Ingersoll and Jack Ingersoll doesn't *work* here anymore! And it was an additional few seconds after that before they saw the little camera snapping away like a tortoise at his left hip (but faster). And by then, Jack was done.

Most of the faces now staring at Jack were familiar ones, it's true, but that didn't mean any of them were friendly. In fact, the four or five guys who jumped to their feet seemed absolutely threatening in their body language as they hurried through the obstacle course of desks and tables and chairs and sleeping photographers, aiming their hands and shouts in Jack's direction.

As rapidly as he'd entered, that's how rapidly he exited, and just as amiably, too. Still shouting hellos to old comrades, still waving the sucker hand without the camera in it, still shooting away with the other, Jack backpedaled, crying, "Well, I won't keep you; I know you're busy. We'll be in touch!" And he was out the door, proceeding at a dead run for the rental.

Two of them actually pursued him out of the house, though they hadn't a hope in hell of catching him before he was in the car and on his way. When last he looked in his mirror, one of them, a true fantasist apparently, was running toward another car as though to turn this into a movie scene, while the other, more sensible, legged it back to the nest to make phone calls.

"Shake in your boots, boys," Jack told the receding figures in the mirror. "*Trend* is on the case. And I do mean your friend and mine, Jack Ingersoll, the All-American Boy."

20

What a day! There was a sense of exhaustion and gloom within everybody else on the team bus rolling back to Branson after a full day of jury selection—not yet completed; only nine good persons and true were now settling into their sequestered quarters at one of the new motels on the hills just north of Branson—but for Sara, the day had been terrific. The others on the bus, driving through the late-afternoon traffic directly into the late-afternoon summer sun, were all too worn out, physically and emotionally, to sing or even to speak, but Sara was dancing inside.

What a scoop! And all her own! If only she still worked for the *Galaxy*—

No, strike that thought. She was happier with *Trend*, more productive, less embarrassed about the very fact of her existence. And what she'd gained today would be extremely useful when it came time to do her Ray Jones piece, whatever Jack might think about the irrelevancy of the underclass.

In the first place, it wasn't all underclass. Ray Jones might make his living off the great unwashed—just as Sara, and Jack himself, used to do, at a much lower economic level, at the *Galaxy*—but he didn't surround himself with those folk, not up close. The people around Ray Jones were smart, talented, sharp, and fun to be with. The musicians weren't very talkative, but they were bright and they appreciated a nice nuance in somebody else's dialogue.

As for Jolie Grubbe, she was great. If I ever have to go to court, Sara told herself, I want Jolie beside me. Once the fat woman had gotten over her natural distaste for the press, it turned out she and Sara had certain things in common beyond gender—attitudes, interests, histories, even some specifics, including a very strange link indeed.

It worked like this. Sara's first journalism job after college had been with a small local paper in New Hampshire. Shortly after she'd been hired, the paper had been sold to a conglomerate, who merged it with some other little papers and fired the redundant staff, principally Sara. Jolie Grubbe, it turned out, had gone to college, prior to attending law school at Columbia, in the area serviced by that newspaper, though years before Sara had worked there. Still, Jolie herself while an undergraduate had written some items for the paper and had maintained her subscription to it after she'd moved away, keeping the connection alive out of some sort of buried sentimentality (any sentimentality Jolie Grubbe might have would be very definitely buried) until the paper became merged, stapled, mutilated, and folded. So she must have read Sara, in Sara's earliest incarnation, though neither of them could pinpoint at this late date any specific item Sara might have written that Jolie might have read.

Still, the link was there, and Sara worked it for all it was worth. It was nice she had Cal Denny on her side, and also nice that Ray Jones permitted her to hang around with the entourage, but it was maybe more important to be pals with

Jolie Grubbe, a smart insider who could be very helpful if she chose.

At least for today, Jolie chose. With nothing else to do but wait, she took Sara around the Warren Thurbridge offices, showed her the conference room being set up for the shadow jury, and explained what a shadow jury was. She made this explanation in Warren's private office, seated at Warren's desk, since Warren was across the street in court and Jolie didn't want anybody else to hear this. Sara should consider the conversation private and the information she was hearing privileged—until after the trial, privileged.

"Absolutely," Sara said, sitting up straight in the seat across the desk.

"What we have here," Jolie explained, "is every potential juror in the county, recorded into the computer, a demographic rundown on sex, age, occupation, race, political affiliation if known, organizations belonged to if known, religion if known, all those things that bundle together to make each and every one of us a unique individual, in a group that can be targeted."

"Like advertising."

"Exactly. As each juror is picked over there, Warren's assistants over here go into the computer to find every other voter who closely fits that juror's demographics. Then we send people out to hire one of those voters as a consultant."

"For all twelve jurors?"

"Fourteen. We do the alternates, too. Then, for the length of the trial, those fourteen people see and hear everything the jury sees and hears, and nothing else. If the jury isn't told something, our people aren't told it."

"They imitate the jury."

"We sure hope so," Jolie said. "At the end of every day's session, we get together with the shadow jury in the conference room there and see what they think of what happened in court that day. We debrief them. And after that, we try different tactics on them for the next day, see how they react. If *they* don't want to see certain pictures, for instance, then the next day we don't show those pictures to the jury. But if they *do* want to see them, and if those pictures make them feel better about Ray Jones, then we bring them to court and flash them around."

"This is an expensive technique," Sara suggested.

Jolie smiled; not a pretty sight. "Our aim," she said, "is the finest justice money can buy."

"But does it work?"

"Ask me after the trial. In the past, it's usually seemed to work."

"You mean, it's common in trials for the defense to have shadow juries?"

"Only among millionaires," Jolie said.

So money could do a lot, but it couldn't necessarily do everything. No matter how much Ray Jones and his team might spend on putting together a shadow jury, the state of Missouri had the resources and the power to put together the *real* jury. For every lawyer, investigator, specialist, and clerk the Warren Thurbridge team could deploy, the state could deploy a hundred. No matter how much money Ray Jones could spend at his most lavish or most desperate, the state would outspend him as a matter of course. And if he were a guy without money, in this situation, the state would still spend just as much and fight just as hard.

At lunchtime, it had been gently suggested that Sara take a walk, which she did, finding a lunch counter out on the main street, half a block from the courthouse. (It must be good; look at all the pickups angle-parked out front.) Back in the office, she knew, they would all be trying to figure out what to do about this brand-new murder charge against Ray Jones, and while she'd love to be there for that discussion, she could understand why they'd be happier—if they could be happy at all under the circumstances—without her.

After lunch, she'd headed for court, and there was the crowd from the bus at last in the spectator seats, a particularly scruffy bunch among all the lawyers and other official types, like a medieval troupe of errant minstrels wandering into Versailles. (Sara wrote that down, then crossed it out.)

The afternoon had been, in a word (which Sara didn't bother to write down), tedious. Lawyers in the process of questioning potential jurors operate from such bizarre mind-sets and follow such complex and arcane private agendas that there's nothing for an observer to hold on to, no story being told, no melody playing out. Every time Sara looked around, the faces of all the musicians had the same inward living-dead look as they quietly beat time with a finger or foot, playing songs in their heads, living in some recording studio or on some blue-and-red-lit stage, light-years from here.

But at last, the day in court came to an end. Riding back to Branson, drained by doubt and monotony and confusion, the gang in the bus sat silent, glumly brooding about life or fate or whatever it is unhappy, frustrated people brood about, and Sara kept her own good cheer—she was the fly on the wall! she *was* the fly on the wall!—absolutely to herself until after they'd dropped her at Jjeepers!, outside the guard shack entrance to Porte Regal, where she'd left the rental. She stood on the parking-lot asphalt in the late-afternoon sun and waved at the bus, and Cal and Jolie and a few others waved dispiritedly back, and she maintained her solemn face as the bus drove on through the gate.

It wasn't until she was in the car and driving away up 165
toward the Lodge of the Ozarks that she permitted herself to
release the broad grin that had been struggling to emerge all
afternoon. Driving along in her packet of silence and air
conditioning, she chuckled, she chortled, and she imagined
the conversation to come with Jack, his astonishment and
admiration at her brilliant good luck. She couldn't help it;
she burst into song: "Baby!" she sang, belting it out at the
top of her voice. "Baby!" pounding the heel of her hand
against the steering wheel. "Baby, would I *lie*?"

21

Jury selection took all of Wednesday and most of Thursday. Warren Thurbridge and his defense team played the voir dire like a Wurlitzer, prying out the prejudices and the eccentricities of the potential jurors, looking for strengths and weaknesses, potential sympathy, potential hostility. At the end of the process, midafternoon Thursday, they were reasonably well pleased with their performance. Nine of the jurors they were not unhappy to have on the panel, three more they could live with, one could probably be neutralized by the interaction of the jury room, and as for the fourteenth, all they could hope was for *that* God-fearing harridan to be chosen one of the two alternates when that cull was made at the end of the trial. In any event, Warren and his team felt they had done reasonably well in this opening round and were slightly ahead of the other side.

The other side, of course, was the people of the state of Missouri, though not all of them were in court. Legally speaking, Taney is a third-class county, which means the Taney County prosecuting attorney is a part-timer, with a private practice of his own to think about in addition to the county's

business. The current holder of the office, Buford Delray, had
requested the assistance of a criminal-trial specialist from the
state attorney general's office, and his request had been granted
in the form of a Lincolnesque gentleman named Fred Heffner,
whose record, so far as the Thurbridge team could discover,
seemed to be limited almost completely to the prosecution of
drug couriers picked up by the state police in the course of
traffic stops along Route 65, a known drug transportation lane
north out of Arkansas, or on Interstate 44, a similar through
route crossing Missouri east-west from Springfield to St.
Louis.

This meant the Thurbridge team did not look upon the
arrival of Fred Heffner as a threat likely to cause sleepless
nights among the partisans of Ray Jones. Of course, Buford
Delray did also have at his command the assistance of the
Missouri Highway Patrol, the Taney County Sheriff's Department, and, since the body had been found in water and with
water inside it, the Missouri Water Patrol—a fairly formidable
array, all in all.

What that array might be doing with itself on Thursday
afternoon, after the close of court, Warren neither knew nor
much cared, but what *he* was doing was getting to know the
shadow jury.

As each actual juror had been agreed upon by prosecution
and defense and accepted by Judge Quigley, the word had
flashed from the courtroom to Warren's offices, where the
staff had at once pored through its computer files, finding the
half dozen or so other Taney County voters who most closely
matched the demographic profile of the just-empaneled juror.
Staff members then hopped into cars and went in search of
these people, with a simple question to ask: How would you
like to take a vacation for the next week or two, live all

expenses paid in a nice motel, have your meals provided, and be guaranteed an exciting, if unpublicized, part in the famous Ray Jones murder trial? Some restrictions apply: You won't be allowed to read a paper or watch TV or communicate with family and friends until the trial is over. But you'll be paid well—better than the state pays its real jurors, who have no choice—and you'll actually get to meet Ray Jones his own self!

Child's play. There were very few turndowns among the potential shadows, partly because everybody likes to have a role in an ongoing drama, but mainly because most people aren't doing much of anything, anyway. Take a couple of weeks off from *this* life? You betcha!

Court adjourned on Thursday at 2:25 P.M., and at 6:30 Warren, bringing Ray Jones his own self along, walked into the conference room in the former furniture store to greet the fourteen people sitting around with grins on their faces as though Ed McMahon had just called them personally to say, "No shit, now, this time you *are* a winner!"

"You all know Ray Jones," Warren said unnecessarily.

"Hi," Ray said generally, waving a casual hand and grinning a casual grin.

"Hi, hello, hi, Ray," they all said back.

Warren said, "I'm Ray's defense attorney in the trial just getting under way here, my name is Warren Thurbridge, and I want to tell you right now, for both Ray and myself, how pleased I am, and how grateful, that you folks have consented to take time from your busy schedules to come in here for the duration of the trial and help us see that justice is done."

They all looked solemn at that, prepared to do their duty come hell or high water. The fact was, however, that even though there's nothing illegal or underhanded about the use of a shadow jury in a felony trial, the jurors all had the sneaky feeling there *ought* to be, and the idea that they were part of the process of pulling a fast one made them feel giggly all over.

Warren went on to explain the concept of a shadow jury, and one woman raised her hand to ask, "Does this mean we're going to be in court every day?"

"No, I'm sorry," he told her. "I wish we could do it like that, but we just can't. What we'll do is, we'll videotape the proceedings every day and then we'll all gather in this room and you'll watch the tape; you'll see and hear everything the jury saw and heard that day. And then we'll discuss it."

A laconic fellow with a big nose and some kind of English or Irish accent said, "You mean, we won't be here in the daytime at all?"

"You're going to have your days free," Warren assured him, "at the motel. There's a nice pool there, a well-equipped game room, and we'll get you any movie at all you want to watch on the VCR. I'm sorry you won't be able to hang out with the other guests or anybody at all except your own group and our staff, but those are the same conditions the regular jury faces, and that's what we're trying for here, to get you people as close to the actual jury as we possibly can."

There were a few more questions of a housekeeping nature, and one woman briefly seemed ready to quit, not having understood the concept of sequestering until about the eleventh time it was explained to her, but a couple of the other shadows assured her the whole thing would be fun and a once-in-a-lifetime experience, so she settled down, and that was that.

Then Ray Jones spoke to the group, while Warren stood

to one side and looked them over, pleased. "After this is all over," Ray told them, "we can get to know one another better, but for right now Mr. Thurbridge here tells me I have to keep my distance from you nice folks, for fear you'll like me more than the other jury over there does." Grinning, shrugging, he said, "Or maybe like me less—that could happen, too. So all I want to say now is, I'm real thankful for your help in my time of trouble and I just hope we can all have a victory celebration together out to my place when this is all over. Thank you."

The woman who hadn't understood *sequester* raised a timid hand. Ray grinned and pointed to her and she said, "Ray, would you sing us a song?"

This was a surprise. Ray and Warren looked at one another, both stuck for a second, and then Warren smiled at the woman and shook his head and said, "Mrs. Carlyle, Ray isn't singing for the regular jury. We're trying to make these groups as parallel as possible."

One of the other jurors, a scrawny little retired postal worker named Juggs, said, "The trial won't start till tomorrow. I bet Ray Jones could sing us a song today."

Warren, not liking loss of control like this, was about to turn down the request a second time, but Ray stepped in, saying, "Well, I think I could. I didn't bring my guitar with me, but let's see if I can carry a tune without help." He smiled at each and every one of the shadows. "You know," he said, "most of my songs are a little comical or irreverent or whatever, but I have my serious side, as well. You may know this song from one of my albums. I don't sing it all the time, just at special occasions, and I guess this is one. If you know the song and feel like joining in, you're welcome."

Warren stepped back, the smile frozen on his face. What the hell was Ray going to do now?

A cappella, Ray sang:

> *Everything we have, we have from Jesus.*
> *Everything we are we are through Him.*
> *Everything we do, you know He sees us.*
> *He sees me when I'm sending out this hymn.*
>
> *He is known to many different people.*
> *Buddha, Mazda, Mithra, all are Him.*
> *From tepee, temple, tower, and from steeple,*
> *Everybody sings this mighty hymn.*
>
> *Are you born in the blood of the Lamb?*
> *I am, oh, I am.*
> *Are you saved in the bosom of Him?*
> *I am, oh, I am.*

There wasn't a dry eye in the conference room.

22

Thursday afternoon, it was Sara's job to play good cop with the *Weekly Galaxy* people, Jack having so spectacularly played bad cop with them the day before by photographing their home base in a drive-by shooting. She couldn't do it before then because she had to wait for FedEx to deliver the peace offering from New York. But when it arrived at the Lodge of the Ozarks, about three that afternoon, Sara immediately put it in her shoulder bag and headed for room 222, Palace Inn.

Where Binx took one look at her and in a flash made a crucifix out of crossed index fingers and glared at her wide eyed through it. Advancing, shaking this fleshy cross in front of her face, he cried, "Out! Out!"

"Oh, come on, Binx," she said. "*You're* the vampire; everybody knows that."

"Not this time." Waggling those fingers more aggressively than ever, Binx chirruped, "We don't want your kind around here, Missy."

"Binx, Binx," Sara said with a girlish laugh and an airy

wave of her hand, "don't you know when Jack's goofing on you?"

Binx lowered his cross, but not his guard, and stood glowering at Sara, while the few people in the nearby crowd who'd noticed his odd actions and paused to see what would happen next decided nothing would happen next and lost interest. Binx frowned and thought and at last shook his head. "Jack Ingersoll does not goof around," he decided. "Jack Ingersoll has *no* downtime. There isn't a civilian bone in his body."

This was true, but Sara was hardly likely to admit it, at least not right this minute. Taking one cautious step closer to Binx so she wouldn't have to shout over the crowd noise— the *Galaxy*'s hospitality suite was as packed as ever, the attendees drunker and louder than they'd been on Monday— Sara said, "Jack's sorry, Binx. He did it as a stunt, honest, just a spur-of-the-moment thing."

"*Trend*'s tried to get us before," Binx said, and shivered all over at the memory. "But to do it to *me*, Sara, to do it on *my* watch."

"Jack was afraid you'd think that," Sara told him, taking from her bag the small black plastic film canister with the gray top. "It takes a lot to embarrass Jack, as you know," she went on, showing the canister on the palm of her open hand.

"Hah," Binx said, but he couldn't keep himself from looking at the canister. He couldn't keep himself, as Jack had known he wouldn't be able to keep himself, from hope. "What's that supposed to be?" he demanded, trying to sound tough and skeptical.

"It's *supposed* to be the roll of film Jack took over at your place," she said, although of course it wasn't. This was what had occasioned the delay; first the original film had to be shipped to New York and developed. Then another roll of film had to be shot, taking pictures of the pictures. Then the second roll had to be FedExed posthaste to Branson and Sara. And here she and it were. "Take it," she said. "Go on."

"That isn't the film," Binx said, though it was clear that every atom of his body, every drop of dew in his every pore, *wanted* it to be the film, wanted to be able to believe it *was* the film.

"Of course it is," Sara assured him. "Jack knows what you're going through over here; he used to go through it himself. He doesn't want you to get all bent out of shape just because *he* decided to play a joke for once."

"It isn't the film," he said. Staring at the canister, Binx looked like a drunk in a silent movie, beholding with desire and repulsion the first drink of the day.

"It hasn't been developed, Binx," Sara said, permitting herself to sound just a trifle schoolmarmish and impatient. "Take it; develop it yourself; see what it is."

"It isn't the film."

This time, Sara didn't answer at all, but let the roar of the crowd enter their cone of space as she stood with her palm out, the canister on it, like someone offering a poisoned sugar cube to a skittish horse.

This was necessary, unfortunately, because Sara still had to maintain her access to the *Galaxy* and its people. She didn't want a persona non grata put out against *her,* not with the entire Ray Jones trial still out ahead, certain to be speckled with *Weekly Galaxy* chicanery. Binx and the other Galaxians would never permit Jack anywhere near them again, joke or no joke, but that was all right—this wasn't Jack's story. This was *Sara's* story, and she was going to get it. "Go on," she murmured, creating a little silence for just the two of them in the midst of the madding crowd. She moved her hand slightly, the canister rolling on her palm. "Take it," she murmured. "It won't bite."

He licked wet lips. He gazed into her eyes, knowing he was being taken but not knowing how, unable to refuse the siren call of hope. He reached out, palm down, and closed his hand over hers and the canister both. "Have dinner with me," he said.

She smiled, sunny and sweet, her hand held in his. "Sure, Binx, I'd like that."

Desire and doubt brewed on his face. "You will?"

"Sure I will," she said. "I'll have dinner with you, and then I'll go to bed with Jack."

He grinned with relief. "Oh, that's okay, then," he said, and squeezed her hand tighter around the canister. "Maybe I'll get you drunk."

"Maybe." Gently she removed her hand from his, leaving the canister behind. "What time?"

He smiled as that hand went into his pocket. "Right after I develop the film," he said.

23

Ray's cook had quit, being a decent patriotic Christian woman who couldn't *wait* to prejudge him, so he arranged to have some kind of edible shit sent in from Jjeepers! for himself and his dinner guests out to his place after his evening show on Thursday, the night before the trial began. These dinner guests were Cal and Jolie and Warren, and the occasion was a combination strategy meeting and pep talk. They all had a drink before dinner, and Jolie and Warren shared a bottle of Italian white—a pretty good Orvieto—over the bland fried chicken, but generally they were light on the booze, though God knows, they all had reason enough to drink.

Warren's primary cause for thirst was Ray's insistence on testifying. *"I'm* the one they're charging with all this bullshit," Ray pointed out. "How's it going to look if I don't stand up there and throw the lie in their fucking faces?"

"Dignified," Warren said.

"Too late for me to be dignified," Ray told him, and conjured up a burp to prove it.

They were dining in the dining alcove, between the spread-out living room and the spread-out kitchen, a roomy hexagonal box stuck onto the golf-course side of the house, wide windows on three angles overlooking the thirteenth tee, where not that much happened after dark.

Warren wasn't satisfied with either Ray's answer or Ray's burp. "You won't keep your cool," he said, twirling the wine in his glass, ignoring the steam-table green beans and wet roasted potatoes. "I know that about you, and you know it about yourself. You don't like authority figures, and that courtroom's going to be full of them, and if our fat friend Buford Delray doesn't have the wit to pull your chain, I assure you the fella from Springfield, that state prosecutor, whatever the *hell* his name is—"

"Fred Heffner," said Jolie, who was good at details. Turning to Ray, she said, "Warren's right, you know. I figure about sixty-five percent of my time is spent keeping you away from places where the only thing you can possibly do is get yourself in trouble."

"I'm *in* trouble," Ray said, which was merely God's own truth. Not over the Bob Golker thing, though; that was just crap. True, the discovery that Bob had not gone to California after all but had gone instead to a watery—and boozy—grave had at first shaken Ray's confidence, made it seem as though maybe his idea wasn't as golden as he'd been thinking. But then he saw that everybody, down to the dumbest deputy, knew that Bob had really died in a drunken accident and that the whole charade this morning had simply been the prosecution taking advantage of a heaven-sent opportunity to play some dirty pool, poison the jurors' minds with images of Ray Jones in handcuffs. Bob's death might complicate things a little, eventually, but there was no reason to give up the original idea.

Ray grinned to himself, a private grin. If Jolie or Warren

were even to suspect what was actually going on here, they'd shit a brick. Well, Warren would shit a brick. Jolie would shit a silo.

Warren said, "Ray, I don't need you on that stand. All the state's got is circumstantial evidence, and not enough of that. I'm talking about Belle Hardwick here. The other thing, the Robert Wayne Golker thing, that's a joke and even the state knows it. If they convict you on Hardwick, they'll just fold Golker into it, and if they lose you on Hardwick, they'll drop Golker."

"It's all bullshit, Warren," Ray said, "and you know it, and I am determined to stand up and tell the world it's so."

"Right on, Ray," Cal said, grinning like an idiot. Well, of course, he *was* an idiot, but a damn good one.

Jolie lowered a bunch of chins at the idiot. "You keep out of this."

"Cal can have an opinion if he wants," Ray said mildly.

Jolie transferred her chins to Ray. "Where would he keep it?"

Warren said, "Ray, the reason you pay a lot of money for a high-priced attorney is because he knows his job. So you ought to let him *do* his job."

Ray swallowed chicken; it wasn't that bad. He said, "Warren, are you threatening to quit?"

"Absolutely not," Warren said. "Whatever damn fool thing you do, I'm in for the long haul."

"Good."

"But if you *do* a lot of damn fool things and get yourself convicted," Warren went on, "I shall protect my own fundament by making it clear in every post-trial interview that you went down only and solely because you failed to follow my counsel."

"Fine," Ray said, and grinned. "Sock it to me, man. At that point, I won't much give a shit, will I?"

"You're saying," Warren concluded, "that I can't dissuade you."

"You got that right," Ray said. "And just to put us out of our misery quick, I want to go on the stand the very first day, tomorrow. Morning."

Warren and Jolie smirked at one another, which Ray didn't like one bit. Then Warren said, "Ray, let me explain a little bit what a trial is, how it works. First, the state tells us why it arrested you. It presents its case, produces its witnesses and its evidence. Then we get our turn at bat, to poke holes in their evidence, cast doubt on their witnesses, and present our own version of events. But they go first, with *their* witnesses. As big a fool as you are determined to be, Ray, you are still not one of their witnesses; you're still on this side of the battle."

"Oh," Ray said, feeling like maybe he was a bit of a bumpkin, like everybody thought. But a smart bumpkin, he was sure of that much. "In that case," he said, "I want to be first up when we get to the bottom half of the inning."

Warren smiled at him. "No."

"Damn it, Warren," Ray said, "it's my goddamn trial, and I can—"

"You can go to hell for yourself, boy," Warren said, and now he glared across his cooling chicken at his fractious client and said, "You can go on the stand against my counsel and advice, if you insist, but you'll go on there when *I* say so. You are not going to alter and confuse and addle my strategy. To continue with your baseball analogy, the player does not tell the coach the batting order."

Time to back down; old Warren was getting pretty steamed. Ray could still work his own agenda, whenever he finally got to the stand. "Okay, pal," he said. "I'll be good, and I'll be patient, and I'll wait for you to point your high-priced finger my way. But don't forget I'm sitting there."

"Hardly," Warren said, and put his napkin on the table. "Excuse me." He rose and left the room, dignified and self-assured and just a little pissed off.

Jolie sipped wine and said, "Let me take the opportunity to present *my* pet peeve."

"Fire away," Ray said. "It's open season."

"Sara Joslyn," Jolie said.

Ray looked blank, though he knew whom she meant. "Who? Oh, Cal's friend."

"She's a nice girl," Cal allowed.

Jolie looked sour. "She's a nice girl *reporter*," she said.

"I kinda like her," Ray admitted.

"So do I," Jolie said. "She's a nice girl, as you say. After the trial, maybe we'll all become pen pals. But tomorrow, we get serious. From here on, I don't want her around."

"Aw gee," Cal said.

Ray said, "Jolie, don't be a pain. The girl works for a nice news magazine up in New York City. They're a weekly magazine; they aren't going to print a word about the case until the trial's all over and done with. What's the harm in having her around?"

"What's the *point* in having her around?"

"Cal's got the hots for her," Ray said.

Jolie gave that the look of contempt it deserved. "Bull," she said.

"Why not?" Ray asked her. "Cal's been married a couple times, he likes girls, he isn't some faggot or anything."

"I think I'm gonna score, too," Cal said, grinning like Ichabod Crane.

Ray, listening, heard a voice. "Is Warren on the phone?"

Jolie said, "Maybe he's calling a psychiatrist."

Ray grinned. "You mean I'm driving him crazy?"

"Calling a psychiatrist for *you*," Jolie said. "If Cal wants to hang out with this girl reporter, at least I don't want her around our strategy sessions."

Ray spread his hands. "Jolie, look at this table. Do you see her here?"

"If I see her where I don't want to see her," Jolie threatened, "I am going to scream until she goes away."

"You do that," Ray said, and Warren came back to the table, looking both grumpy and satisfied. Taking his seat, putting his napkin on his lap, he said, "The next couple of minutes should be rather interesting."

"Why's that?" Ray asked.

Instead of answering, Warren looked around at them all and said, "What were we discussing?"

"Reporters," Jolie said with a curl of the lip.

"What a coincidence," Warren said as a whole lot of really *bright* floodlights flashed on, out there on the golf course, impaling from half a dozen directions a golf cart stopped on the little golf-cart road out there, midway on a line between these windows and the little ball-washing box on the thirteenth tee. On the golf cart were two shabby men and a lot of expensive equipment: infrared cameras, high-definition long-range microphones, shortwave radio scanners to monitor police calls, professional-quality earphones.

The men on the golf cart, in the middle of that sudden glare, tried to do thirty things at once, and accomplished none of them. They tried to shield their eyes from the blinding light, they tried to get the golf cart started and run *away* from there, they tried to keep their equipment from falling off the cart, and they tried to pretend they weren't doing any of those things. So, for about ten seconds out there, the clumped mass of golf cart and men and equipment looked like some sort of windup toy gone bonkers.

Then the Porte Regal security cops arrived, running in from all directions, waving nightsticks and Mace cans and handcuffs, and collected up the windup toy gone bonkers, then took the whole tangle away from there. And the lights went out.

"There," Warren said. "Wasn't that fun?"

"You saw something," Jolie said to him.

"I saw light reflect from something shiny that moved," Warren explained. "Probably a camera lens. I doubted there were many golfers out there in the pitch-dark, so I phoned security. I assume they were reporters of some sort."

Jolie raised a significant eyebrow at Ray. "Reporters," she said.

"Jolie, have some more wine," Ray suggested.

24

Binx wanted to talk about Marcie. Sara wanted to talk about what the *Galaxy* was up to in connection with Ray Jones, but she couldn't ask that question head-on, so they talked about Marcie. That is, Binx talked about Marcie. Sara could have sung the whole song right along with him, but she didn't, because he thought he was making it all up. So she let him take a solo.

"The thing is, we were too young when we got married, we didn't know our own minds, we didn't know who we *were*. I'm not blaming Marcie, I think it's just as tough on her as it is on me, and she's stuck just the same way I am. And now with the kids, you know, and that drives us even further apart. We were just kids ourselves, somebody should have told us, 'Don't do it! Find out who you are first, don't tie yourself down before you ever even tested those wings.' I'm not blaming Marcie, I know it's hell on her, too, and she's got the kids more than I do. We came together and we thought it was love, you know, love for the ages, but what did we know? It was just sex, that's all. We were just kids, and sex was like a new lollipop, you know, in those days we couldn't keep our hands off each other, and then the kids started coming. I'm not blaming Marcie, we made all the decisions together, but we were *wrong*. What did we know? Nothing. We met in college, and her folks were all over her to marry me, and my folks were just as bad. I'm not blaming *them*, it was our own decision, but we weren't ready to make a decision, neither of us. I'm not blaming Marcie, I'm as responsible as she is. More. It was up to me to be the mature one, and I just wasn't. And then the *Galaxy* job came along, and the money looked so good, and we just spent it, we just bought stuff, and everything you buy it winds up you still owe on it, we've got all these mortgages, and paying off the cars, paying off the furniture, paying off the swimming pool, paying off all this *stuff*. I'm not blaming Marcie, I wanted that stuff as much as she did, or almost as much. But it means we're stuck again, all over again. The kids, and all the debts, and when I was fired for a while we *really* fell behind, taking out loans and I don't know *when* we're gonna get caught up. I'm not blaming Marcie, it's the whole lifestyle, you get it, you spend it, you know how it is at the *Galaxy*, the money isn't real, so you spend it as soon as it comes in, and then you're behind the eight ball, and you don't know what the hell you're gonna do. You're stuck, that's all. You and Jack were right to get out, you really were, but I'm *stuck* in it. I got Marcie, and the kids, and the house, and the cars, and the pool, and all this *stuff*, so I can't make a move. I wanted life, you know? And I got the Sargasso Sea. I'm not blaming Marcie, but if only I could get away from *her* at some point, find somebody that understands me, has confidence in me, faith in me, I *know* I could turn my life around, get out from under all this *shit*. And I have to tell you, I'm not blaming Marcie, but she's no help at all, she doesn't try to *save* any money, give me any *encouragement,* act like she's gonna stand by me, you should have heard her when I was fired for a while, *no* support, nothing. And sex. On a *good* day our sex is down to something that looks like an illustration in a plumbing manual, but when I was fired for a while it was hopeless, she had Krazy Glue in there, I swear I couldn't—"

"Maybe," Sara interjected, "you shouldn't tell me about your sex life."

"Well, it isn't what you'd call a sex *life,*" Binx said. "It's more like your dance of the dead, if you know what I mean. Now, I'm what I think I'm a pretty passionate guy, if you know what I mean, I mean in terms of like technique and understanding what a woman likes, you know, what she'd like a guy to—"

"I don't think you need to tell me about that," Sara said, definitely not wanting to hear an offer of cunnilingus.

"I'm just saying," Binx explained, "what I'm saying, I'm not a turnoff. In bed. I give good orgasm, I really do, but I gotta have a *partner,* it's been so long since there was any kind of *satisfaction* in the marriage, I mean *any* kind of satisfaction, I honestly believe if I could meet a woman who would *appreciate* me and *encourage* me and give me the kind of boost of the ego that I just don't get at home, I honestly believe, Sara, I'd even be a better husband for it. Better able to go home, better able to face the problems, put up with Marcie and the kids, maybe see my way clear at last, figure out some way *out* of this mess. I mean, I'm not blaming Marcie, but I can't do it all on my own, and I'm on my own, Sara—in every way that really matters, I'm on my own. I'm not blaming Marcie, but she isn't *satisfying* in the way that a woman ought to be and could be and most of the time *is* in the life of a man. You know what I mean. We've known each other a long while now, Sara, and—"

"Mr. Radwell?"

Binx, having just hurtled from the roof in this mad attempt to teach himself to fly, now faltered, fluttered, wings collapsing, as he looked up at the waiter. Rage and hatred seethed so fully in Binx's red-rimmed eyes that the waiter, a slender chap, took a nervous step back. Through gritted teeth, Binx said, *"Yes?"*

"Telephone for you, sir."

Binx was torn. He was shredded. Sara could see it in the clench of his jaw and she felt a kind of amiable pity for him. This must be the *Galaxy*, his master's voice, and both he and Sara knew it. But he didn't want to stop, not when he was— he apparently believed, or desperately hoped—at last getting somewhere, just starting to make his pitch, just about to dream the impossible dream, scale the unscalable mountain, bed the unbeddable broad. No; not the *Galaxy*; not now.

But yes. "I'll be right back," Binx threatened Sara, in a new voice, low and guttural, as he rose, trembling all over, to follow the waiter to the phone.

Binx, in his pursuit of Sara, had brought her to Branson's only attempt at a prestige restaurant, the Candlestick Inn, high on the cliff directly across Lake Taneycomo—a river-narrow Lake Taneycomo—from downtown Branson, whose lights, both in themselves and in their reflections in the water, were the view. The Candlestick was hushed, dim, candlelit instead of fluorescent-lit, and there was no buffet table at which you could have all you could eat. Therefore, the tourists weren't here, the bargain-seeking families who didn't care what they ate just so long as it was cheap and there was lots of it. What was here on a Thursday night, fairly late, therefore, were locals of the professional class, in pairs and quartets, eating slowly, chatting quietly, drinking wine, and looking only occasionally out the plate-glass window at the seductive lights of Branson.

With no Binx before her, singing his aria of the hog-tied husband, Sara sat back, observing the people at the other tables, watching the Branson lights shiver and shatter in the waters of Lake Taneycomo, and thought about what weird places one found oneself in if one were a reporter. This is not a place Sara would come to on vacation, but that hardly meant much of anything, since *vacation* was not a word in Sara's personal lexicon, anyway. Vacation? What do you *do* when you're on a vacation? If you love your work, if you derive your sustenance and your heartbeat and your very air from your work, what's a vacation for? What's the difference between vacation and exile?

That's what separates me from the Branson tourists more than anything else, Sara thought. They're happy when they're away from their lives, and I'm happy when I'm in my life. She turned that thought over, found it good, and decided not to share it with Jack.

Binx returned, a troubled man—more troubled, in a different way. His nose-to-the-ground trailing of Sara was off for now; that was obvious. Looking sunny and innocent, Sara said, "Good news?"

Binx drained his wineglass, reached into the bucket for the bottle, found it empty, and waved it energetically over his head at the waiter, who nodded calmly and retired. Then Binx plunked the bottle back into the ice and water, sighed deeply, and said, "They arrested Don and Chauncey."

Two of Binx's reporters. "*Who* arrested them?"

"The police. When it's time to do an arrest, that's who you get."

"Binx," Sara said, "don't make it tough on me. Just tell me what happened."

"We had Don and Chauncey outside Ray Jones's house," Binx said. "With gear, you know."

"Infrared cameras."

"Gear, yeah."

"Microphones."

"*Gear*, all right?"

"And the police got them?" Sara shrugged that off as the waiter arrived with a new bottle.

"Yes," Binx said to Sara. "Yes," he said, less patiently, to the waiter, who insisted on showing the label for approval rather than merely opening the damn thing so Binx could pour it all straight down his throat.

"So what is that, after all?" Sara said carelessly. "Trespassing. The *Galaxy*'s used to trespassing."

"They got the gear."

"The *Galaxy*'s lost gear before."

"Well," Binx said, "we weren't broadcasting it, too tricky, you know. It was just on tape, right there."

"The police have the tape, you mean."

"They turned it over to Ray Jones."

"Pity," Sara said.

"There is no pity," Binx said. He tasted the wine, at the waiter's silent behest. "Yes," he said again.

Sara said, "So you lost one conversation and a few green-and-black pictures. You must have other things set up, other ears and eyes in place."

"Oh sure," Binx said, watching greedily as the extremely slow waiter poured first Sara's wine—as though *she* needed the stuff—and then at last his. He drank off half the glass before the waiter could put the new bottle in the bucket. Rolling his eyes slightly, the waiter carried away the empty bottle, and Binx said, "But this alerts them. And they're keeping Don and Chauncey in jail overnight. And Florida is going to *hate* all this."

"They had *Galaxy* ID on them?"

"Don't remind me," Binx said, and drank down the other half glass.

As Binx poured for himself again, the neck of the bottle chattering against the rim of the glass, Sara said, "Still, you have other things going."

"Thank God." *Splunk*, bottle away.

"What kind of thing do you have?" Sara asked, as casual as a spring day.

Binx drank deep. He put the glass down. He gazed upon Sara more in sorrow than in anger. "Oh, Sara," he said. "You're gonna do it, aren't you?"

"Do what?"

"Shoot me down."

"Binx! What a thing to say."

"I know you are," Binx said, as forlorn as a poodle in a rainstorm. "I can't stop you, and maybe it doesn't matter anyway, but at least I'm not gonna help you."

"Binx, these are awful things to say."

"At least I'm not gonna slit my own throat," Binx said, and used that throat to down more wine. "And maybe it's just as well, anyway," he said.

Sara looked at him carefully. "Maybe what's just as well?"

"Get thrown out of the old life entirely," he explained. "Take the decision out of my hands. No more excuses, no choice, nothing. Like those army guys—what are they?—Rangers. Get dropped naked on a mountaintop—"

"I don't think they're naked."

He ignored that. "Have to figure it out, start all over, don't carry a thing from the old life."

"A naked person on a mountaintop," Sara cautioned, "is most likely to just die."

Binx smiled wanly and spread his hands. "See? No downside."

25

Friday was the first day of the actual trial, and Sara was there, but only through the intercession of Cal Denny. The court was being quite strict with the press, which by its very nature prefers the circus of celebrity to the bread of jurisprudence. Only three pool reporters were allowed in the courtroom itself, though the rest of the flock could preen and honk all it wanted in the hall outside and in the stairwell down to the main entrance. Remote-TV trucks now girdled the courthouse, as though they'd formed a circle there against an attack by the Atlanta Braves, but no media cameras were permitted anywhere in the building. Other cameras were present, however, small video cameras discreetly on black tripods by the side walls of the court, one placed there by the prosecution, the other by the defense.

Sara was not seated with the press contingent, three shaggy reporters and three intense sketch artists jammed together in the rear row on the prosecution side, but with the defense partisans across the aisle and down front, between Cal Denny and Ray Jones's "secretary," Honey Franzen, a woman so laid-back and sure of herself, she probably didn't even bother to have a pulse. Jolie Grubbe, on the aisle, had given Sara one brisk nod upon meeting but then grimly avoided her eye ever after; so whatever good fellowship had developed between them last time, Jolie still didn't like the idea of a reporter, any reporter, hanging out inside the tent.

Well, she was right, wasn't she?

The Ray Jones trial was a hot ticket, but the courtroom was small, with four benches on each side of the public area that you could maybe squeeze six people onto apiece, which meant fewer than fifty spectators could be accommodated, of whom six—rear row, left—were press and six—front row, right—were with Ray Jones. How the court had decided to allocate the rest of the seating, Sara didn't know, but the benches were jammed with civilians of every sort—except children—all of them trying to look solemn and sober and mature, but all of them actually so agog, they looked mostly like those fish with both eyes on the same side of the head.

Judge Quigley entered the court promptly at 9:30—*swish*, everybody rose; *swish*, everybody at the judge's order became seated again—and in no time at all, reality set in. Intensity and expectation drained out of the room like crankcase oil; you could feel the deflation everywhere. And Sara's own delight at being an insider didn't last long; very soon, what she was mostly thinking about was how hard this bench was and how very long it still must be before lunch.

This first day of the trial being on a Friday, there would be a long two-day hiatus before they all got rolling again on Monday, so the state had chosen not to lead off with anything particularly interesting or dramatic. Since the jury could reliably be counted on to forget by the end of the trial whatever happened here today, the state used this time to fill the record with all the necessary boring background stuff, the forensics:

the medical examiner's testimony; testimony of the police officers who first responded to the report of the dead woman in the lake; testimony of the old geezers who'd found the body; testimony of various experts on the condition of the body, the meaning of the water in the lungs, the length of time in the water, the approximate time of death, the casts of tire tracks taken at the murder scene, the analysis of the bloodstains found in Ray Jones's Acura SNX sports car, and on and on and on. By the time Judge Quigley banged her gavel for lunch, Sara had begun to feel she was trapped forever in the world's slowest mystery novel.

Apparently, Cal felt the same way. They'd all trooped over to Warren's offices to eat take-out sandwiches in the conference room, and Cal, after consulting with Warren and Jolie and Ray, came over to say, "They tell me this afternoon's gonna be just like this morning."

"Goody."

"If you want to stay, you know, for your job and all—"

Sara sat up straighter and looked up at Cal, standing beside her. "What's the alternative?"

Cal took the empty seat next to her, resting one bony elbow on the conference table now littered with little white paper bags and Saran Wrap and Styrofoam coffee cups and aluminum Diet Pepsi cans. (Product placement.) "I was talking to Ray," he said, "and, you know, he'd like for you to get to know him and understand him, for that piece you're gonna write in your magazine after the trial—"

"I've had the feeling, to tell the truth," Sara said, "that Ray's been avoiding me."

"Well, yeah, he is," Cal agreed.

"He is?" She hadn't expected that blunt an answer.

"See, the thing is," Cal explained, "Ray hopes, you know,

he'll come out a good guy in that piece of yours in the magazine. But if everybody sees like you and him are buddies all through this, nobody won't care what you think. So you and *me* are pals, but Ray's gonna keep his distance. You know, till after the trial."

"When he may be keeping his distance from everybody."

"We sure hope not," Cal said.

"I'm sorry, Cal, but I just don't get the point."

"Ray says to me," Cal told her, " 'Cal, you know what I'm like, who I really am. *You* tell that friend of yours, let her get to understand me without all this regular press stuff.' You know what he means. You do an interview, photo op, all of that, you don't get to know somebody that way."

"You don't get to know them by staying away from them, either," Sara pointed out.

"You aren't *away,*" Cal said. "You couldn't get much closer, now, could you? It's just, Ray's got a lot on his mind these days. He don't want to have to put on his publicity face just because you're here, you see?"

"I guess so," Sara said dubiously.

"So," Cal said, "if you don't want to be in the court there this afternoon, when Ray's *got* to be there, you wanna go see his house?"

Sara stared at him. *"What?"*

"It's that keep-your-distance thing again," Cal said. "Ray wants you to know how he lives, but he can't invite you to the house. That's too close; that gives you—what do they call it?"

"Conflict of interest?"

"Maybe," Cal said. "Anyway, I talked it over with Ray and it's okay with him, so *I* could show you the house while he's in court here. If you want to see it."

Sara considered, frowning at this big open friendly face, wondering just what the hell was going on here. This is the way, she thought, Binx felt with *me* last night. She said, "What are we gonna do there, Cal? Just the two of us, huh?"

Cal blushed. Tomato red, looking like a really bad sunburn, the blush came up out of the open neck of his yellow shirt and suffused his face. "Oh no!" he said, and his big bony hand nervously lifted, then quickly pat-pat-patted the tabletop between them as though gentling a horse. "No no," he said. "Uhh—I don't even know how to say this."

"Just go ahead and say it," Sara suggested.

"Well, uh, you and me, I mean, I *like* you, and I think you like me, like friends, but, uh, I'm not the kind of guy you're gonna *go* for. You're a very pretty lady, and you're a New York lady, and a reporter and all, and we can get along with each other, but, you know, not *that* way. I'd be embarrassed to even, even, uh . . . Nothing."

There was no way not to believe that protestation. Cal is who he seems to be, and if this whole situation is weird, so what? Most situations are weird, if you stop to look at them. "I apologize," Sara said with absolute sincerity. "I didn't mean to make you uncomfortable. I just wasn't sure."

"I imagine," Cal said as the red sea receded from his face and he tried a tentative smile, "you get a lot of fellas expressing interest."

"Some," Sara admitted. "I'd like to see Ray's house this afternoon. Very much. Thank you."

26

And what has Jack Ingersoll been up to all this time? Plenty. Plenty.

For one thing, he's been on the phone a lot with Hiram Farley, his boss at *Trend* back in New York, explaining that while everything is all right here and Sara Joslyn has not lost her marbles after all, nevertheless it seems to Jack that he ought to stay a little longer in Branson, just a little longer, to nail this story down here. Going to be an interesting story, maybe two stories.

"What two stories?" Hiram, on the phone, sounded just as dour and unimpressed as he looked in person.

"Time will tell, Hiram," Jack said, breezy but serious nonetheless, "I think we may have a little something to say about our friends on the *Weekly Galaxy*. I don't want to spoil it for you—"

"Go ahead, I don't mind."

"But *I* do, Hiram. I don't want to promise what I can't deliver. Just give me a couple days here to be sure I've got what I think I've got."

"We have a reporter on the scene."

"And she's doing the job, she's doing fine. Hiram, you'd be proud of her, she's linked up with Ray Jones's *best friend*, his actual real-life best friend, she's on the *inside*, she's going to bring us *so much meat*!"

"Then leave her to it. I believe you have one or two things on your desk back here in New York."

"I'm taking care of all that, Hiram, I'm taking care of everything. I just need a couple more days here to—"

"You and Sara have an extracurricular association, do you not?"

"Hiram! What are you saying? Do you think I'd stay away from the office for nothing better than *sack time*? Hiram, we know each other!"

"Oh, very well," Hiram said, because, in fact, he did know Jack. "A couple more days."

"You're going to be so happy, Hiram."

"Don't promise what you can't deliver."

"Okay. You won't be *un*happy. You won't be *too* unhappy. You won't be any more unhappy than you can stand, how's that?"

"See you next week, Jack. In New York."

So that was part of Jack's adventures on the telephone. The rest of his phone surfing concerned his other projects for *Trend*, those items that were, as Hiram had so delicately mentioned, on his desk back in New York. With an encouraging call here, an apologetic call there, an explanatory call somewhere else, Jack managed to keep all his current Indian clubs in the air by long distance, and then he grabbed his cameras and went outside.

To take pictures. Many pictures. Pictures, for instance, of Louis B. Urbiton at lunch in a Forsyth diner with the prosecution team of Buford Delray and Fred Heffner. Pictures of various scalawags entering and leaving the *Galaxy* nest on Cherokee. Pictures of Harry Razza, drunk with various other drunks, all of them members of the fourth estate, including pictures of Harry handing great wads of money to bartenders to keep the other drunks drunk.

And this morning, pictures of a very disheveled Don Grove and Chauncey Chapperrell being transported in handcuffs from the holding cells in the back of the Branson police station and around to the Branson municipal court, where there was no problem of overcrowding in the spectator seats. And even, illegal though it might be, pictures (taken when nobody was looking) of Don and Chauncey in court itself, being tongue-lashed by a judge while a black-suited *Galaxy* lawyer who looked remarkably like a ferret stood silently to one side, eyes darting this way and that, searching for rats.

This sequence was followed by further pictures of Don and Chauncey looking abashed in the city hall parking lot with the ferret attorney, after that creature had paid their fine and agreed they would be out of the state of Missouri by the end of this calendar day. And *these* were followed by pictures of Don and Chauncey snickering together in that same parking lot, once the company ferret attorney had left. And the last in the series, just a split second before Jack went away from there to seek for greener pastures, was of Don staring open-mouthed directly into the telephoto lens—lovely tonsil shot.

Jack knew the Binx Radwell reporter team, or most of them. They'd been his own team, once upon a time, in those happily dead bygone days of yore when he himself had been a *Weekly Galaxy* editor. The few additional members of the team, added since his reign, had been easy for him to pick out and become familiar with. He was determined to get each and every Galaxian in Branson on film, to get each and every one of them doing something he or she shouldn't.

It was working, too. Still, as Jack drove away from the gaping-mouthed Don Grove, it occurred to him there was one member of the team he hadn't seen for some little while. One-third of the Down Under Trio, the indomitable Aussies. Louis B. Urbiton and a photographer were hanging out with the prosecutors. Harry Razza was continuing to ply the world's press with drinks.

But where was the lanky, laconic Aussie with the big nose? Where was Bob Sangster?

27

The automobile that Sara and Cal shared, he driving, as he took her out to see Ray Jones's house, was a maroon Jaguar town car with the steering wheel on the right instead of the left. So the car had been built for use in Britain and its Commonwealth, or maybe Japan or some other part of the world where traffic keeps to the left, and it had either originally been driven in that country or had been bought this way by Ray Jones to show off. Whichever the case, Sara found it unsettling to be in the driver's seat, looking out through the windshield at the uneven and nerve-racking traffic of southern Missouri in tourist season, and have neither steering wheel nor foot controls for comfort. Her foot kept stabbing for the brake, her hands kept twitching in her lap, and it wasn't until they were in Hollister, where everybody had to slow down a bit, that she could divert enough attention from the road to say, "This is a nice car. How come Ray happens to own it?"

"He bought it from Jeremy Irons," Cal said, laconic and open, both eyes on the road.

Pursue that? No. Clearly, it was one of those facts that was best left alone. The *whole* story, even if she managed at last to mine it out of Cal, would have as its connecting core something commonplace like a shared agent or a booking manager's mother's next-door neighbor. Leave it where it is: A country singer in Branson, Missouri, owns a right-wheel Jaguar that he bought from Jeremy Irons.

All of which led Sara to remember the first rule of life, a rule that all reporters and many other people are well aware of. The first rule of life is: Everything is either mysterious or boring—that is, either unknown or known. The unknown is mysterious and the known is boring. This postulate explains everything and is therefore boring. (The corollary is that insecure people prefer to be bored because it's safe.)

Everywhere you go in the vicinity of Branson, Missouri, the vehicle driving ahead of you is either a cement mixer (because of the massive amount of cheap construction going on) or a Ride the Ducks open-top bus. This time, as they drove from Hollister around to Table Rock Dam, just down to the right from where Belle Hardwick had been so furiously murdered, it was a Ride the Ducks bus leading the way. Tourist children leaped and bounced on top of the thing as though it were a popcorn maker and they the corn, while their parents excitedly jabbed one another and pointed at trees.

At the turnoff to Jjeepers! and the Porte Regal golf course/ condo/luxury-living complex, the Ride the Ducks bus went straight ahead, taking the tourist families to wherever it is the tourist families go (someplace with fried food), and Cal turned the Jaguar right. He slowed for the speed bump by the guard shack and waved at the guard. Sara noticed that the guard never looked at her, in the normal driver position, but looked straight at Cal to wave back, which meant this was a known vehicle here and suggested the guard turnover was slow enough so they'd learn the residents' cars. A question, of course, that would eventually come up in the trial: Was that definitely Ray Jones's red Acura SNX coming through the gate shortly after the murder, and who was behind its wheel?

Porte Regal was as artificial and well maintained as Disneyland. The earth will have to live another 3 or 4 million years before it naturally produces a surface this smoothly rolling and evenly unscarred. Real trees here somehow looked slightly smaller than life-size, and therefore not real. The low buildings were all in earth tones, suggesting that had there been any scenery, they would have blended in with it. For most of the drive, the golf course was visible, just beyond a condo complex or through a mustered platoon of trees.

Cal drove almost to the far end of the complex, slowly, braking with care at each spot where the golf-cart track crossed the road. The occasional large American car passed, going the other way, and at times golfers were close enough to the road to have recognizable faces, but Cal didn't do any more waving after the front-gate guard. There wasn't much of a sense here of a community.

Ray Jones's house was wide and low, a southwestern ranch style on an extremely flat parcel of land nicely furred with very green and very short grass. Beyond the house, the land dipped just slightly as though curtsying, then swept up past the golf-cart track to the golf course. Shrubbery had been planted at the hem of the house by a professional in such matters, but the rest of the land had been left open, as though in fear of Indian attack. The broad blacktop driveway leading to the three-car attached garage looked liquid, almost molten, and Sara was disappointed when the Jaguar's tires didn't sink into it at all, didn't even leave a wake.

"Here we are," Cal said, of course, and cut the engine. They got out of the car, and the air seemed nicer here somehow, as though the thoughtful operators of Porte Regal had installed a massive dehumidifier somewhere.

"This way," Cal said, and Sara walked around the Jag to follow him along the curving path of large round fake stones to the front door.

Cal had a key. He unlocked the door, opened it, and said, "Gimme a second here."

"Sure."

An alarm keypad was mounted on the wall a few feet to the left of the door. Cal went to it and punched in a number, too fast to follow. Grinning at Sara, he said, "If I don't do that, we'll get all *kinds* of security around here."

Sara nodded at the keypad. "You know a funny thing?" she said. "Most people, it turns out, use their own birthday as their code number on those pads."

Cal blinked a lot but otherwise merely looked politely interested. "They do?"

"A person like Ray Jones," Sara said. "His birthday's public knowledge, isn't it? Listed in *People* or *USA Today* or some fan magazine somewhere?"

Cal thought about that. The blinking stopped. "Huh," he said.

"Just thought I'd mention it."

"You're real good," Cal allowed, and beamed upon her. "I'll tell Ray he oughta change it."

"Make it *your* birthday," she suggested.

"Or yours."

"No, you'll want to know the year." Sara stepped forward from the entryway, looking at a large, airy, well-furnished, comfortable, pleasant, impersonal living room. "Nice place."

"Ray worked with the architects and the designers and all them people. Every step of the way."

"You can see his personality in it."

Cal gave her a sharp look; so the zingers didn't zing by him after all, did they? So she fessed up, grinning and saying, "That was just a joke."

"When you lived in as many hotel rooms and motel rooms and buses as Ray Jones," Cal said, "this here *is* your personality."

"I suppose it is."

"Come on, let me show you around."

The house was comfortable, God knows, and maybe Cal was right. After years on the road, maybe deep impersonal comfort, clean uncluttered comfort, simple low-maintenance comfort, *was* Ray Jones's personality—or, in any event, his ideal.

Cal expected Sara to particularly admire the kitchen, being she was a woman, and she accommodated him by admiring it with extravagant ignorance, being a woman who felt that the first step in any recipe at home was to pick up a Chinese menu and the second step was to pick up the phone. She also admired the hexagonal dining room, with its air-traffic controller's view of—what else?—the golf course. And also the big game room downstairs with its bar *and* its pool table *and* its Ping-Pong table *and* its giant built in TV screen. She admired the master bedroom, large enough and with a deep-enough wall-to-wall shag carpet so a person could sleep on a different rectangle every night for a year. And the two guest rooms, too, both of which were modeled after better-quality motel rooms and showed not the slightest indication of recent—or any, come to think of it—use.

"No children?" Sara asked.

Guarded, Cal said, "Ray's estranged from his two daughters."

"How old are they?"

"Twenty-three and twenty-six."

"Did the estrangement begin when he started going out with girls younger than them?"

"Before that," Cal said. "When Cherry took them away."

"The ex-wife. I'm remembering."

"Ray's trying to forget," Cal said. "He give Cherry a lot of money to just go away and leave him alone, and he told the girls to see him anytime they wanted, but Cherry turned them against him."

"What are their names?"

"Christy and Charly," Cal said, and spelled them both, then added, "Their real names are Christine and Charlotte."

"And Cherry's real name is Shirley."

Cal's brow furrowed. "I don't think so," he said.

The tour finished, the nonprobing questions shallowly answered, they wound up back in the living room, where Cal said, "Want to see a tape?"

Always a surprise from Cal. "What kind of tape?"

"Ray working, here in the living room."

"What do you mean?" she asked, looking around for gym mats or Nautilus machines. "Exercise tapes?"

"Naw," Cal said, amused by her. "See, what the thing is with Ray, he had so many years running late at night, he has trouble to go to sleep early, and this is an *early* town."

"I noticed," Sara agreed.

"So he set up equipment in here," Cal explained, "and when he can't sleep, he comes in and practices songs, works on new songs, and puts it all on videotape."

"In here?"

"Let me show you," Cal said, and crossed to the inner living room wall, opposite the front door, beyond the baby grand piano that jutted out from the right. The space back there was dominated by a mahogany built-in structure with open shelving to display memorabilia, plus some sections closed off by heavy dark ornate Mexican-looking doors. Opening a couple of these doors, Cal revealed a large TV monitor, a VCR, extra sound equipment, and a small TV camera mounted and fixed in place, pointing straight ahead.

Resisting the impulse to flinch away from that TV eye, Sara said, "Is that thing on?"

"No, no, there's a red light up here on top, tells you when it's recording. And these two show lights here come on, or the picture'd be too dark."

Cal opened another of the Mexican doors, to reveal rows of videotapes, each with pen-and-ink notations on the spine. "Ray saves his tapes," Cal explained, "in case there's something good on them he can use later."

Sara went over to look at the tape boxes. Each was dated in spidery but firm writing, and most included a word or two under the date, probably to indicate what song Ray had been working on that night. A lot of the tapes were marked "IRS," which must be the song she'd heard him sing on the bus, and which suggested his tax problem had been looming large in his mind for some time now.

Sara said, "Now I get it. I know he said one time, he was sorry he didn't tape the night of the killing, and I didn't know what he meant."

Pointing, Cal said, "Sure. You see? Nothing for July twelfth. And that would have proved he was here instead of out anywhere with Belle or anybody."

"Well, the prosecutor would say he'd altered the date, wouldn't he?"

"Then why didn't he?" Cal asked reasonably, and pointed to another tape, saying, "Just put a one in front of July second."

"Maybe he should have," Sara said.

"Too late now," Cal said, and reached for a tape. "Want to see one?"

"Sure."

Turning the equipment on, inserting the tape, Cal said, "I'll play you this one because it's a song you won't know."

"Why not? I've been to his show."

"He's still working on it; he don't feel like it's a hundred percent ready. Well, you'll see. Sit down there, why don'tcha."

Sara sat in one of the low well-padded armchairs facing the screen from across the room. Cal started the tape and moved to a similar chair, saying, "Let me know when you had enough."

"Absolutely."

Snow. An image. This room, this identical room, but at night. What must be the show lights Cal mentioned made deep shadows in the background, so that the chair Sara was sitting in made a shadow in its screen persona that reached almost all the way back to the door, which was hardly visible at all.

What was mostly visible, standing about halfway between Sara's chair and the screen, was Ray Jones, in black T-shirt and jeans, barefoot. He'd brought out a dining room chair to put one foot on, with his guitar resting on that raised leg. At first, he didn't look at the screen at all, but at his fingers working out chords on the guitar. Then he hummed a bit, then he sang a few words, then went back to his guitar work some more.

"Takes him a while to get into it," Cal said.

"It's fascinating," Sara said. And it was. She watched Ray

Jones work out notes, chords, progressions, then fit the words into the music, sometimes changing a word, sometimes a note, sometimes merely an emphasis.

After a while, Ray put the guitar down on the chair and went over to the piano, which was barely within camera range and quite poorly lit, so that he almost disappeared when he sat down to play. Four or five minutes, he spent at the piano, and during that time he did no singing, merely tested his melody, altering, changing, changing back, pounding away with varying accompaniments in the left hand. He was an accomplished pianist, which was a surprise to Sara, but with no delicacy of tone; every note came out with the same thudding precision.

After the piano, Ray went back to the chair and the guitar, and for the first time he looked at the camera and acted like a performer. He sang part of the song, a longer and more coherent stretch of it than before, but then broke off and did some more second-guessing. And so on.

When it was all over and done, Sara was astonished to discover she had just spent an hour and five minutes watching that tape. It had all been disjointed and frustrating, one false start after another, but fascinating as well, as she had said to Cal at the beginning, to watch the determination and the knowledge of the man, to watch a workman good at his work *doing* his work.

It hadn't been until the very end of the session that Ray had put the chair off to one side, stood flat-footed facing the camera, strummed the guitar, and sang the song all the way through:

> *There's rules and regulations,*
> *Worse than the United Nations.*

It seems to me that it's only for fools
To obey those regulations, and those rules.

It's hard at times to stay within the law:
If I got my freedom, why can't I be free?
So what's those rules and regulations for?
They haven't got a thing to do with me.

I'm speedin down the road at ninety-two,
Though the signs all flashin by say fifty-five;
I want to see what this old car can do.
This car can kill . . .

                         someone who was alive.

There's rules and regulations,
Worse than the United Nations.
It seems to me that it's only for fools
To obey those regulations, and those rules.

You love 'em, and you leave 'em, that's the way,
They get a kid, there's nothin' else to do;
You pack your ditty bag one sunny day,
Don't leave a thing . . .

                         except a part of you.

We need these regulations
To hold together all our nation;
You know it's only greedy men and fools
Who ignore the regulations and the rules.

America's the greatest land on earth.
The smartest move I made was be born here;

Where every man and woman knows their worth,
A land of hope, and not a land of fear.

At which point, Ray segued into "America! America! God shed his grace on thee, and crown thy good with brotherhood from sea to shining sea." Then he stopped, and yawned, and said, "Enough." He walked forward toward the camera, hand reaching out.

The tape went to snow. "Wow," said Sara. "And he didn't mention taxes once."

"Nor murder, neither." Crossing to the equipment, just as Ray had done, to rewind the tape and shut it all down, Cal said, "That's gonna be his next release, after the trial."

"If *he's* released, after the trial."

"Well, yeah," said Cal.

28

Leon "The Prick" Caccatorro, chief negotiator for the Internal Revenue Service in its ongoing discussion with Ray Jones as to just how many pounds of flesh he owed Uncle Sam, had borrowed a hive for himself and his team from the U.S. Department of Energy's offices at the substation at Table Rock Dam. Had Ray cared to, he could look out Leon "The Prick's" office window and see the spot where he was supposed to have done all those things to Belle Hardwick. But he didn't care to.

Jolie didn't care to have him here at all, but he'd insisted. After court let out at 3:40 on Friday afternoon, while Warren and his team went off to show the tape of day one to the shadow jury, Ray took Jolie to one side and said, "Get hold of Leon 'The Prick.' I want to meet with him this weekend."

She reared back, causing seismographs to flutter all over the state. "*You* want to meet."

"This whole thing's been done arm's length, Jolie."

"Damn right."

"Damn wrong, you ask me. I hate having this damn trial

and the IRS hanging over me at the same time. That guy with the sword, who was he?"

"Damocles."

"No, that was the sword. Anyway, you know what I mean, and he only had *one* sword hanging over him. I got two."

"Ray, let sleeping dogs lie."

"Leon 'The Prick' is not sleeping, Jolie. We got the weekend, no trial going on. Call him and set us up a meeting tomorrow, anytime he wants."

"For God's sake, Ray, why?"

"I wanna know what the details are."

"You never did before."

"I do *now*. I want to know what our position is, and I want to know what their position is, and I want to know what's between them."

"A space the size of the solar system."

"So maybe we can move inward a couple planets, get some *motion* going here."

"Ray, you'll say the wrong thing, you know that. That's why you let *me* handle all this—"

"I won't, Jolie, I swear to God, I promise on a stack of Bibles, Boy Scout's honor, whatever you want. This time, I'll be good."

"I don't like it, Ray."

"That's okay, Jolie. Just do it."

So she just did it, frowning massively all the way, and that meant, at 11:00 A.M. on Saturday, with the world outside a massed and colorful chorus of tourists in polyester, Ray and Jolie entered the Table Rock Dam substation offices and were shown to Leon "The Prick" Caccatorro's lair, where Leon himself awaited them like a vampire.

Leon "T P" was a cadaverous man in his forties who wore

his dead father's dark suits, cut down to more or less fit. He wore his father's white shirts, too, and his father had had twice the neck of Leon "T P," so behind the tight knots of his father's wide dark ties, the old frayed white cloth could be seen to bunch and pucker, well in front of T P's Adam's apple.

This apparition's bat cave, on the second floor of the substation offices, somehow never seemed to draw the sun. There were three rooms set aside here for T P and his crew of three: The Prick's own den, an outer reception office, and a small conference room. The other three members of The Prick's gang were a secretary, an accountant, and a guy who stood around a lot, maybe waiting for a bus, but none of them mattered. Only Leon "T P" Caccatorro himself mattered.

The Prick ushered Ray and Jolie into the conference room, where they all sat around the oval table, The Prick and the accountant on one side and Ray and Jolie on the other. The secretary stayed in the reception office, and the other guy was somewhere around, waiting for a bus.

Jolie got the ball rolling: "Ray here, as you know, doesn't have much of a business head. That's how he got into this mess in the first place, taking bad advice from people who should have known better. So he's let me try to handle the situation for him, but you know he's got other problems as well—"

"We know," Leon "The Prick" acknowledged.

"And I think it's getting to him," Jolie said. "So he wanted to come here today, meet with you, find out exactly what the situation is."

"It's a quite simple situation," T P said. "Ray Jones owes the government money, and the government wants it."

"Well, it's not quite *that* simple," Jolie said. "Let's not go back to square one here. On the one side, we've got the original indebtedness, plus judgments, interest, and penalties, all still piling on. On the other side, we have reality."

T P's lips moved in what might have been a smirk. "And what," he asked, "is reality?"

"Ray Jones is finite," Jolie said. "He has only so much money; he has only so many more songs in him; he has only so much life expectancy. The government, speaking realistically, is *never* going to get the full amount of tax owing, plus interest, plus penalties, and you know it as well as I do. The question is, then, What will the government accept as full recompense, and in what form will the government accept that recompense?"

Ray said, "Jolie? What do you mean, what form? Money's money, isn't it?"

"Copyrights in songs are an asset," she told him. "Royalties, future royalties from past records, that's another asset. Royalties from performance of your songs by other artists, that's another."

T P added with ghoulish relish, "Box-office receipts from your theater. Product-endorsement payments."

"Don't have any of those right now," Ray said.

"You have had in the past," T P reminded him. "Beer, at one point, I believe, and wasn't it sausage?"

"And the Interstate Bus Company," Ray said. "They'd be real distressed if you forgot that one."

"I won't forget anything, Mr. Jones," T P said, and smiled that smile again. His teeth were small and narrow and crooked, but they looked sharp.

Ray felt Jolie's warning eye on him, and he didn't respond anymore, just sat back and nodded and tried to look like a sober businessman. The conversation went on without him, mostly Jolie and T P batting it back and forth, with occasional footnotes from the accountant, and what it all came down to was: Ray Jones's money, for the purposes of this discussion, separated into three categories. First, there was money still coming in on songs he'd already written and/or recorded, and small residuals from reruns of TV shows he'd been on. Second, there was whatever money he was earning right now, at the theater in downtown Branson and through his *Best Hits* album sales on late-night TV. And third, there was future income, from those first two sources and also from any new songs Ray might take it into his head to write and/or record.

The difference between Jolie and T P was that Jolie wanted to pay the government mostly out of the first category of money, earnings derived from the past, with a little topping up of the tanks for a while from present earnings, while T P wanted a part of anything Ray might do in the future. In Jolie's plan, in other words, which Ray liked insofar as he could like anything to do with this cock-up, the government would get half a loaf and then be out of Ray's hair forever. In T P's plan, the government would be in his pocket for all eternity, his partner. The impasse was caused, on the one side, by Jolie and Ray's absolute refusal to let the government be Ray's permanent partner and, on the other side, by the government's greedy belief that the real gold was in them thar future hills. Until T P could be distracted from the future by a demonstration that the past would eventually generate enough income to satisfy the bulk of the debt, the impasse would continue.

As it did today, for close to an hour, back and forth, Jolie and T P clearly disliking one another but both being formal, both finding endless ways to restate the same old positions, endless ways to try to make the same old positions sound like new positions, like compromises of some sort. Round and round the maypole they went, and then Ray decided it was time to make his move. "Leon," he said, "let's cut through the crap, okay? Mind if I call you Leon?"

"Not at all," Leon said, squinting and showing those sharp little teeth.

"I'll put you a proposition," Ray said.

Jolie, alarmed, said, "Ray? We haven't discussed this."

"That's okay, Jolie," Ray said, giving her a look of exasperated sincerity. "But none of you people's getting anywhere, and this whole thing's running me down. It's bad publicity, for one thing, on top of the bad publicity about the trial, and I've had enough bad publicity; it's gonna hurt me with the fans. And it's buggin' me, too, goin' on for years, affecting how I sleep, how I eat, how I digest my flapjacks."

Jolie said, "Ray, for God's—"

"No, Jolie," Ray said. "That's why I wanted this meeting, get myself an idea when this thing is gonna be *over*, and I can see right now, the way it's going, it ain't never gonna be over." Looking at T P, Ray said, "It ain't ever gonna be over because you can't go into court and enforce a judgment against me while we're still in this bullshit good-faith negotiation, because if you *could* go into court and whomp me, you'da done it last year. You wanna correct me on that, Mr. Leon?"

"The government is patient," T P said.

"I know it is," Ray said. "And I know I'm not, but that's why I hire a whole passel of people that are patient by profession. People like Jolie here. So here's my proposition. You people all talk about money from the past and money from the future, right?"

"Essentially," T P agreed.

"So here's my offer," Ray said, "and it's a onetime deal,

the last offer you're gonna get that isn't bullshit string-'em-along stuff. You can have fifty percent of one or the other."

Jolie looked as though she'd just been shot in the forehead. T P floundered, then said, "I'm not certain I know what you mean."

"Fifty percent of money that comes from the past," Ray said, "or fifty percent of money that comes from the future. You pick."

"By future," T P said, "you mean any new song you might write, anything that is not as of this date copyrighted?"

"Right."

"Plus future income from the theater and record sales?"

"But only on those future songs," Ray said. "Royalties on old copyrights, that's the other kind of money."

"But a new album, containing a mix of old and new songs, would generate new money, would it not?"

"Sure, throw that in, too. If that's what you want the fifty percent of, fine."

"*Ray!*"

"Shut up, Jolie." To T P, Ray said, "Or you could go the other way. Money that comes in for anything I did before a certain time, before . . . well, pick a date. I tell you what. July twelfth. The day Belle Hardwick went down. If that's the way you decide to go, then any money at all that comes in on stuff I did before the twelfth of July this year, you get half of it. Simple, clear, something a country boy like me can understand."

T P had a canary feather stuck in the corner of his mouth. He licked it away and said, "I'll have to check with D.C. on Monday, of course, but if that's the proposal that you and your advisers agree on—"

"It's the proposal *I* agree on," Ray said grimly. Beside him, Jolie had turned into a mountain of marble awaiting a sculptor, but that was okay. Ray had his own agenda here, and it was all going according to plan.

"Then I don't see why," T P said, smirk now in plain sight, "sometime in this coming week we can't come to an agreement."

"Good. Get this thing out of the way."

"Choose the one," T P said, and giggled a little, "or choose the other."

"Just let me know which," Ray said. "But remember, I'm serious about this. This is the last shot. We come to an agreement on this now or I'll stonewall you forever. I'll cost the government millions just to hire file clerks to pack all the paper away; my grandchildren will stonewall your grandchildren. It's now or never, and I mean it."

"I don't see any problem at all with your proposal," T P said.

"We're gonna have a deal? Guaranteed?"

"I still must check with D.C.," T P said, "but I think I can guarantee, within the parameters you've just given, we will definitely have a deal."

"When?"

"I should think by the middle of the week," T P said, "we could be generating the paperwork."

"Just tell me where to sign," Ray said, and got to his feet. T P also rose, wiping his right palm on his father's pants, but Ray didn't offer to shake hands. "I won't take up any more of your valuable time," he said, deadpan, and turned to say, "Jolie? You ready?"

Jolie struggled into consciousness from a coma. She stared

numbly at Ray, then at the preening T P, then at last heaved herself to her feet and silently followed Ray from the conference room and from the building.

It was as they were approaching the Jag, parked in bright sunlight amid the tourists' campers, that Jolie found her voice. "Do you know," she demanded, "Ray, do you have any *idea*, what you just did in there?"

"I cut through the bullshit."

"You gave away the store!"

"I gave away half the store," Ray corrected. "No, half of half. I can live with that. Whichever way he picks."

"Whichever *way*? The one thing we've been trying to do, for months now, more than anything else, is keep the feds away from future earnings, and you just *handed* them future earnings! On a silver platter! Months of negotiation down the drain!"

"Well, we'll see," Ray said. "Come on, I'll buy you lunch. Or are you dieting again?"

29

"What's going to happen to Binx?" Sara asked.

Jack looked at her in surprise. "Binx? Why should anything happen to Binx?"

It was Saturday night and Sara and Jack were having dinner at the Candlestick Inn, where she'd been Thursday with Binx, so that hapless fellow had been intruding into her thoughts the entire meal. She said, "Well, he's the one we're going to expose, isn't he? Him and his team?"

Jack snapped a bread stick as though it were Binx's neck. "So?"

"So what if they fire him?"

"They fire everybody," Jack said. "Sooner or later, they fire everybody."

"I know, I know," Sara said, tired of that excuse, "but when they fire everybody else, I'm not responsible."

Jack put down the halves of his bread stick. "You're responsible for Binx Radwell? Responsible for his life? Responsible for his decisions?"

"No, of course not," Sara said, frustrated and helpless. It didn't help to be told her guilt feelings were irrational. *All* guilt feelings are irrational, in that with sufficient sophistry all actual guilt can be reasoned away, but so what? Sara didn't want to bury her sense of shame toward Binx; she wanted to wallow in it, and she wanted Jack to wallow in it, too, and the bastard just wouldn't cooperate. "The only thing is," she said, still hoping to explain herself somehow, break through his leather skin somehow, make him feel *bad* somehow, "we all used to be friends, in the old days, Binx and us."

"That's the way you remember it, eh?" Jack smiled at her. "That's nice."

"All right, we had friendly competition," Sara said, and Jack laughed out loud, and Sara hated him, but had to grin and duck her head and say, "Oh, all right."

She pretended to eat for a couple of minutes, aware of Jack's eyes on her but determined to say not another word on that or any other subject, and then Jack said, "Two things."

She looked up at him, expectant. Two things was two things more than she'd anticipated. "Yes?"

"The story is two stories," Jack told her. "I was on the phone with Hiram again this afternoon, and we've agreed on that. The *Weekly Galaxy* is one story and the Ray Jones murder trial is a different story."

"What does that mean, exactly?"

"It means I'm going to do the *Weekly Galaxy* story," Jack said, "so if any rain falls out of that cloud onto Binx's head, it's my fault and not yours, okay?"

"That helps," she admitted. "Not a lot, but some."

"So that means," Jack said, "you're doing the Ray Jones trial story as the Ray Jones trial story—country celebrity on trial in a country setting."

"Good," she said. "I can do that, no problem."

"Just go a little light on the salt-of-the-earth stuff, okay?"

"I won't mention gingham once," she promised.

"Glad to hear it."

"You said two things," she reminded him. "Was that both of them?"

"No. The other thing, I didn't know when exactly to tell you."

"Uh-oh."

"Not that bad," he said, and grinned at her. "We're still the dynamic duo."

"The unholy two."

"Now and forever. However, Hiram says I gotta go back."

"When?"

"Tomorrow."

The feeling that came over Sara now was much more real and much harder to take than her crocodile guilt over Binx Radwell. She'd enjoyed having Jack around, enjoyed sharing with him her reactions to this weird place, enjoyed sleeping with him. "What's the hurry?" she asked.

"Well, it isn't exactly a hurry," he said. "I've been here almost a week as it is, and Hiram's wanted me back since Wednesday. I stalled it as long as I could, but now I gotta go. I said to him, 'Why don't I stay till the end of the trial?' and he said, 'We have somebody covering the trial.'"

"Me."

"That's who he had in mind, all right."

"I'll miss you," she said.

His face was really very attractive, in those rare moments when he permitted an honest expression to cross it. "We'll miss one another," he said with a rueful smile. "But then we'll be together again."

"I'll hurry home."

"You do that. The instant the trial's over."

"In the meantime," she said, pointing at his wineglass, "don't drink too much of that stuff. I'll want you at your best tonight, for the farewell scene."

30

Binx Radwell slept, when he slept, humidly, curled on his side, arms and legs bent, hands and feet twitching like a dog chasing a rabbit in his dreams—only, in *his* dreams, Binx was the rabbit. And Binx awoke, when he awoke, in terror, eyes staring, heart pounding, listening for horrors in the dark. Then he'd get up and work a while on the project until he was calm enough to go back to bed.

No one in the world knew about Binx's project, and perhaps no one ever would. No one knew that Binx was a changed man, and perhaps no one ever would, but he was. The change had begun during the time when he was fired, when his fear and despair were at their most acute, and when he had nothing but time on his hands. He'd started the project then, partly to distract himself from reality and partly as an excuse to close himself into his study, away from Marcie and the kids.

Then, when he was rehired, the project languished, he returning to it only occasionally, usually when on assignment on the road. But when Massa died, and the Pure Reef Development Corporation took over control of the *Galaxy*, Binx knew immediately and instinctively that change was coming and that the change could not possibly be for the good. He went back to the project, then, more seriously than he'd done anything in years, and it had grown.

He still worked on it, but only at night, when the great tides heaved him out of sleep onto the stony shore of consciousness. By day, he was either too busy or had been drinking too much; only at night, in the sharp edge of night's terror, did he have the clarity to work on the project.

Saturday night, Branson, Missouri. Binx's bedroom in the *Galaxy* house on Cherokee is the only room in the house to remain what it had been, all the rest having been converted to the purposes of communication. Three times he clawed out of sleep, shaking, sweating, and calmed himself with half an hour or so of further work on the project. The fourth time he jolted awake, scared, staring, surrounded by enemies, there was daylight beyond the drawn window shade and the sounds of voices on the other side of his closed door.

It was Sunday, and there was no rest for the wicked. Binx arose, locked the project away in the attaché case under the bed as usual, spent some time in the adjoining bath, and went out to see what fresh mischief had been occupying his troops. Later today, he'd have to go over to 222, which still sailed merrily on like a ship of the heedless condemned in an allegory, but not yet; he wasn't up to 222 just yet.

The kitchen was now a darkroom, so for breakfast Binx had to get into a *Galaxy* car and drive downtown, ten minutes away, to eat various kinds of grease. Then he went back to the house on Cherokee and prepared himself for his two required awful phone calls to Florida, the daily obeisances— to the *Galaxy* and to Marcie—but as he sat there, tasting this morning's grease and thinking about what he might say to the citizens of Florida, the front door opened and a diseased

Englishman entered, his pale and poxy face open in a smarmy smile. "Happy time, ladies and gentlemen," he announced. "You must all think happy thoughts now. Boy is among you."

It was true. Boy Cartwright, the most successful of the *Weekly Galaxy*'s editors because the most loathesome, a sickly, pasty creature in his mid-forties, who had lived most of his adult life on champagne and Valium, who would sell his mother for a nickel and beat her up for you as a favor, was *here,* here in Branson, here in the *Galaxy* house, here on *Binx's turf!*

Binx leaped to his feet from his chair of pain, squawking: "This is *my* story!"

Boy gazed upon him with superior pleasure: "Ah, Binx, lad," he purred, with that voice like a fur-coated tongue, "what a bundle of energy you are. Come walk with me and talk with me, and tell me of many things." Boy crooked a finger, smiling like a road-show Oscar Wilde, and turned to go back outside, fouling the morning air by his presence.

Binx had no choice but to follow. He did, trying to look stern and manly and in charge, to bolster the morale of the onlooking troops, but inside he quaked with fear and rage. He knew what this was; he knew what this meant. Don Grove and Chaunccy Chapperrell had been arrested, had spent a night in the Branson bastille and been fined and tongue-lashed by a local judge, and it was going to be *Binx's* fault. Unfair, unfair, unfair; but who ever expected fairness, after all? (Binx did, and couldn't help it.)

Boy wanted to stroll up and down, though there were no sidewalks, and the *Galaxy*'s cars lined both curbs. So they walked in the street, on which, fortunately, there was rarely any traffic, and Binx said, "Just tell me one thing straight out. Am I fired again?"

Boy smiled like a gargoyle made of bread dough. "But of course not, dear boy," he said. "Our lords and masters admire your persistence; they esteem you. Really."

"They sent you here."

"To assist, dear boy, assist, nothing more." Gazing around in mild amusement, he said, "What a charming corner of Americana this is, every bit. One will enjoy working here, rubbing elbows with the hoi polloi, taking the pulse of the great unwashed."

"What's going to happen to *me*, Boy?"

Boy looked at Binx as though a bit surprised to see him still there. "You, dear boy? Why nothing. Everything's already happened to *you*."

"Why do they think I need to be assisted?"

"Oh, well, our employees in Newgate overnight, you know, there was the feeling, just the slightest feeling, you know, that perhaps the hand on the tiller was not quite so *firm* as it might be."

"How can that be *my* fault? How?"

"No one's talking about fault, dear boy, blame, all that sort of thing. You take these things too much to heart, if I may say so. Take the long view, lad, take the long view."

"I will," Binx said grimly, his mind hardening. "I definitely will."

"We're closing down, you know, that little bacchanal of yours over at that hovel called the Palace," Boy said.

"We are?"

"Its effectiveness has diminished. We'll retain the space, however; in fact, I'll be staying there." With a pouting little smirk, Boy said, "One has always wanted to live in the Palace."

"When do you want me to shut it down?"

"Oh, it's done, Binx," Boy said, and showed his awful

rotting teeth. "What I'll want *you* to do, gather so much of your team as is not in durance vile—"

"Nobody's in jail now."

"Praise heaven for small favors. I'll want to see them all this afternoon, in my digs at the Palace, at fourteen hundred hours."

Binx added and subtracted: "Two o'clock, in Two-two-two."

"Felicitously phrased." Boy yawned, a dreadful sight, and stretched his diseased soft body. "I take it you've breakfasted."

"Or whatever it was."

"Such a long drive," Boy said. "I believe I'll nappy-doo. Ta ta till two, in Two-two-two."

"Ta ta," Binx said, smiling on the outside, gnashing his teeth to slivers on the inside. He stood in the street while Boy clambered into the anonymous gray *Galaxy* sedan he'd driven all the way from central Florida, then drove off one-handed, ignoring the road to consult his map of Branson. His wobbling departure did not hit any parked cars, but it came close.

Binx remained where he was, like Lot's wife, until Boy and his gray chariot disappeared. Outside, there appeared to be no change in him, but within, Binx had annealed. A particular fantasy that had always been too terrifying to consider transmuting into the real world had now become marginally *less* terrifying than reality. Action, daring action, had suddenly become possible.

With a firmness of step and a clarity of eye that would have astounded anyone who knew him, Binx turned and marched back into the house and over to the phone farthest from prying ears. He dialed the Lodge of the Ozarks, folded his shoulder down between his mouth and the rest of the room, and said, "Jack Ingersoll, please."

It was Sara's voice that answered, warm and sleepy from bed. "Mmm? Yes?"

Binx's resolve stumbled. If only I had a Sara, he thought in a regression to the former self, as sexual arousal worked through him like hot-pepper sauce in his blood, then I wouldn't have to do what I have to do. Voice trembling with more emotions than he understood, he said, "Sara, it's me. Binx."

"Oh, Binx, hi." Rustling sounds in the background. She's sitting up, the covers falling from her breasts. Binx managed not to moan. "What can I do for you?"

Many answers swirled in his head. He said, "Is Jack there?"

"Sure. You want to talk to him?" Off, she said, "Jack, wake up. It's Binx." Muffled mumbling. "He says, 'What's it about?' "

"I have to talk to him, Sara."

More muffled conversation, then Sara back. "He has to drive to Springfield this morning, fly back to New York. He says why not call him at *Trend*?"

Panic and dread. "*No*. Back to New York? I have to see him *now*. It's important."

Mutter, mutter. Sara: "Important to who? Whom?"

"All of us. I'm not kidding."

Mutter, mutter. Sara: "How about the coffee shop here in twenty minutes? But he can't stay long."

"He shouldn't stay," the new Binx said, "any longer than he's interested. When I'm boring him, he should go away."

Surprised, Sara said, "Why, Binx. What's gotten into you?"

"It isn't in, Sara," Binx told her. "It's out."

And he hung up, went to the bedroom, got out the attaché case with his project in it, and carried it with him out of the house, into a *Galaxy* car, and through the Sunday-morning traffic jams of Branson to the Lodge of the Ozarks, where Jack—without Sara, damn it—lounged over muffins and coffee. From somewhere, he'd obtained a Sunday *New York Times*, but to show he was still a regular guy, it was the sports section he was reading.

Binx slid into the booth across from Jack and ordered from the nice waitress three glasses of grapefruit juice. Jack raised an eyebrow. "What's that supposed to do?"

"Increase my acid."

Jack closed up Sports and gave Binx his attention. "What's going on, Binx? You're looking clear-eyed."

"Boy arrived this morning," Binx said. "To assist me."

"Boy? That guano dweller?"

"He's going to live in the Palace now."

"I'm sorry, Binx."

"Two of my people spent Thursday night in the Branson jail."

"Yeah, I heard."

"They didn't say it yet, but they're going to fire me again."

"Sooner or later," Jack said, "they fire everybody."

Binx's upper lip curled. "I'm not everybody, Jack," he said. "I'm *me*. They're going to fire *me*."

"Your problem is," Jack said, "you take things too personally. Besides, maybe they won't."

"You're going to do us in *Trend*."

Jack looked away, shrugged, crumbled a muffin. "Maybe, maybe not. Nobody's sure yet."

"If I'm not fired already, I will be then."

"Well, you know, Binx," Jack said, "every once in a while in life, there comes this opportunity for a career change."

"That's right," Binx said.

Jack peered at him. "It is?"

Binx said, "The last time I was fired, I had time on my hands, you know."

"That's what happens, when you're fired."

"I thought I'd do a *Galaxy* exposé myself," Binx said.

"I bet you'd do a good one, too," Jack assured him.

"It's hard, though," Binx said, "without something to drive you. The paycheck, the boss, all that."

"Sure."

"Still, I did some. I kept it up, too, ever since."

"Good for you."

"And the approach I took, I focused on the different editors."

"That's one way to do it, I suppose."

"The things they did, the reasons. I've got a lot of it done. I thought maybe you—"

"I do my own pieces, Binx," Jack said. "And my own research."

"Still," Binx said, and opened the attaché case on the bench beside himself. Leafing through the sets of typescript, each set with its own paper clip, he chose one and brought it out. "You might find some of this useful," he said, and handed that set to Jack, who reluctantly took it. "That one's you," Binx said.

Jack frowned. He looked at the top page, scanning, skimming, then began to read more slowly. The waitress brought Binx his three grapefruit juices. He drank the first one down at a gulp, the cold sharpness a pleasure on his tongue, in his mouth, in his throat. "Did I really do all this?" Jack said mildly.

"Afraid so."

"Some of it's quite outrageous, isn't it?"

"Some of it's felonious."

"But not very provable, Binx."

"Oh, I don't know," Binx said. "I know where the witnesses are, and I know how to get them to talk."

Jack hefted the thin manuscript. "What do you want to do with this?"

"I thought I'd send it to *Trend*."

"Not interested. Wouldn't publish it."

"That's all right. I'll make multiple submissions. *The New Yorker*, *Vanity Fair*, *GQ*, *New York*, the *Times*."

Jack disdainfully dropped the manuscript onto the table. "Don't be stupid. Nobody's going to want to publish this parochial crap."

"But they'll all read it," Binx said. "They'll make copies and pass them around the office. There's great anecdotes in there, Jack. You were quite a scamp."

Jack was clearly controlling fury, with some difficulty. "What would *you* get out of it?"

"Everybody gets fired, Jack, isn't that it? Sooner or later. What happens when *you* get fired? Time for a career change?"

Jack thought that over, then looked at Binx with something different in his eyes, something Binx didn't recognize. "Binx," he said, "you're a changed man."

"I am," Binx said, and couldn't help but smile. That's *respect* in his eyes! No wonder I didn't recognize it.

Jack nodded. "So what do you really want?"

Binx reached into the attaché case, brought out the rest of the papers, leafed through them, handed a set to Jack. "Here's Boy." The rest he dropped on top of the Jack history, already on the table. "All told, nine editors. A lot of stuff there, Jack."

Jack had been smiling over the Boy story. Now he looked at Binx and said, "You're giving me this."

"Yes."

"Why? What's in it for you?"

"That's background for your piece, research. It's worth something."

"Money won't solve your problems, Binx."

"It can help. But money isn't all I want."

"I didn't think it was. What else?"

Binx gestured at the manuscript. "That's my résumé. That shows you what I can do, professionally speaking. On the basis of that, *Trend* can make me a roving correspondent."

Jack slowly nodded. "Spell it out," he said.

"A little money, not a lot. I've given up being greedy," Binx said, and smiled in a new way. He drank the second grapefruit juice; it was just as good as the first. He said, "I have an idea for a story that's right up *Trend*'s alley. I'll need travel expenses, some living expenses."

"What is this story?"

"Eastern Europe," Binx said. "The coming of democracy and capitalism, and all of a sudden there's a free press. Magazines and newspapers being born all over those countries, raw and new and learning how. And *free*. A survey piece. The free press, behind what used to be the Iron Curtain."

Jack sat back, fingering a muffin, thinking it over. Binx drank his third grapefruit juice. It was the best of all. Jack said, "*Trend* pays your expenses to Prague, Sofia, Warsaw, somewhere. You've got an assignment letter, letters of introduction. You're connected."

"Sounds good, Jack."

"A survey piece for us, but you're job-hunting. And they'll like you; they'll take you on. Not much money."

"Don't need much money, Jack. Not anymore."

"Over there, you're the old pro, the guy who knows how. Girl reporters at your feet."

"Oh, better than that, I hope."

A broad smile crossed Jack's face. "I'm happy for you, Binx," he said.

Binx's heart leapt. "You're going to do it."

"Of course I'm going to do it. Even without the blackmail, I might have done it."

"We'll never know."

"So you're getting out," Jack said. "And you might even turn in the survey piece."

"Stranger things have happened."

"Not much stranger," Jack said, and looked intently at Binx. "What about Marcie and the kids?"

Binx returned Jack's gaze with his own level look. He'd never felt better in his life. He said, "Who?"

31

When Sara learned, in the Branson *Beacon* (reading the local newspaper was both good sense and good manners), that Ray Jones would be among the stars to appear on Sunday afternoon at a charitable fund-raiser for the local hospital, rather alarmingly named Skaggs, she knew she had to go. The setting was a big tent in the parking lot of the Grand Palace, the four-thousand-seat theater and video complex that was an elaborately pillared and porticoed white Dixie plantation house fronting a huge, sinister, featureless gray box big enough to hold all the world's Scud missiles, as though Tara had been attached to a nuclear plant. The huge yellow-and-white-striped tent in front of this harridan with a painted face flapped in the fitful breeze, and at 12:40 Sara joined the line of families snaking slowly forward toward the volunteers at the folding tables, who took their money and peeled off little orange tickets from giant rolls. Hand-lettered red-on-white signs taped to the front of the folding tables read SUGGESTED DONATION $4.

"Press," Sara said, an automatic reaction, when she reached the volunteer, and showed her *Trend* ID.

The girl, who was probably herself named Skaggs, gave Sara a look of deep dislike and mistrust. "Jested donation four dollar," she said.

Oh well. Sara dug a five out of her wallet, handed it over, waited for change, and got an orange ticket instead. The volunteer looked past her at the next in line, and Sara said, "Could I have a receipt?"

The volunteer's antipathy increased. "A what?"

"Oh, never mind," Sara said, and proceeded to the entrance to the tent, where a scraggly Skaggs volunteer who was possibly trying to grow a mustache ripped her ticket in half, gave her back one part, and she entered the tent.

It was merely an open space, without seating of any kind, except for the folding chairs under the people selling T-shirts behind the trencher tables along the rear. Families milled on the blacktop under the tent, and at the far end a temporary stage had been set up, flanked by enough giant speakers and amplifiers to send a message to Mars.

Sara was lithe and slender, a rarity in that crowd. She slithered through the families, intending at first to establish herself all the way up front, but then she took another look at those speakers and amplifiers and veered off instead to a fairly quiet spot midway down the right side.

Already, children were bored and crying. Already, fathers and mothers were holding fractious infants in their arms and bouncing leadenly from foot to foot. Already, people everywhere looked as though they'd been on this death march for months. But none of them would sit down. A rock-and-roll audience, or a jazz audience, or even a classical music audience, in this situation, would arrange newspapers or jackets or *something* on the blacktop and sit down, but there's a sweet instinctive formality to the country fans. Sitting on a blacktop parking lot would not be seemly, so they wouldn't do it. They would stand, no matter. After all, suffering is the human condition, as the country families well know, here below.

The show was supposed to start at one and last an hour and a half, so as not to steal any audience from the regular commercial three o'clock shows in the theaters up and down the Strip. And by God, at exactly one o'clock, a fellow in a black frock coat and a black string tie came bounding up onto the stage, grabbed a microphone, grinned, and waited while all those hundreds of people who'd recognized him and wanted to applaud their recognition gave him an (necessarily standing) ovation. Sara realized she was undoubtedly the only person inside this tent who did not know who Mr. Frock Coat was.

She missed Jack; already she missed him. His plane out of Springfield would have been airborne for about half an hour now, on its way to St. Louis—for the change of equipment, as the airlines say, for some reason not wanting to acknowledge that they use airplanes to move people from place to place. The new equipment would take Jack to New York and their dear little apartment on West Eleventh Street. She missed him. She missed the dear little apartment. She missed New York. But mostly, she wished he were right here in Branson this second, this instant, standing next to her here inside this tent, so there'd be *somebody* around she could share her reactions with, someone she could understand who would understand her. It's never an entirely comfortable feeling to be alone deep inside another tribe's territory.

Mr. Frock Coat thanked everybody for the warm welcome. He reminded them how much Skaggs Community Hospital had done for folks over the years and he thanked them for helping to support that good work. He thanked the performers who were about to come out here and give selflessly of their time and talent so the good work of Skaggs Community Hospital could go on. And he said he didn't want to take up any more of everybody's time; he'd just introduce the first artist, who was *Soandso*!

Soandso was a somewhat hefty, tall woman dressed entirely in vermilion, head to wrist to toe, covered with bugle beads. Her hair, of which she had a lot, was a clashing orange in color, and the electric guitar she carried displayed most of the other shades of the red section of the spectrum. Her eyelashes were long enough to hang laundry on, her smile would light Central Park, and when she thanked everybody for the applause that had welcomed her, she had a voice like a backhoe.

But it was powerful, all right, and even melodic when used for purposes of singing. Soandso was a belter; she stood well back from the microphone and delivered two songs about hard times on the field of love. Both songs were clearly well known to the crowd and well liked by them. After the applause following the second, Soandso said, "You're all gonna see Ray Jones in a little while," and that got its own rush of fervent applause, following which Soandso said, "Ray's havin' more than his share of troubles these days, but he's always been a good friend to me and he's a *fine* songwriter. I'd like to dedicate this to Ray and wish him the best." And she did a gravelly honky-tonk version of the song Ray had sung to Sara in the bus: "It's Time to Write Another Love Song (This Time, The Song's for You)."

Big applause. Soandso blew kisses, waved her guitar, disattached the guitar from the amplifiers, and jounced away, revealing a behind that looked like the world's largest candy apple. Mr. Frock Coat bounded back and introduced somebody else, and Sara spent her time watching the audience, trying to think about Ray Jones and his trial—trials, there was also the income-tax thing—and his relationship with his audience, these people here. What did it mean? What could she make it mean, in a piece for *Trend,* that wouldn't make Jack, or Hiram Farley, throw up?

Then at last, Ray Jones was introduced, and he got a whole lot of applause. When it died down, he said, "You know, Branson's my home, been my home for a while now, and if I feel like maybe I can do something to help Skaggs Community Hospital, it's mostly a selfish act, because it's my community and my community hospital, and I can't tell you how happy I am, as a local boy, that they are there. So thank *you* all for supporting their good work. And now"—*strum* the guitar— "I'd like to sing about my favorite girl. Anybody out there with that name? My favorite girl's name?"

Squealing, absolute squealing, from the crowd. Girls and women of all ages jumped up and down, waving their hands over their heads, yelling, "Me! Me!"

And yelling something else, too: a name. Their own name, it must be, and Ray Jones, like so many songwriters before him, must have written a song to a particular girl's name. A popular name among the country fans, from the agitation in the crowd. What were they shouting?

Fllrrumm went the guitar, and Ray Jones sang:

> *Tiff-fa-nee, you're pretty as a picture.*
> *Tiff-fa-nee, you're sweet as berry jam.*
> *Anywhere you are, I'll be right witcha.*
> *Anywhere you go, that's where I am.*
>
> *Tiff-fa-nee, you're good as golden apples.*
> *Tiff-fa-nee, you're nice as apple pie.*

In your eyes, the light of lovely chapels.
In your eyes, the blue of heaven's sky.

When we met, I heard your name so sweetly,
Ringing like a bell, a chandelier.
You know you have captured me completely.
You know I will always be sincere.

Tiff-fa-nee, your voice is like a robin.
Tiff-fa-nee, you move with such sweet grace,
I can feel my heart within me throbbin'.
Every time I gaze upon your face.

When we met, I thought you were above me.
Your sweet lips were open in a smile.
Tiffany, if you could only love me,
How I'd love to walk you down the aisle.

Tiff-fa-nee, if we could live forever,
Tiff-fa-nee, I'd live life by your side.
Beautiful, you know I'd leave you never.
Come with me, my love, and be my bride.

Sara couldn't make a sociological statement out of that one
at all.

32

Monday, the trial got into high gear. Sara sat between Cal and Honey Franzen again, watching, remembering, wishing she could take notes but afraid it might just be the gesture to drive Jolie's forbearance beyond endurance. And anyway, what was happening was memorable enough.

Over vociferous defense objections, the jury was shown photos of the dead Belle Hardwick, as well as of the scrubby lakeside land where the murder had taken place and the blood-stained interior of the red Acura SNX. The prosecution wanted to bus the jury over to the actual murder site—on a Ride the Ducks?—but even Judge Quigley realized that was going too far, both figuratively and literally, and ixnayed it.

Still, the prosecution made its approach clear from the opening salvo. Their two-pronged attack was first to demonstrate the absolute depravity of the crime and second to establish the absolute depravity of Ray Jones, thus linking him to the crime by making him the only person in the vicinity vile enough to have committed it. Since all they had in real terms was circumstantial evidence, and rather shaky circumstantial evidence at that, this was clearly their wisest approach. As the old legal dictum has it: If the facts are with you, pound the facts; if the facts are against you, pound the table. The prosecution pounded the table.

There was a lot of stuff they wanted to pound the table with, and the defense blocked them at every turn. They wanted to bring in the Ray Jones tax problem. They wanted to introduce supposedly cynical or unchristian lyrics from his songs. They wanted to talk about his marital life. They wanted to talk about a previous legal record that seemed to consist of the various things that can happen when you combine alcohol with automobiles. They even wanted to mention a decades-old song plagiarism suit against Ray that had been dismissed as frivolous and without merit the first time it had reached a court.

Every time one of these unacceptable side roads appeared on the horizon, Warren Thurbridge was at once on his feet, objecting loudly, eloquently and unceasingly, drowning out the offending matter, seeing to it by his volume and vocabulary that not one extraneous syllable tainted the jurors' ears. And each time, Judge Quigley would pound her gavel and order the jury removed while she consulted with the attorneys at the bench, and the technician running the defense team's video camera would switch it off, not to switch it back on until the jury returned.

The jury did a lot of marching back and forth Monday morning and the video technician did a lot of switching off and on. Sara, watching all this, thought there wasn't going to be much tape for the shadow jury to look at later today, which made her realize she wanted desperately, hungrily, voraciously to watch the shadow jury in action.

At lunch, which she was permitted to take with the defense team in the conference room of Warren's offices, presumably because all strategy had already been worked out and nothing of dangerous importance was likely to be said over the ham-and-American sandwiches and really sweet coleslaw, Sara began to wheedle Cal for permission to sit in on today's shadow jury session, "even for just one minute, just to get the idea of it."

At first, Cal didn't even want to broach the subject with the lawyers in the room, not wanting his head bitten off, but then Sara said, "Ask Ray. If he says yes, they'll have to go along with him. If he says no, I'll give up."

"Well, I'll try it," Cal agreed, and went away around the conference table to hunker down beside Ray and engage in muttered conversation for a while. Ray raised an eyebrow in her direction at one point (she smiled like a sunny schoolgirl back at him), then muttered with Cal some more, then turned to mutter at Jolie on his other side, and from the great light-ning-flash thunderclouds that immediately formed all over Jolie's head, Sara knew the answer was good news even before Cal came back and said, "It's okay. Ray'll fix it."

"*Thank* you, Cal. And thank you, Ray." She smiled and nodded in his direction, but he wasn't looking at her.

"Only for a minute, though," Cal warned.

"That's all I want; that's all I ask. Boy, I appreciate this, Cal."

"Sure," Cal said, looking dubious but relieved.

The afternoon session in court brought more meat but not less controversy. A skinny rat-faced young woman, Jayne Anne Klarg, identified as an ex-employee of the Ray Jones Country Theater, had allegedly been called by the prosecution to testify that she had seen Ray Jones in what appeared to be intimate conversation with Belle Hardwick on more than one occasion (not including the night of the murder, unfortunately, which was not emphasized), but it soon became clear that she was actually on the witness stand to suggest she'd left Ray Jones's employment because he'd made unwelcome sexual advances and had frightened her when she had rejected him.

Warren was getting a lot of exercise today, popping to his feet at every other word, objecting all over the place, while Jayne Anne glared. Fred Heffner, the state prosecutor from Springfield handling the testimony, did his best to insert the information into the ears and brains of the jurors despite Judge Quigley's reluctant agreement that he really shouldn't do that.

Sara had expected Warren to chew Jayne Anne to bits when it came time for cross-examination, but he had a different tack in mind. Mildly, he said, "You quit your job at the Ray Jones Country Theater?"

"Because he was all the time—"

"I asked you," Warren overrode her, "if you quit your job."

"Of course I did! Nobody likes to be treated—"

"You weren't fired, is that right?"

She blinked. She looked wary. "I was quittin'," she insisted, which was an odd locution, all in all.

Warren returned to the defense desk, picked up a piece of paper—a business letter, it looked like—and returned to the witness. Holding it up in front of her, he said, "Is this a copy of a letter that was sent to you by the box-office manager at the Ray Jones Country Theater?"

She squinted. She didn't like that. "I guess so."

Fred Heffner was on his feet. "May I see that letter?"

"After Judge Quigley, I think," Warren told him. He handed the letter to the judge, who read it, frowned with disapproval at the witness, and handed the letter to Fred Heffner, who read it, looked extremely expressionless, handed the letter back to Warren, and returned silently to his seat.

Warren: "You were dismissed, were you not?"

Jayne Anne: "I was quittin'."

Warren: "You were not dismissed for any reason having to do with Ray Jones or unwanted overtures, were you?"

Jayne Anne: "What?"

Warren: "You were dismissed for—"

Heffner (rising): "Your Honor, the reason for Miss Klarg's dismissal is immaterial to the matter at hand. We do not dispute the defense contention that Miss Klarg did not resign, as she earlier suggested to us, but was dismissed."

Warren: "Thank you, counselor."

Quigley: "The reason for the dismissal need not concern us."

Warren: "Agreed, Your Honor." To the witness (smiling): "But you did pay it back, didn't you?"

Heffner (rising, wounded): "Your Honor!"

Warren: "Withdraw the question. I've finished with this witness, Your Honor."

The next witness was the gate guard at Porte Regal, who for Fred Heffner was absolutely positive it had been Ray Jones's red Acura SNX he'd waved through into the compound late that night, and who for Warren Thurbridge was equally absolutely positive he couldn't be sure who'd been at the wheel, or indeed how many people had been in the car.

And there, astonishing everybody, the prosecution rested. It was barely three in the afternoon. Warren agreed with the suggestion from the bench that the defense didn't feel like starting its presentation today and Judge Quigley gaveled the court closed until 9:30 the following morning.

A quick phone call was made to the motel in Branson where the shadow jury was being sequestered and then the defense team plus Sara crossed the street to Warren's offices to await the jurors' arrival.

The feeling in Warren's offices was cheerful, even smug. What had the prosecution presented, after all? Their circumstantial evidence, boring, easily forgotten, all last Friday. This morning, the jury had essentially seen nothing but the judge agreeing with the defense and chastising the prosecution, and this afternoon the prosecution's principal witness had exploded in their faces. The state had shot its bolt, it hadn't laid a glove on Ray Jones, and now all the defense had to do was establish the principle of reasonable doubt and they'd be home free.

The self-congratulatory sense of well-being was infectious. Sara felt the lift of it herself, though it wasn't her fight and, realistically speaking, the outcome didn't matter to her one way or the other. She was an experienced reporter and an experienced magazine writer. Whatever the conclusion of the trial, Sara would find within it a larger meaning, a mirror in which America could gaze upon itself with perhaps a new understanding, blah blah blah. Nothing to it.

About twenty minutes later, the shadow jury's bus—not a Ride the Ducks, but a charter from Interstate, for whom Ray used to do promos and, who knows, might again—arrived out front. Through the curtained former showroom window, Sara watched the people, who looked remarkably like the actual jurors she'd been observing in the courtroom across the street, climb down from the bus, squint in the sunlight— the bus windows were tinted—and cross the sidewalk toward the building.

"Oh my God!"

Sara jumped away from the window as though it had

grown teeth and bitten her. The jurors were beginning to enter, to file past her toward the conference room. There was a secretary's desk behind her; she dashed to it, sat down, swiveled the chair halfway around so her back was to the jurors, and became very interested in the contents of a bottom file drawer.

Immediately, Jolie was at her side, reaching down as though to slam that drawer, barking, "Get out of there! What do you think you're doing?"

"Shut up!" Sara hissed, with such commanding urgency that Jolie stepped back, startled, and stared at her as though Sara were foaming at the mouth.

Sara risked a look over her shoulder. The last of the jurors was passing, was gone. Straightening, she said, "Jolie, get Warren out here. *Now.* Before anything else happens."

"Have you lost your—"

"Don't be a *fool*, Jolie. You can tell when I mean it."

Jolie could. She gave Sara one last glare—this better be good, kid—then turned and bustled off to take Warren away from his jurors.

Which gave Sara a minute to look around and think, so that when Warren came back with Jolie, distracted and irritated, saying, "What's this?" Sara merely rose, put her finger to her lips, and motioned for them to follow her outside. They didn't want to—they wanted to believe she'd gone crazy—but they followed.

Hot humid sunlight beat down on the sidewalk. Sara turned, and as Warren and Jolie both started to demand something or other, she said, "One of your jurors is a ringer."

That stopped them. They frowned. They stared at one another. Warren said, "What do you mean, a ringer?"

"I mean one of your jurors is not a bona fide Taney County

voter. One of your jurors is actually a reporter for the *Weekly Galaxy.*"

Jolie nearly squeaked: "That *rag*?"

"You know it, eh?"

"The things they've said about Ray over the years—"

"Are nothing," Sara interrupted, "to what they mean to say about him. And about all of you."

Warren said, "What do you mean, all of us?"

"I've had a minute to think it out," Sara said. "I know how those people think; I've had experience with *Weekly Galaxy* reporters before." It seemed to her, all in all, better not to mention that she'd once been such a reporter. "And how did they get the information about the shadow jury?" she asked. "How did they get to know what you know fast enough to slip one of their own people in instead of the person you were going after?"

Jolie stared at the building with horror. "They bugged us!"

A man for whom light had suddenly dawned, Warren said, "The telephone repairers!"

"Sounds good," Sara said.

Warren explained, "After everything was installed, these two came back and said there was a problem, and fixed it."

"They sure did. Where did they work?"

"In my office," Warren said, his usually robust voice gone hollow. His tan had faded, too.

"Everything you've said in that office," Sara told him, "is now on a *Weekly Galaxy* tape."

"My God."

To Jolie, Sara said, "Aren't you glad now you let me come along?"

Warren didn't have time for good fellowship. He said, "Which one? We have to get rid of—"

"No no no, not that fast," Sara said. "Jack Ingersoll, my boss at *Trend*, it happens he's working on a *Weekly Galaxy* exposé right now. I want to call him, see how he wants to handle this."

Outraged, Warren said, "How *he* wants to handle it?"

"You wouldn't know a thing if it weren't for me," Sara pointed out.

"If what you say is true," Jolie said. "If you aren't just trying to scare us for some reason of your own."

Sara looked at her. "You want me to walk away?"

Warren said, "Miss Joslyn, Sara, tell us who the ringer is."

"Right after I find a pay phone and call Jack," Sara told him. She turned away, then turned back. "And I suggest, if you don't mind, that *you* find a pay phone and call a debugger."

33

Branson is an early town. That was a real jolt for some of the performers, who were used to the pace and timing of the road, where your two shows would usually begin at eight and eleven, or Vegas, where some of the shows on the Strip started at nine and midnight. In Branson, where the families and the retirees bed down early and rise early—PANCAKES! ALL YOU CAN EAT!—the shows begin at 3:00 and 8:00 P.M. Some of the performers have trouble for a while, getting up to speed in the middle of the afternoon and then being required to turn off in the middle of the evening. But eventually, even the most night owl of the show folk adapt to the slower rhythm, and even come to enjoy it.

Ray Jones was one who had the hardest time shifting gears. In the old days, he'd toured 250 to 300 days a year, sleeping by day in the moving bus, rising like a vampire as the sun went down to perform into the night for the people out front, then partying back till it was time for Cal and the boys to pour him back onto the bus; occasionally stopping a town or two away to eject a lady friend who hadn't realized the party was over.

The last few years, in Branson, he'd grown used to sleeping in a bed that wasn't traveling at sixty miles an hour, he'd grown used to the concept of being up and about in direct sunlight, and he'd even grown used to performing the three o'clock matinee—pretending, on the rougher days, that it was a rehearsal or a record date. But the hardest mental shift had been the idea that by 9:30 in the evening, the day was *over*— no more shows, no more people out front, and even the members of the band yawning and scratching themselves and looking bleary-eyed. By midnight, even Honey Franzen would have gone home to her little ranch style on Mockingbird Lane, north of the Strip, toward Roark Creek.

That's why he'd set up his little videotape operation out at the house: to give him something to do on those long nights when there weren't any shows to perform, there weren't any people, and there wasn't even any bus. (In fact, there was a bus, stashed at the farthest corner of the parking lot out behind the theater, and sometimes, in the deepest winter, when the Branson tourist business at last dried up, Ray still did a southern tour or two, mostly out of nostalgia, his as well as the customers. But it would be six months at least before he rode that bus again—or maybe, if things went wrong with this Belle Hardwick thing, a lot longer than six months.)

The Belle Hardwick thing had been a disruption in a number of ways, but now that the trial had started, the disruption was even more complete. Because he had to be in court all day long, showing his honest citizen's face to the honest citizens of the jury, he couldn't do a 3:00 P.M. show, only the 8:00 P.M. That had now become the first show, and his mind and body just *craved* a second show three hours later, just when everybody else in his world had gone to sleep.

God, it was tough. He was raring to go, ready to let performance soothe his shattered nerves and battered psyche, ready to let those hours under the lights on the stage clean out all the bad thoughts and bad vibes, fears and apprehensions, but the world was *shut down*. Meantime, with the trial going on and all, the pressure from the fans who wanted to see that one and only show per day was *extreme*. Flouting the fire laws, his people had put a row of folding chairs in front of the first row of regular seating and two more folding chairs at the top end of the aisles. They'd even dropped the Elvis gag so they could sell the Elvis seat; the girl reporter and her editor wouldn't be able to get in at *all* these nights.

With all those people out front, laughing and applauding and approving and adoring, it was hard to stop. The shows got longer and longer. Songs he'd decided for reasons of personal image not to perform until the Belle Hardwick thing was over, he had begun to sing again. (Not all of them; "My Ideal," for instance, he still wouldn't touch, maybe never would again.)

But the fact of the matter is, the fans *wanted* Ray to be a rogue, if a lovable rogue. He was one of their outlaws, like Willie Nelson and David Allan Coe, and they wanted that whiff of brimstone they knew he could if he chose deliver. So that was why (in addition to the fact that he didn't want to get off the damn stage) he was bringing back into the repertory songs like "L.A. Lady" and "The Dog Come Back." The people who knew "L.A. Lady" was about his ex-wife, Cherry, liked that one, but just about everybody liked "The Dog Come Back":

Oh, things seemed pretty bad, but now they're not so black.
It's true my wife has left me, but the dog come back.

I've been drinkin' pretty heavy since I lost my job,
Been lookin' for an easy 7-Eleven to rob.
But now I'm not so broke up that I got the sack.
The missus may have walked out, but the dog come back.

The girls down at the pool hall never meet my eye.
I just can't find me a woman, however hard I try.
But I don't mind the silence in my solitary shack.
The little woman's run off, but the dog come back.

The pickup's got an oil leak, and the rifle's choked with
  rust.
Instead of boomin' right along, I go from bust to bust.
Still I keep it in my memory, when things get out of whack,
The battleship has sailed off, but the dog come back.

Oh, a man can face a lot of woe, and not get thrown off
  track,
If his wife will only leave him, and the dog come back.

Oh, if that could only be the whole of life. To get up here and sing the songs, backed by the good old pals and terrific musicians of the band, with the cheering fans out front, everybody happy, everybody simple and clean, the good music flowing out, the good times happening, *these* are the good old days.

If only.

34

For Bob Sangster, the big-nosed Aussie from the *Weekly Galaxy*, permanent member of the Down Under Trio, life as a shadow juror was one long vacation. All he had to do was laze around the motel all day: in and out of the swimming pool; in and out of the special dining room set aside for the jurors and stocked at all times with a working buffet; in and out of the common room full of magazines and board games and VCR movies, where he flirted dispassionately with three of the five female jurors—shadowettes, he called them—the other two being just too ridiculous. Then, late in the day, all fourteen shadows would get into the bus and be driven from Branson over to Forsyth to look at the video of that day in court, or, that is, as much of that day in court as the real jury had seen, which tended to be not very much.

Bob was known to his fellow shadows as Jock O'Shanley, a naturalized American citizen originally from Galway Bay, brrrrightest jew-wel aff the Umerald Aysle. The actual Jock O'Shanley, a night cook at Skaggs Community Hospital, a divorced loner living in an amazingly filthy cottage down by Ozark Beach, and a dedicated alcoholic, was at the moment having his own vacation, at *Weekly Galaxy* expense, in San Diego, where most of the alcoholics are seamen and therefore expected to stagger a little on land.

Jock O'Shanley wasn't the sort of amiable Irish drunk who made friends easily, or at all, so it was unlikely any old pal of good old Jock's would suddenly pop up and say, "*You* ain't Jock O'Shanley, bugger me eyes!" Nor were Jock's employers at the hospital surprised when he'd called to say he was taking a couple weeks away from the job; well, actually, they were surprised he'd *called*. Physically, Bob Sangster and Jock were alike enough, both being rangy gnarly guys consisting mostly of bone and gristle marinated for a good long time in booze, and in Taney County an Australian accent can pass for an Irish accent with no trouble at all.

For the two days of the trial so far, Friday and Monday, Bob was conscientious enough in his simulation of Jock O'Shanley the shadow juror. Over in Forsyth each day, after the fourteen of them had watched the videotape of that day in court, Warren Thurbridge and his assistants would ask questions and solicit opinions, and Bob, not wanting to invalidate the process by his presence any more than was absolutely necessary, did his best to give responses a Jock O'Shanley might give. In the second part of each afternoon's exercise, when the lawyers discussed with their shadow jurors various strategies and ploys that might be put into play on the morrow, Bob again let his knowledge of the beliefs and prejudices and ignorances and knowledges of such a fellow as Jock O'Shanley guide his tongue, and all was well.

His actual work, though, the work he did for the *Weekly Galaxy*, came at the end of the day, when the jurors were bused back to the motel in Branson. There, in the semiprivacy of his room—two jurors per room, each juror with a king-size bed, Bob's roommate being a retired upholsterer from Cleveland named Hacker—Bob would remove the cassette recorder taped to his side—ouch—take out the cassette, and pass it to the maid named Laverne. In the morning, she would bring him the blank to take the used one's place, which he would install in the machine and tape the machine again to his side.

And that was that.

The maid named Laverne had been suborned on Friday morning, the first day of the trial, by a fierce young *Weekly Galaxy* reporter named Erica Jacke, whose flaming red hair and hard aerobics body distracted attention from her gaunt-cheeked face and icy hazel eyes. As Erica approached Laverne in the parking lot that first morning, it was hard to believe both belonged to the same species, Laverne being soft and round and sweet and sloppy and kinda dumb. "Hi," Erica said, with what might have been good fellowship.

"Hi," questioned Laverne.

"You work here, don't you?"

"Yes'm, I do." Laverne looked at her Goofy the Dawg watch. "And I'm gonna be on time for once, too."

"That's great," Erica said. Then she said, "You know about the people sequestered in there?"

"The what?"

"Well, you do know about the Ray Jones trial."

"Oh, sure!" Laverne said, and grinned widely and leaned forward to half-whisper with bubbling excitement, "Do you think he did it?"

"Men," Erica said. "What do *you* think?"

"I just bet you're right," Laverne said.

"You're going to find out, when you go to work in there,"

Erica told the girl, "there're people in there that are off in their own section, can't see anybody else or anything—"

Wide-eyed, suddenly afraid of her place of employment, Laverne said, "What did they *do*? Is it a *jail*?"

"No no no, they're helping with the trial; they're the extra jury."

"Extra jury? There's an extra jury?"

"Oh, they always do that," Erica said. "In important cases, they do. So if something goes wrong with the first jury, they always have an extra jury that can step right in."

"I never knew that," Laverne said, smiling broadly again, happy at the accumulation of knowledge.

"The thing is," Erica said, "my boyfriend's one of those people on the jury, and they're not allowed to see *anybody*, and I miss him *already*."

Now, this was a palpable lie, Erica Jacke being as far as you could imagine from girlfriend material, but there are natural romantics in this world, most of them overweight, and Laverne was one. Her heart softened even more at this image of lovers wrenched apart by the inexorable processes of the law. "Gee, that's awful," Laverne said.

"And I know he misses me, too," Erica said. "We've never been away from each other before."

"Gosh," Laverne said.

Here it came. Out of her shoulder bag, Erica drew the tape cassette. "I just did a letter on tape," she explained, "because I just *know* Jock would like to at least hear my voice."

"Is that his name?"

"Jock O'Shanley."

"That's a pretty name!"

"I love it," Erica admitted, trying to look like a person

melting in love, but failing miserably. "What's *your* name?"

"Laverne. Laverne Slagel."

"*That's* a pretty name, too! I'm Erica Peterson," Erica Jacke lied.

"Erica?" Laverne's eyes lit up. "Like on 'All My Children'?"

"I was *named* for her!"

"*Really*? Has she been around *that* long?"

"Oh sure," Erica said, blithely maligning a fine actress named Susan Lucci. "My mother told me, in the early days, that show was actually in black and white."

"I never knew that!"

"Anyway," Erica said, calling attention to the cassette by waggling it in front of Laverne, "I did this letter on tape, and I so much want Jock to hear it, and I know he has his Walkman in there so he can listen to his Merle Haggard records, so I was wondering if you could give him my letter for me."

"Well, sure," Laverne said, bighearted girl that she was. "But why don't you just give it to him yourself?"

"Because they aren't permitted to see anybody," Erica explained, with what looked like patience. "The extra jury. They're not allowed to talk to anybody, or watch TV, or read the papers, or anything."

"Oh, that's *awful*! No TV?"

"I know," Erica said. "It seems un-American."

"It *does*!"

"But Jock came here from Ireland and he wants to be a good citizen, so he's going to go through with it, going to do this extra jury thing, so all *I* want is to let him hear my voice while he's stuck in there."

"That's *nice*."

"Thank you. So would you give him this tape?"

"I'd be very happy to," Laverne said, simple and sincere and pleased as punch to be a character in a love story.

"Thank you," Erica said, and handed Laverne the cassette.

Laverne looked confused, turned the cassette over, and saw the twenty-dollar bill Scotch-taped to the bottom. "What's *this* for?" she asked, wide-eyed again.

"Well, I know you get most of your money in tips," Erica said.

Not hardly, not with the tourists of Branson, but Laverne was just barely smart enough to say not a word at this juncture, to smile and lift both eyebrows, and wait.

And Erica went on: "You'll have to *sneak* that love letter of mine to Jock, so nobody sees you do it, and that ought to be worth something, shouldn't it?"

"Well, thanks," Laverne said. "Gee, thanks."

"What time do you get off work?"

"Seven," Laverne said. "Sometimes a little later."

"I'll be here at seven," Erica suggested, "just in case Jock wants to send me a love letter back."

"Oh, you think he might?" Laverne was thrilled. "And I could bring it to you!"

"You could!"

"Why," Laverne said, "it's, it's like something in the movies!"

"It is, isn't it?" Erica agreed, as though noticing the similarity for the first time.

"*You* know," Laverne expanded, "the lovers are separated, and there's this trusted person that carries their love letters back and forth and later helps them to escape."

"Well, Jock won't have to escape," Erica said, returning

them, if not to reality, at least to its vicinity. "We'll just listen to each other's love letters," she said, "until he can come home to my arms."

Laverne sighed, smiled, wiped away a tear, and slipped the cassette into her purse.

Friday evening, with another twenty bucks in her kick, this time from Jock O'Shanley, Laverne delivered his audio billet-doux to Erica in the parking lot. Erica thanked her and blessed her, then hurried away to the *Weekly Galaxy* nest on Cherokee, where Binx—still then an active coconspirator—and the rest of the team eagerly listened to the discussions among the shadow jurors and the defense team.

Monday morning, Erica was in the parking lot again, with another cassette for the faithful Laverne to carry to Erica's love (and another crisp twenty-dollar bill for Laverne herself), and Monday evening, Laverne brought out to the parking lot and to Erica the lover's reply. The only difference this time was that two photographers hired by *Trend*, "The Magazine For The Way We Live This Instant," photographers whose usual assignments were in war-torn parts of the Third World, under fire and frequently missing presumed dead, were concealed hither and yon—one hither, the other yon—to record the entire transaction.

And later, having trailed their prey to the house on Cherokee, their telephoto lenses picked up Boy Cartwright, in for the now-missing Binx, in full hideous close-up as he gloated over this clear evidence of his wickedness.

35

They all talked it over Monday night, Ray and his defense team, after the shadow jury (and its ringer, damn the son of a bitch to hell) had been bused back to Branson, and it looked as though Ray was going to get what he wanted, after all. Warren put it this way: "The prosecution's case was even worse than we thought. The car means nothing; we can demonstrate that half a dozen of Ray's pals regularly borrowed that car to impress their bimbos."

"Lady friends," Ray said.

"Bimbos," Warren repeated; he hated to be reversed. "There's no direct evidence to connect Ray with the killing," he went on, "and their circumstantial evidence is laughable. So all we have to do is be quiet and polite, and we'll get our verdict, no problem."

Jim Chancellor, the local lawyer who'd been helping out in the preparation of the case, said, "Warren, what about resting the defense? Right away, no witnesses at all. Just to point up how little prosecution case there is to rebut."

"I would do that if I could, Jim," Warren said, and nodded

his heavy head in Ray's direction, down at the end of the same conference table where late the shadow jury (and its cuckoo bird) had been in deliberation. "If Ray here would let me."

"No way," said Ray.

"As you see," Warren said to Jim.

Ray said, "We've been over it and over it, Warren. I'm not disputing your smarts, you know that. All I'm saying is, if I don't stand up there and look those people in the eye and *tell* them they're full of shit, I'll never be able to live with myself."

Jolie said, "Using slightly different language, I presume."

"Come on, Jolie," Ray said. "I know how to talk in public, you know that."

Warren turned back to Jim, saying, "So we won't do the sensible thing, I'm afraid. Our principal is determined to testify."

"Mm mm," said Jim, expressing the most profound of misgivings.

"Agreed. And yet, here he is." Warren turned again in Ray's direction. "You wanted to go first," he said. "Okay, you've got what you want. Tomorrow, you'll be our first witness."

"By God, Warren, thank you," Ray said, grinning from ear to ear. "I feel like a kid on Christmas Day."

"You're welcome, Ray," Warren said with just a hint of irony.

Jim said, "First of how many witnesses, Warren?"

"That depends how badly Ray performs," Warren said.

"And thank *you*, Warren," Ray said.

Ignoring his client, Warren told Jim, "If Ray does reasonably well, we may stop right there, while we're still ahead. If he makes a really true mess of things, I'm afraid we'll just have to keep calling witnesses until the jury forgets. No matter how many months it takes."

"It's support like that," Ray said, "that's kept me going all these years."

36

The tiny container of Mace that Sara kept in her shoulder bag was about the size and shape of a lipstick, which made it very convenient to carry but a little tricky to find in the dark in the middle of the night, with somebody coming through the motel door. On the other hand, this time it was just as well she came up with the wrong tube in her haste and panic, because she was already aiming the thing and pressing the top of it with a shaking thumb when Jack's voice said, "Is that you? Are you awake?"

Sara lowered the fatal lipstick. "Jack? What are *you* doing here?"

"Okay if I turn on the light?"

"I think you'd better."

Lights burst into existence, causing Sara to squint and to shield her eyes with the hand holding the lipstick. And there was Jack, with his suitcase and some sort of dumb grin, saying, "So that's what you wear when I'm not with you. I *like* that shorty kind of stuff."

"Do you."

Peering more closely at her, at her hand, he said, "You're putting on lipstick in the dark?"

"I was trying to Mace you. From now on, call first."

"Mace me with a lipstick?"

"Oh shut up," she said, and turned to put the lipstick back in her bag; *there* was the damn Mace. And when he ran a hand up inside her shorty nightgown, she irritably slapped it away. "Don't scare me in the middle of the night."

"I thought you'd be pleased to see me."

Then she was. All at once, she remembered how her last thought before falling asleep was how much she missed having Jack in the bed beside her.

Which didn't mean she wasn't still mad at him for scaring her. Forgiving, and not forgiving, she turned and said, "What are you doing here at this hour, anyway? What hour *is* it?"

"A little after one."

"What are you—How can you *get* here this late?"

"This time," Jack told her with an almost boyish eagerness, "we can get the *Galaxy* on a number of *felonies*, with people who would be very happy to prosecute. Hiram wanted me here to set it up. It was too late to make a connection to Springfield, so I drove down from St. Louis."

"And didn't pass a single telephone along the way."

"I wanted to surprise you."

"You succeeded. Leave Sunday morning, come back Monday night—that's fairly surprising." All at once, Sara wrinkled her mouth like a rejected page of copy and said, "Uk. What's that?"

"What's what?"

"That *taste*, it's like—I don't know what it's like."

He looked at her with real concern. "It just hit, just this second?"

"No, it's—" She made a series of disgusting mouths, with sound effects; he looked away, not wanting to know this. She said, "It's been building the last few days. I didn't notice, really, but waking up just now it hit me; it's"—smack-smack—"salty, nasty, kind of—not rancid, exactly . . ."

"Wait a minute," he said. "I've been getting it, too. You know, you don't pay attention, but you're right."

They both went smack-smack, tasting their mouths. Jack said, "Is it something in the water?"

"No, it's . . . I almost remember; it's—" She stopped, mouth and eyes wide open, and stared at Jack. "Bac-O Bits!"

"What?"

"Bac-O Bits! You know, that fake bacon stuff. You shake it out; it's like coarse pepper, only it's—what color is that? Cordovan!"

"Cordovan? And it's a *food*?"

"Kinda."

"This," Jack said, "is a part of Americana I don't want to know."

"Bac-O Bits," Sara repeated, then nodded and tasted some more. "It's the redneck's garlic," she said. "They put it on everything; we've been getting it in every meal. They put it on the eggs in the morning, on the sandwich at lunch, in the salad at dinner."

Jack, belatedly wary, hunched his shoulders and said, "I had a Bloody Mary."

"Bac-O Bits!"

"Does it build up in the body," he asked, "like PCBs?"

"It builds up in the *mouth*," Sara said, and turned toward the bathroom, saying, "Excuse me while I brush."

"Me second."

In the bathroom doorway, she turned back to say, "What did Binx want?"

"Oh, it's great," Jack assured her, chortling. "Wait'll you hear. Binx has pulled the greatest caper; he's home and dry, you'll be proud of him."

"Tell."

He studied her, eyes gleaming. "Just as soon as you brush your teeth and I brush my teeth, and just as soon as I complete my *exhaustive* study of that appealing garment you're wearing, I'll tell you all about it."

37

Tuesday morning, while Jack was off tightening the noose around the collective *Weekly Galaxy* neck, Sara was in her usual seat in the courtroom over in Forsyth, Cal on one side of her and Honey Franzen on the other. There was more of an air of expectation in court today, a sense of everyone waiting to be thrilled in some way. As Cal had explained to Sara, Ray was going to testify in his own defense this morning, over the objections of his high-priced defense attorney. "Then why is he doing it?" Sara asked as they waited for Judge Quigley to enter and gavel the crowded courtroom into session.

"He's got his reasons," Cal said. "He wants to tell his side of it."

Good drama, bad move, Sara thought as the judge did come sweeping into the room in her black robe and gavel everybody back into their seats and into silence.

Seated now at her high desk, Judge Quigley looked severely around for somebody to reprimand, found no one, and snapped, "Is the defense ready?"

Warren rose. "We are, Your Honor. The defense calls Ray Jones."

A stir, and a murmur, and a muffled hubbub—all went through the room as Ray got up from the defense table and went over to the witness seat to be sworn. Judge Quigley rapped again with her gavel. "There will be no disturbances of any kind," she announced, "or I will clear the court. Mr. Thurbridge?"

"Thank you, Your Honor," Warren said, and looking only slightly like a man who believes himself to be on a fool's errand, he approached the sworn-in Ray and the morning began.

Ray started well enough; but of course, it was his own lawyer asking the questions, and those were real easy ones he was tossing over the plate. With Warren's gentle guidance, Ray at last got to tell his side of the story to a hushed and fascinated courtroom, including fourteen hushed and fascinated jurors. He wanted all present to know that he had never had any kind of sexual or emotional relationship with Belle Hardwick, who was merely another employee in his theater; that he hadn't driven the red Acura SNX that night; that he'd been home from the theater, absolutely by himself, before 10:30 that night; that he'd been asleep in his bed by midnight; that he had not thrown away any clothing in the last month or so, nor burned any clothing, nor given away any clothing, nor lost any clothing; and that he had no idea who might have been angry enough at Belle to have done all that awful stuff to her. "Though," he added, while Warren looked just a teensy bit nervous, "it seems to me, when you get into excess violence like that, more likely than not somebody's been drinking."

"Do *you* drink, Ray?" Warren asked. But of course, Sara realized, he had to ask that and not leave the subject to the prosecutor.

"Sometimes," Ray answered. "Not when I'm working; it throws off my timing. But after a show sometimes, if there's a little party goin' on, a bunch of people kickin' back, sure, I like a taste or two. But I'm not a solitary drinker, never was."

As the testimony went serenely along like that, Sara could see Warren gradually becoming less tense. Ray wasn't being defensive; he didn't have a chip on his shoulder; he wasn't caustic or mean. He was just a reasonable, normal person who happened to be innocent of the charges against him and who would like people to know and understand that.

Warren stretched it out, and Sara could see him doing it and she knew why, but once Ray had told his story two or three times, there really wasn't much left to say, so there did have to come that moment, about an hour into day three of the trial, when Warren had to step away from his client, flash a nervous smile at the judge, and say, "No more questions, Your Honor."

Now it was the prosecutor's turn. Fred Heffner, the Lincolnesque gun from Springfield, was handling interrogation of witnesses, that being a task rather beyond the capacities of the local prosecutor, Buford Delray. (Sara was happy to see Louis B. Urbiton in a privileged seat directly behind Buford Delray. She was happy for Louis B. She wanted his impersonation of a reporter from *The Economist* to last and last, right up until the dramatic unveiling. Gotcha! Gotcha *both*, Buford.)

Fred Heffner started small and easy, saying, "Mr. Jones, I want you to know I'm pleased and happy you've decided to come forward and tell your story like this. If I tend to go back over one or two details, I hope you won't mind. It's my job, you know, just to make sure everything's crystal-clear for the jury. Okay?"

"Sure," Ray said. He seemed easy and calm, half-smiling

at the prosecutor, unworried. But was he truly the confident, well-prepared witness he appeared to be, or was he a lamb, gullible and trusting, led to slaughter?

Well, we'll see, won't we? Fred Heffner said, "Now, Mr. Jones, I noticed in your testimony a little earlier this morning, in referring to what happened to the late Belle Hardwick, you used the phrase "excess violence." Do you recall using that phrase?"

"In connection with drinking, yeah."

"In connection, I believe, with the death of Belle Hardwick. You considered her manner of death to be, in your words, 'excess violence.' Isn't that so?"

"I think we can all agree on that part," Ray said with a little grin.

Fred Heffner didn't grin back. Raising an eyebrow, he said, "Can we? What is your definition, Mr. Jones, of *excess* violence?"

Lifting himself wearily to his feet, as though he really was above this sort of foolishness, Warren said, "Objection, Your Honor. This is just some sort of semantic game. Everyone in this court knows what Ray Jones meant."

"Well, I'm not sure we do," Fred Heffner said. "That's why I'd like Mr. Jones to tell us, in his own words, what he had in mind with that phrase."

Judge Quigley, smiling upon the prosecutor, said, "I think that's a legitimate question. The phrase was introduced by the defendant; he should certainly expect to have to answer as to what he meant by it."

"Thank you, Your Honor," Fred Heffner said, while Warren shook his head at the folly of humankind and resumed his seat. Fred Heffner turned back to Ray, saying, "Let me try to make it easier for you, Mr. Jones. I take it you were saying that *some* level of violence is acceptable, until it reaches a point you—"

"Objection, Your Honor," Warren said, on his feet again. "The prosecuting attorney is putting words in the witness's mouth that are clearly *not* anything he said or meant or implied."

"Your Honor," Fred Heffner said, "all I'm asking the witness to do is define his terms."

"Then I think," the judge said, "we'll let him do so." Gazing down at Ray without love, she said, "Mr. Jones?"

Ray directed his answer straight to her. "Your Honor, I'm not in favor of violence at all. If I wanted to knock this prosecutor here down," he said, still looking at the judge but pointing at Fred Heffner, who smirked, "that would be a bad thing to do; I'm not condoning it. If I hit him and he went down, that would be a bad thing, but it's what I wanted to do and I did it. Now, if all I want to do is knock him down and I start hitting him with chairs and desks and microphones and all sorts of stuff, that's *excess*. Anyway, that's always what I thought the word meant. Whoever killed poor old Belle there, they killed her three or four times, according to what *I* read. If I call that excess, I don't mean I think it would've been all right if he just killed her once. I'm against violence, all kinds of violence. I'm a musician, not a boxer."

Bravo, thought Sara, taking sides for just a moment. You're not just a musician; you're a songwriter, and that was a good song. Well done.

Judge Quigley seemed to think so, too, reluctantly. "Thank you, Mr. Jones," she said, and she looked over at Fred Heffner, who, during Ray's answer, had gone back to the prosecution table and found a photograph, which he now held. "Mr. Heffner, are you satisfied?"

"Indeed I am, Your Honor," Fred Heffner said, approaching the witness. "In fact, that was very eloquent, Mr. Jones. What you say about Belle Hardwick having been killed several times seems to me a pretty accurate description of what happened on the night of July the twelfth. This is a picture of the victim's body after it had been taken from the water."

"I've seen it," Ray said, not taking the picture.

"Take another look at it," Fred Heffner suggested. "Go ahead. Take it."

Slowly, with evident revulsion, Ray took the photo and looked at it. From back here, Sara could see only that it was a glossy eight-by-ten, and in color. She felt that was probably all she wanted to know about that particular photograph.

"Are you looking at the picture, Mr. Jones?" the prosecutor asked.

"Yeah," Ray said, his voice heavy, "I'm looking at it."

Leaning toward Ray, lowering his voice but still clearly audible throughout the courtroom, Fred Heffner said, "Tell me, does she look like a pizza to you?"

As though he'd been hit by a cattle prod, Ray jumped in his seat, glared, and threw the photograph at the prosecutor. *"You cocksucker!"* he yelled. *"That song doesn't have a goddamn thing to do with it!"*

38

Ray over there was the one who'd stumbled, but Warren was the one sitting at the little bare desk with his head in his hands. They and Jolie and Jim Chancellor and Cal, but nobody else, were crowded into the small office behind the courtroom set aside for the defense during breaks, where they were allegedly trying to figure out what to do next. Judge Quigley had just about broken her gavel pounding it into the stunned silence that had followed upon Ray's outburst, then had shouted out an order for a thirty-minute recess "to permit the defendant to regain some measure of self-control, and to permit his extensive legal counsel, both attorneys from within Taney County and attorneys from somewhere outside the state of Missouri, to attempt to explain to the defendant something of the concept of decorum in a court of law." All of which was said within the full hearing of the jury.

Fifteen minutes of the thirty had gone by, and except for some mumbled condolences toward Ray from Cal, nobody had said much of anything. Ray stood it as long as he could and then he said, "The son of a bitch blindsided me, that's all."

His head still within the bowl of his hands, his words muffled, Warren said, "Defeat from the jaws of victory."

"It isn't over yet, Warren," Ray said.

Warren lowered his hands at last. His eyes were bloodshot. He used them to look at Ray. "It *was* over," he said. "Now I don't know."

"That judge was pretty snotty to me in front of the jury, that's what *I* thought."

Jolie said, "I noticed that, too. Warren, could that be grounds for reversal?"

"Possibly," Warren said, "though, given the provocation, I seriously doubt it."

Ray said, "Whadaya mean, reversal? I'm not gonna get *convicted*."

"You're a good deal closer to that eventuality than you were when you got up this morning," Warren told him.

"Because I said *cocksucker*? That's not a death-sentence offense."

"It may be," Warren said. "But to be honest with you, although I do regret that word having been placed into the record in that fashion, that's not the word you used that really bothers me."

Ray frowned at him. "Why? What else did I say? I didn't say anything else. I was doing pretty good up till then."

"I was proud of you, up till then," Warren agreed.

"So what word didn't you like?"

"The word *song*," Warren told him.

Ray shrugged, shook his head, scratched his elbow, pulled his ear. He looked like a base coach with three men on. He said, "I don't get it. *Song*? What's wrong with that?"

"You may have noticed," Warren explained, "when the

prosecution had its innings, they tried from time to time to include lyrics by you into the record and into the jury's ears, and in every instance we beat them back."

"Sure," Ray agreed. "We don't want me tried on my attitudes, but on what I did or didn't do."

"Very good. You'll be a professor of tort one of these days, the way you're going. But, Ray," Warren said, elbows on the table, hands spread wide, body bent forward, face pleading for comprehension, "when you mentioned *song*, you gave the prosecution the opening it wanted. When we go back in there, Fred Heffner is going to ask you, innocent as pie, just *what* song you were referring to. I happen to know the song in question, Ray. I did my homework on your repertoire, and I must say, of all your compositions, those lyrics are the ones I would *least* like the jury listening to."

"I haven't sung that song in years," Ray said. "It's out of my repertory, for the very reason that it's a kind of a male chauvinist thing."

"I'll have to go along with that, Ray," Warren said.

"Well shit," Ray said. "I don't want to testify anymore. I told my story, now the hell with it."

Warren sighed. He could be seen to grapple with the concept of excess violence in re Ray Jones. He said, "Ray, it doesn't work like that. You go up there and tell your story, and that means the prosecution gets to ask you questions for as long as they like. They can't *call* you; they can't make you testify against yourself. But once you agree to be sworn in and testify at all, you have to answer *their* questions, as well. And once you claim that a certain song of yours is not germane to the case, they have every right to question you about *that song*."

"Shit," Ray decided.

Jolie said, "Warren? Can we limit it to just that one song?"

"Possibly," Warren said. "I'm not that hopeful, but possibly. But my heaven, Jolie, after—Ray? What's it called?"

" 'My Ideal,' " muttered Ray.

"Charming." Turning back to Jolie, Warren said, "After listening to 'My Ideal,' I really doubt the jury could be swayed much further, in any direction at all, by any other song of Ray's, or all his songs together in a medley."

"Well, I guess I stepped on my dick this time," Ray admitted.

Warren looked at him. "If only," he said, "it were possible to execute your mouth and leave the rest of you alive."

"Hey, wait a minute," Ray said. "I *need* my mouth."

"I don't," Warren told him without sympathy, and the bailiff arrived to say it was time to go back to court.

39

It was not turning out to be a good month for Jolie Grubbe. On her latest diet, she'd gained seven pounds. Her doctor kept telling her *he* didn't like the sound of her heart. Her one and only client, Ray Jones, whom she also happened to like on a personal level, was about to get himself executed by the state of Missouri for a murder he might actually have committed. And to put the icing on the cake, as she and Ray and Warren and Jim Chancellor and Cal Denny headed back for court, there was Leon Caccatorro waiting for them in the hall, amid the journalists encamped around the courtroom door.

Warren was at that moment murmuring something in Ray's ear about some sort of statement he ought to make to the judge—an apology, no doubt—so it was up to Jolie to deal with the creep from the IRS. As journalists up and down the corridor snapped to attention—or as close to attention as a journalist can snap—yapping out dumb questions at the moving clump of Ray and his advisers, questions that were unheeded and unanswered and asked for God knows what reasons of personal ego gratification, Jolie veered off to say to the taxman, "Not now, for God's sake."

Caccatorro was a happy man, far too happy for Jolie's bad mood to bring him down. "No rush," he assured her. "At the lunch break, your client might want to sign a few papers."

"You have them ready? That was quick."

Caccatorro showed his small sharp teeth in a Cupid's bow smile. "It was an easy decision to make, actually," he said. "Between earnings from past endeavors and earnings from future endeavors."

"Let me guess which one you picked."

"We feel," Caccatorro allowed, "that Ray Jones is still a vibrant and creative force in the country-music industry. I hope he'll be pleased by our vote of confidence."

"He'll jump up and down," Jolie predicted. "Excuse me."

The others had gone on ahead into the courtroom, leaving the squall of journalists to blow itself out in muttered asides to one another. Jolie bumped her way through them like a beach ball through bowling pins and made her way to her seat in the front row, near Cal and the ever-present ever-present *ever-present* Sara Joslyn. Looking back just before taking her seat, Jolie saw that Caccatorro had come in as well and was showing some sort of ID to the bailiff back there. Another ever-present son of a bitch. Gloat, you bastard.

Warren was on his feet at the defense table, saying, "If the court please, Mr. Jones would like to make a short statement before resuming his testimony."

"He already made a short statement," Fred Heffner commented. He was so pleased at having rattled Ray Jones that he was beside himself over there, grinning and winking at Buford Delray and the distinguished little man whom Sara had said was some sort of journalist. Takes one to know one.

Warren had ignored Fred Heffner's remark and kept his eyes and attention on Judge Quigley, who pondered a moment, pushing her reddened lips in and out in a disgusting fashion before saying, "Very well, Mr. Thurbridge. A short *temperate* statement."

"Thank you, Your Honor."

Warren sat, and Ray stood. "I want to apologize to everybody in this courtroom," he said, "and especially to you, Judge, and to the prosecuting attorney, Mr. Heffner, who was just doing his job. And I hope the jury will remember that a weak man isn't necessarily a killer. Thank you."

Good boy, Jolie thought. You do come through, Ray, more often than not. Ray's manner was so offhand and shitkicker, it still came as a surprise to Jolie every time he revealed the good and devious brain tucked away inside there. Ray was deep, and he was always playing his own deep game, and Jolie had to keep that in mind.

Now he was going back to the witness stand, where Jolie was sure he wouldn't let himself be caught out again. As the old saying goes: Fool me once, shame on you; fool me twice, shame on me.

The judge assured Ray he was still under oath, Ray thanked her and sat down, and here came Fred Heffner, grinning like a fox, looking less like Lincoln now and more like John Wilkes Booth. "Mr. Jones," he said, "before the break, we were just about to discuss a song, I believe a sing you wrote. Is that right?"

"I've written some songs, yes, sir."

"I'm referring to a specific song, Mr. Jones, as I believe you know. You did have a specific song in mind, just before the break, did you not?"

"Yes, sir, it's called 'My Ideal.' "

"And what is the name of— Um, yes."

"It's called 'My Ideal.' "

"Yes. Thank you."

"I wrote it a long—"

"Thank you, Mr. Jones, I don't need your professional biography at this point."

"I haven't sung that—"

"The song is called 'My Ideal.' Do you happen to remember the words to that song, Mr. Jones?"

"I haven't sung that—"

"Do you *remember* the words?"

"No, sir, I don't believe I do. It's been so many—"

"It's your own song, Mr. Jones. But I take the point. You've written so many songs, it wouldn't be reasonable to expect you to remember every word of every one of them."

"No, sir, I'm saying—"

"And yet, Mr. Jones, you have a sufficient memory of that song, of its subject matter and terminology, let us say, that the photo I showed you recalled the song to mind, did it not?"

"No, sir."

"Excuse me, Mr. Jones, but it was on seeing the photo that you—"

"You said that poor dead woman looked like a pizza. I thought that—"

"Mr. Jones, I asked *you* what she looked like."

"—was a disgusting thing to say about a poor dead—"

"Mr. Jones, I would ask you to be responsive to the question."

"—woman. I didn't think she—"

"Your Honor, would you ask the witness to be responsive to my question?"

"—looked like a pizza. I thought she looked like a poor

dead woman that was being made fun of when she couldn't defend herself."

Judge Quigley said, "Mr. Jones, have you quite finished your speech?"

"Your Honor," Ray said, "somebody ought to defend poor Belle Hardwick from being made fun of when she can't stand up for herself. If the state of Missouri won't defend her, I guess it's up to me."

Judge Quigley pounded her gavel, outraged. *"Mr. Jones!"*

Now Warren was on his feet, and Jolie thought it about goddamn time. "Your Honor, I've been a patient man," Warren said, with which Jolie could only concur, "but it seems to me we've all heard enough by now of the prosecutor's bizarre ideas of what a dead body looks like. Perhaps some in this court have cast-iron stomachs, but I do not."

Judge Quigley raised an eyebrow in Fred Heffner's direction. "Counsel, is there a purpose to this line of questioning?"

"Your Honor, when the court hears the song to which Mr. Jones and I have been referring, the direction and intent of my examination will be made clear."

Surprised, the judge said, "You aren't going to ask the defendant to *sing*, are you?"

"Alas, no, Your Honor," Fred Heffner said. "I am sorry to miss the opportunity to hear Ray Jones live, in person, but I can understand that he might be reluctant, under the circumstances, so we have brought into court a recording, which, with the court's permission, we will now play."

Buford Delray was already on his feet, holding up the cassette player, but Warren, who hadn't sat down, said, "Objection, Your Honor. A song written eighteen years ago and not performed by the defendant for some eleven years can hardly be germane to a crime that occurred in July of this year."

Good, Jolie thought. They wouldn't let Ray make that point, so Warren made it for him.

Fred Heffner said, "Our purpose is to establish character and motive. The jury cannot have a clear idea of Ray Jones or of his attitudes—particularly when he's being just a bit less gallant than he was a moment ago in this courtroom—unless we are permitted to hear him express himself in his own words."

"I'm going to overrule your objection, Mr. Thurbridge," Judge Quigley said. "A published article written by the defendant, or a book, if relevant to the subject matter at trial, would certainly be admissible. By that standard, a song written and performed by the defendant can be equally illuminative of attitudes and state of mind. You may proceed, Mr. Heffner."

"Thank you, Your Honor."

Heffner smiled at Buford Delray, who pressed PLAY on the little cassette player, then held it over his head as the music began.

It was an old song and an old recording, heavy on the electric guitar and the fake Hawaiian sound of that era. The machine was not at all high fidelity, but when Ray Jones started to sing, the words came through loud and clear.

Jolie, who knew the song—she knew all Ray's songs—watched Sara Joslyn's profile next to her to see how the song would go over with somebody hearing it for the first time.

Not well.

I'd like to tell you how I feel,
And what I think is my ideal.

Her face is like an angel's is, but the devil's in her eyes.
She dances like a panther, with lightning in her thighs.

She's Ali Baba's treasure room, all without a lock,
And she turns into a pizza at three o'clock.

She listens to my jokes like she thinks they're all brand-
new.
She's sunny all the time, and she never does get blue.
Wherever birds assemble, she is the pick of the flock,
And she turns into a pizza at three o'clock.

Come closer, girls, while I reveal
The shapely shape of my ideal.

She doesn't know a word like no, it's always yes;
And when she comes to call, she would never overdress.
Her door is always open, just every time I knock,
And she turns into a pizza at three o'clock.

It's too bad nobody dropped a pin; you would have heard it. The *click-click* of the little machine as Buford Delray switched it off and the *foom-squll* of his trousers as he sat down were audible to every stunned ear in the room.

Jolie looked at the jury. They looked as though *they* had been condemned to death.

Fred Heffner milked the silence beautifully. Jolie watched him do it. She had to admire the slimy bastard. It wasn't until Ray had actually opened his mouth and just started to make a sound—Don't do it, Ray, she thought; nothing you can say will make anything better—that Heffner, as though letting Ray off the hook (though he wasn't; he was fixing Ray more firmly than ever onto the hook), said quietly, somberly, "No further questions."

"Perhaps it's time to break for lunch," Judge Quigley said,

and when there was a gasp in the room, a sudden intake of many breaths as though the awful tension was about to be broken by even more awful laughter, she reared back, glared the assemblage into ongoing silence, and announced, "Court is adjourned until two P.M."

Into the sudden rush of comments, shiftings, chair slidings, Warren called, "We reserve a right to redirect."

"Of course!" Judge Quigley cried, and almost ran from the room.

Ray's friends in the front row continued to sit there as the jury was led out, stumbling, like trauma cases off to rehab. "I don't feel much like lunch," Jolie said, and thought that was probably the first time in her life she'd ever made that statement.

"I may never eat again," Sara said, which Jolie considered extreme.

On Sara's other side, Cal leaned forward to tell the row of people, "You know, that was just a joke. Back then, when Ray wrote that, that was just a joke goin' around. So he turned it into a song. Like 'If It Ain't Fried, It Ain't Food.' It was just a joke, that's all. And he don't even sing it anymore."

"It isn't a joke now," Jolie said. "Every single member of that jury is thinking, Belle Hardwick was turned into a pizza at three o'clock."

"Please," Sara said.

A shadow fell across Jolie—another shadow. When she looked up, Leon Caccatorro was standing there with the strangest and most wrinkled smile Jolie had ever seen. "As it turns out," he said, "the paperwork *isn't* quite finished. We won't be able to have our signing today, after all."

Well, *here's* a hell of a silver lining. "Back on your branch,

buzzard," Jolie said, and when Caccatorro faded away like
Bela Lugosi, she looked around at all the long faces and
suddenly, for no reason at all, felt better. "It isn't over," she
announced, "until *I* sing. Let's go eat, I'm starved."

40

"I don't care," Ray said. "I'm not goin' onto that witness chair again."

They were gathered around the table in the conference room in Warren's offices, Ray and his defense team, but none of them except Jolie could actually be said to be eating lunch. The rest of them pushed sandwiches around on their plates, not quite looking at the food.

Warren said, "Ray, you dug yourself into this hole; now it's up to you to dig your way out again."

"Not a chance," Ray said.

"Ray, stop and think for a second. Is that really what you want in the jury's minds when they go in to their deliberations? 'My *Ideal*'?"

"They've heard it," Ray pointed out. "It's over and done with."

"If you go back on the witness stand," Warren told him, "I'll be the one asking the questions. Heffner already said he was finished with you."

"He sure was," Ray said, and ruefully shook his head.

"So," Warren went on, "I'll take you through your history, the evolution of your thinking *away* from that song."

"Aw, come on, Warren," Ray said. "What are you gonna do, start playin songs yourself? Play 'The Hymn'? You're not a disc jockey. Anyway, then Heffner gets another crack at me, doesn't he? If you take a double dip, he gets to do the same thing, doesn't he?"

Reluctantly, Warren said, "Yes, he does."

"So then *he* plays 'The Dog Come Back.' It isn't a trial anymore; it's a greatest hits. Warren, I made a big-enough fool of myself out there. I'm not gonna go do it again, and that's that."

Warren looked deeply pained. "It's the wrong image to leave with the jury," he insisted.

Jim Chancellor said, "Warren? Don't we have other witnesses?"

"Oh sure," Warren said. "I was going to put on half a dozen character witnesses, but how can I, in the teeth of that song? I'll be maligning *their* characters instead of boosting Ray's. Milt Lieberson flew in from L.A. to testify, and wouldn't that be great, a Hollywood Jew agent telling these fine folk what a great character Ray Jones has."

Jolie, around a mouthful of sandwich, said, "Forget character witnesses."

"They're forgotten," Warren assured her. "And I also had three Ray Jones Theater employees to say there was never anything between Ray and Belle Hardwick, but so what? A guy who prefers his women to turn into pizzas at three in the morning isn't likely to be known for his *long-term* relationships."

Ray said, "What about my ex-wife?"

Warren gave him a look of deep mistrust. "What about her?"

"Put Cherry on the stand," Ray suggested. "*There's* a long-term relationship for you."

Jolie was heard to groan. Ray turned to her, saying, "Come on, Jolie, you know that's true. I've kept up with my alimony payments, and I was never a minute behind in my child support." To Warren again, he said, "How's that for character?"

"Ray," Warren said, "do you really want Fred Heffner asking questions of your ex-wife?"

Ray thought about that, his eyes shifting back and forth. "Probably not," he said.

Jim Chancellor said, "We have other witnesses, don't we?"

"Oh certainly," Warren agreed. "We have three scruffy shifty-eyed no-fixed-abode musicians ready to testify that they borrowed Ray's sports car for short-term assignations with loose women all the time. Won't Fred Heffner love *them*."

Jolie said, "Forget the car. The car isn't what it's about, not anymore."

Jim said, "Warren, a little earlier you said, if Ray did badly—"

"And at that time, I had no idea," Warren interjected, "just *how* badly our friend Ray could do."

"Thanks," Ray muttered.

Determined to make his point, Jim said, "You said you'd put witnesses on until the jury forgot Ray's testimony, no matter how long it took."

"Not this testimony," Warren said. "Our *grandchildren* will remember this testimony."

Ray said, "Oh, come on. One song?"

"Circling in their heads," Warren said, "with those ukuleles."

"Electric guitars."

"Electric ukuleles, for all I care," Warren told him. "If I'd had my wits about me, I must admit, I would have insisted you *recite* those lyrics. Awful as they are, they wouldn't have stuck quite so forcefully in the jury's mind. But now, as those jurors sit there trying to determine your guilt or innocence, that *song* is going to circle in their heads, twang twang twang, and she *turns* into a *pizza* at three o'-*clock*."

That line, delivered with that much savagery, pretty much silenced everybody in the room for a couple of minutes, until Jolie said, "Warren? Is there anything else to do?"

Warren didn't answer. He was gazing across the room as though there were something he really despised on that wall over there.

Ray cleared his throat. "Warren," he said, "if you really want me to go back on the stand . . ."

Warren roused himself. "No," he said with a long and pessimistic sigh. "I realize now, that would merely be waiting for the other grenade to drop."

"You're probably right," Ray admitted.

"My entire defense strategy," Warren said, "is in ruins around my feet."

"I'm sorry," Ray said.

Jim said, "Warren? What are we going to do?"

"The only thing we can do," Warren said. "The defense rests."

They stared at him in astonishment. Ray cried, "What? *I'm* our only witness?"

"Let us hope," Warren said, "I'm brilliant in summation."

41

Judge Quigley decided to end the court day with Warren's announcement that the defense would rest, so the summations would be given by both sides on Wednesday, giving everybody one more night to think it over.

Then Wednesday arrived.

Fred Heffner, in his summation, quoted the lyrics of "My Ideal"—all of them. A little later, he quoted parts of it again. He talked about Ray's car, found in front of Ray's house, stained with Belle Hardwick's blood. He talked about depravity. He talked about rootless show-business people. He talked about Belle Hardwick as a God-fearing working person with a history in this community, a person about whom no one had found one unkind thing to say. He talked about Belle Hardwick trying to fend off the unwanted advances of a brutal and no doubt drunken suitor. He talked about that suitor having the arrogance of fame, show-business fame, leading him to believe he could have whatever he wanted in this world, that he was too important to be denied and that, in any case, he could get away with anything. Heffner talked about that suitor's increasing fury at Belle Hardwick's refusal to give in to his lust, a fury that had at last turned murderous. He asked the ladies and gentlemen of the jury to consider just who that suitor might have been. Who *else* could it have been? Who else had the qualities of depravity, rootlessness, arrogance, social apathy, and disregard for convention that had led to the assault on Belle Hardwick and then her murder? "Ladies and gentlemen, you see him before you, seated at the defense table. If you see *anyone else*, in or out of this courtroom, anyone at all who might have been responsible for this depraved and wanton destruction of a young woman's life, then that is reasonable doubt and you must find this fellow innocent. But if he is the only one you see, the only one who *might* have done it, the only one who *could* have done it, the only one whose failings of character made such an outcome even possible, then there is no reasonable doubt, is there? Of course there isn't. Raymond Jones is a murderer, a foul, foul murderer, and it is your duty, your privilege and your duty, to see that he is put away in such a fashion that he will never never *never* be in a position to wantonly attack anyone else's daughter. Your daughter. Or mine."

Heffner, finished, moved toward the prosecution table, and Ray called out to him on his way by, "If Belle Hardwick was a saint, I'm the Pope."

Heffner gave Ray a small gratified smile and went on to his seat as the jury box turned into an iceberg, from which twenty-eight horrified eyes stared at Ray Jones. And Warren Thurbridge, with the longest and most heartfelt sigh of his career, rose and approached the iceberg. "Ladies and gentlemen of the jury," he said into the cold gale-wind force of their disapproval, "Belle Hardwick is not on trial here today. Her trials are over, poor lady. Ray Jones is on trial here, and I am in the unhappy position of being his defense attorney."

Warren sighed again. He had at least diverted the jury's attention from Ray to himself. He said, "My client, as you may have noticed, is an idiot. He has these moments of seeming rationality, when you almost think you can depend on him to have at least some small sense of self-preservation, but then he does it again. Foot-in-mouth disease."

No one laughed; no one even smiled—not that he'd expected much jollity out here. He said, "After his last outburst, Ray apologized to the court, and to you, ladies and gentlemen. He described himself as 'weak,' and I guess that must be accurate. Ray is an artist, as you know, a singer and a songwriter, as well as a businessman operating his own theater over in Branson. The businessman side of him makes him sensible at times, but I'm afraid the artistic side is what you might call dominant in Ray Jones's personality."

Warren walked away from the jury to gaze down gloomily upon his client, who scowled back, not liking to be called an idiot, and liking even less to be called somebody who was an idiot because he was an artist. Warren didn't much care what expression was on Ray's face. He looked at it a while, then looked back at the jury and said, "If you're looking for a fool, I have one for you right here. If you're looking for a loudmouth, here he is. If you're looking for a self-destructive buffoon, I've got the guy. But."

Warren left Ray and moved again toward the jury. "But," he said. "If you're looking for a killer, look again. I don't know who killed Belle Hardwick, and neither do you and neither do the police and neither does my friend Fred Heffner. The evidence they have against Ray doesn't exist. A car with the keys in it. *You* could have taken that car. The victim knew Ray Jones. The victim knew hundreds of people. Where are the eyewitnesses? Where are the people who saw Belle Hardwick and Ray Jones get into that car together? Nowhere, and believe me, the police *searched* for an eyewitness to that event, and they came up with nobody, because Ray Jones and Belle Hardwick did *not* get into that car together that night."

Warren went over to the witness box and leaned on the rail there. Gesturing at the empty witness chair, he said, "Where are the experts to testify as to the blood found in Ray's *house*, or on his *clothing*? You didn't see such experts. Do you think that means no such experts were employed by the state in their efforts to pin this terrible crime on Ray Jones? Of *course* those experts were there. They went over Ray's house with the latest scientific equipment. They took his clothing away to their laboratories. They used sniffer dogs on his property, looking for evidence Ray might have buried. And what did they find?"

Warren turned and looked at the empty witness chair. He appeared to be listening. Then he turned back to the jury, spread his hands wide, and shrugged. "Nothing. Believe me, ladies and gentlemen, if the state's experts had found anything at all to bolster their miserable case against Ray Jones, they would have been in this chair, testifying under oath. Their absence testifies, too. It testifies to Ray Jones's *innocence*."

Warren moved away from the witness chair. "An idiot," he told the jury, "but an innocent idiot. So why did the police and the prosecutors and the whole mighty array of law enforcement press so *exclusively* on Ray Jones? Well, didn't Mr. Heffner tell you why? Isn't it because Ray Jones is a celebrity? Didn't Mr. Heffner say so himself? Isn't that why the hall out there is packed with reporters? Isn't that why the television news all across this country shows Mr. Heffner's face and

Mr. Delray's face every single night? If Belle Hardwick were murdered by some brutal anonymous drunk—and *she was*—where would be the television time for these gentlemen?"

Warren stopped his pacing and faced the jury flat-footed. "Ray Jones is not a murderer," he said. "Ray Jones is a fool and a celebrity and an easy target for ambitious prosecutors, but don't let yourselves be led astray. The prosecution has no case. If they had a case, they'd have showed it to you, and they didn't. What did they show you? Eighteen-year-old song lyrics! Eighteen years old! *That's* their case? Ladies and gentlemen, end this farce."

Warren turned around and crossed to the defense table and took his seat, where Ray clapped him resoundingly on the back and announced, "That was terrific!"

Warren wheeled around, about to lose his patience for good and all, and found himself looking deep into the bright, innocent, mocking eyes of his unknowable client.

Innocent?

42

It took Jack nearly five minutes to attract the secretary's undivided attention, but once he got it, he *had* it. "Oh my goodness," she said, her typing forgotten, her filing forgotten, her phones forgotten, all her standoffish busywork forgotten. Looking at the photographs, pale beneath her makeup, rattled beneath her former display of competence, she said, "This is terrible."

"That's what I thought, too," Jack agreed, as serene as a monk on a mountaintop.

"None of us had the slightest idea."

"I didn't think you had."

"Duford has to be told," she said, staring at Jack with watery blue eyes. She was a decent lady of forty-something, and though she worked in a lawyer's office, she had been till now essentially unfamiliar with the depths of human depravity.

"Yes, he must be told," Jack said, agreeable as ever. "Privately," he suggested. "Quietly. Don't you agree?"

"Let me call over to the courthouse," she said, and reached for the phone. Her finger trembled like a whip antenna as she punched the number, but apparently she hit all the right buttons, because she spoke briefly, in a hushed voice, with some-body named Janie, then cupped the mouthpiece to say to Jack, "The jury's just gone out."

"Ah," Jack said, having timed himself to that event.

"So he should be able to come right— Buford?" she asked the telephone. "It's Del, Buford. I think you ought to come over to the office right away."

"By himself," Jack suggested.

"Yes! By yourself, Buford. Don't bring—don't bring any-body with you. I don't *want* to tell you on the phone, Buford! All right." Hanging up, she said to Jack, "He'll be here in five minutes."

"Eight minutes," Jack said, nodding at her desk clock. "See if I'm not right."

It was seven minutes, actually, so Jack was closer, not that it mattered. Buford Delray the butterball rolled into the front office of his law firm, down the street from the courthouse, looking both worried and irritated, hating to be taken away from what was beginning to look like a really major feather in his cap, a tremendous victory in a capital case—the fact that Fred Heffner from upstate had done all the work wouldn't matter a rap around Taney County, where Buford Delray had his private practice—but at the same time having to take seriously the undoubted sound of alarm, even panic, in his secretary's voice. "Yes?" he asked. "What the heck's so important, Del?"

Mute, Del pointed at Jack, who came forward, smiling amiably, and held up a photo for Delray to look at. "His name," Jack said, "is Louis B. Urbiton. He's Australian originally, and he's a reporter for the *Weekly Galaxy*."

"What?" Delray blinked but clung to previous certainties.

"He is not. His name is Fernit-Branca. He's with *The Economist*; that's an English magazine."

Jack held up a second photo. "Here's Louis B. Urbiton with his *Weekly Galaxy* editor, a man named Boy Cartwright." Another photo. "Here are Louis B. and Boy entering the house on Cherokee the *Galaxy* rented for the duration of the Ray Jones trial. Here's another picture of the house; that's a fellow named Bob Sangster, also a reporter with the *Galaxy*. Here's a picture of the shadow jury the defense has been using. I guess you know about that. Recognize that fellow there?"

"Let me see that!"

While Delray stared at damning photo after damning photo, many of them with his own dumb and happy face clearly identifiable, Jack took from his inner jacket pocket a slender document, which he dropped on Del's desk: "Here's an affidavit from a maid at the Mountain Greenery Motel in Branson, named Laverne Slagel, stating that she was paid bribes by Bob Sangster and by a woman employee of the *Weekly Galaxy* named Erica Jacke to pass on to Miss Jacke from Mr. Sangster the audiotapes he was making at the shadow-jury sessions. She was told they were love letters. You have pictures there of the two women exchanging tape and money in the motel parking lot."

"My God!" Delray spread photos out on his secretary's desk, then leaned on the desk, the better to hold himself up while studying them. "What were these people *doing*?"

"Going too far, I hope," Jack said. "By the way, I'm Jack Ingersoll. I'm an editor with *Trend*. We're a magazine up in New York. You've heard of us?"

Delray, too late suspicious, frowned at Jack. "I'd like," he said, "to see some identification."

"Louis B. showed you identification," Jack said, grinning

cheekily at him. "You don't want identification; you want to know what's going to happen next."

"All right," Delray said, being guarded and wary now that it was all over. "What's going to happen next?"

"One of two things," Jack told him. "As you can see from those pictures, all the other people the *Weekly Galaxy* dealt with were completely taken in. Either I write the story that way, that *everyone* was taken in, or it turns out that you knew what was up the whole time and were just stringing them along until the time was right to make a number of arrests."

"I see." Delray turned and leaned his butt on his secretary's desk. He thought a while. "There are certainly some misfeasances here," he decided.

"Mmm."

Delray squinted at Jack. "When am I going to think the time is right to close in on these people?"

"*Trend* publishes on Friday. My deadline is nine A.M. Thursday, tomorrow morning. If you planned some predawn raids and arrests, I could have *Trend* staffers and photographers ready to accompany your men."

"You want an exclusive."

"Oh, I've got an exclusive," Jack said, "one way or the other."

Delray pondered, scratching some of his chins. "We'll need a judge tonight, give us the warrants. We'll need to do a bunch of paperwork between now and then, without letting the word get out."

"I stand ready to assist in any way I can," Jack assured him.

Suddenly decisive, Delray rose from his secretary's desk and said, "Come into my office."

"I'll bring the pictures," Jack said, starting to gather them up.

"God yes! And Del?"

"I know," Del said. "Mum's the word."

"Double mum," Delray told her. "And hold all my calls."

He was already going through into his inner office, Jack following, when Del called after him, "You'll want me to tell you if the jury comes back, won't you?"

Delray couldn't have cared less about any jury. Pausing in the doorway for a fraction of a second, he said, "Uh . . . uh . . . yes, of course. Come on in," he said to Jack. "What did you say your name was?"

"Jack."

"I'm Buford." And the door closed.

43

The change in the atmosphere of the shadow jury had come, of course, with "My Ideal," on Tuesday, which was probably a worse experience for them than for the real jury, because, in fact, one significant difference between the two juries was that the shadows knew they were being paid by the defense, had been hired by the defense to help in their strategies, their efforts to win a verdict of *not guilty.* However dispassionate they might try to be, the shadow jurors couldn't help but think of themselves as part of the defense *team*, rooting for their side to win.

This had not been a problem for the shadows at first. Riding over to Forsyth from Branson in the bus Tuesday afternoon, they'd still been cheerful, chatting, optimistic. Riding back Tuesday evening, after seeing and hearing "My Ideal" on the day's videotape of the court proceedings, they had been as silent as, well, as the tomb.

And Wednesday was worse. As several of them commented after watching the tape, they hadn't thought much of Fred Heffner's summation, they'd seen pretty clearly that he was blowing smoke, and though they'd found Warren's arguments interesting, they weren't really all that persuasive; sorry, Warren. No, what they all remembered, not happily, was Ray's interjection in the middle of the sandwich: "If Belle Hardwick was a saint, I'm the Pope."

It just stuck in everybody's craw. "I'm sorry Ray said that," admitted Juggs, the retired postal worker, and several of the other jurors nodded agreement, more in sorrow than in anger, among them the fellow not really named Jock O'Shanley.

Yes, the cuckoo bird from the *Weekly Galaxy* was still among the shadows. On balance, despite the shameful falsity of his presence here, he was pretty much giving good weight, doing a credible Jock O'Shanley imitation, commenting as that Irishman would, reacting as O'Shanley might be expected to react. It had finally seemed that to remove him would be more disruptive to the jury as a whole than to leave him in place and leave the rest of the jurors ignorant as to the truth about him, so that's what had been done—for now.

Warren led a brief discussion, briefer than usual because there was no more strategy to be considered. The war was over. All that was left was to choose which brow would get the laurel.

So, after just a few minutes of chitchat, Warren said, "Let's see if we can get a sense of where we are here. I want to do a first, very preliminary vote. Not a show of hands. I want this one to be anonymous, so you can make your decision without being asked to defend it. You've all got your pads and pencils. I'd like each of you to write one letter on a sheet of paper and fold it so the rest of us can't see it. Then toss it into the middle of the table. If you were on the regular jury, across the street there, would you vote guilty or not guilty? Write *G* if you'd vote guilty; write *N* if you'd vote not guilty."

They did it. A few of them had to think it over first, but a depressingly large majority had no trouble at all deciding which letter to write. Then, when all fourteen folded pieces of paper were in the middle of the table, Jim Chancellor gathered them and opened them and tallied the vote.

Five *N*. Nine *G*.

NG: not good.

44

Meanwhile, the real jury had less than two hours to deliberate on day one before being gathered into their own bus and driven back to their own motel in Branson, all of which was exactly what the shadow jury was doing, except that the shadows were still fourteen, while the real jury had been weeded to twelve. The last thing the judge had done before charging the jury—in which she had been somewhat less proprosecution than expected, probably because she felt it wasn't needed—was reach twice into a box containing all the jurors' names on separate sheets of paper and draw out the names of the losers, called alternates. These two were necessary in case anything happened to an actual juror, but if *nothing* happened to an actual juror, which is usually the case, then there wasn't a blessed thing for these two ex-jurors to do but keep their opinions to themselves.

(The slightly raffish ex–Merchant Mariner the defense had particularly loved was now one of the alternates, while the born-again harridan in the flowered dresses that the defense had *prayed* would be an alternate was now firmly a juror. Sometimes you can't win for losing.)

The alternates, however, were still sequestered. And, since it is known that jurors who discover, at the end of a tense or otherwise deeply interesting trial, that they are mere alternates, that thcy will not even get to be in the *room* where the deliberation is going on, tend to become terribly depressed, even full of feelings of guilt and self-contempt, counselors stood ready to assist these two washed-out jurors in any way they could. Of course, being counselors employed by the state, they weren't worth much, but it's the thought that counts.

As for the shadow jury, it was agreed they would stay together for one more night at the Mountain Greenery Motel in Branson, then come back tomorrow to join the defense team in awaiting the verdict. There were also more debriefings to be done on the morrow—in case worse came to worst and appeals had to be readied. Did any of the shadows feel improper manipulation had been practiced by the prosecutors? The judge? The prosecution's witnesses? In the meantime, for tonight they could still eat and sleep at Ray Jones's expense; enjoy.

In his room at the Mountain Greenery, Bob Sangster, the false Jock O'Shanley, sequestered himself from his roommate by going into the bathroom, where he once again removed the cassette recorder from his side and extricated the tape, which now included the results of the first shadow-jury vote. Then he went out into the hall, where he did not make the expected rendezvous with Laverne Slagel.

Hmmmmm. Bob roamed the portion of the motel set aside for the shadows, and when at last he saw another maid and asked her about Laverne, she merely said, "Laverne isn't around."

"But she was here this morning"—when she'd given Bob the then-blank tape he wanted to pass back.

"I think she got sick or something," the maid said, and went back to her work.

Unfortunate, Bob thought, but not critical. There was still plenty of space on this tape for whatever might happen tomorrow. So thinking, he went back to his room, hid the tape in his underwear drawer, put on a bathing suit, and went for a swim, followed by dinner, followed by cribbage with another juror, followed by a showing of *Support Your Local Sheriff*, followed by sleep, followed by a rude awakening at 4:30 in the morning by rough-handed Missouri state troopers here to make an arrest. They were delighted to find that Bob Sangster still had that tape in his possession.

Ten minutes earlier, Boy Cartwright and his guest for the night, Erica Jacke, had been awakened just as rudely, at the former hospitality suite in the Palace Inn, by even more state troopers.

"Who are *they*?" wailed Boy, pointing a flabby finger at the *Trend* photographers popping flashcubes in his face.

"None of your business," a trooper said, and jabbed Boy painfully in the side with a gloved knuckle. "You wanna get dressed, or you wanna come along like you are?"

The residents of the 1000 block of Cherokee (nearly its only block, by the way) were not surprised to be awakened at 4:30 in the morning by many glaring lights and blaring sirens, and not at *all* surprised when the center of this sudden official attention turned out to be their new neighbors at 1023. A few of the good residents had already phoned their suspicions about those new people to the local police, with, as usual, not a damn thing being done, grumble, grumble. Their suspicions had generally involved Satanists, Arab terrorists planning to blow up Table Rock Dam, a coven of child abusers from out East, or possibly—though no motorcycles had as yet been seen—Hell's Angels.

Whatever the deviltry would turn out to be, it had been clear from the instant of the arrival of those people that they were up to no good. They took all the parking spaces on the block, for one thing, including right in front of your own house. And there were so *many* of them, and they looked so *strange*, not like normal people at all, who, as everybody knows, are fish-belly white, drastically overweight, clad in pastel polyester, and shyly smiling unless your back is turned. These people weren't normal in any particular, weren't like *us*, and therefore must be up to no good.

As a result, the arrival of several platoons of state troopers at arrest hour—4:30 A.M.—was no surprise and no inconvenience to the neighborhood, but was, in fact, a source of gratification. Even more gratification was provided by those photographers, who, having been rousted from sleep under tables, chose to resist arrest for a while. It was a fine hullabaloo over there, well lit, intelligently cast, imaginatively costumed, with good production values all around and the kind of minimal script that works best in an action flick of this sort. Afterward, a lot of residents could kick themselves that they hadn't taped it.

(And much afterward, there was a moment of bewilderment when it was learned by some of the residents that those people had, in fact, been employees of their favorite newspaper. Ah well, not everything is understandable in this life. Think about something else.)

* * *

At 5:15 that same morning, the phone rang in a dark and pleasantly musky motel room. Jack awoke first and rolled over Sara (who then awoke) to answer the phone, saying, "Yuh?" Then he said, "Ah." Then he said, "Oh ho." Then he said, "Mmmm." Then he said, "Right," and hung up. Rolling back over Sara to his side of the bed, still in the dark, he said, "My story's just about closed up. How's yours?"

"The jury's still out," Sara said, and went back to sleep.

45

The jury began its second day of deliberations Thursday morning at nine. Among the news items they were being protected from, there now could be added the tidbit of the excitement early this morning among their shadow compatriots and the rather astonishing number of *Weekly Galaxy* employees crowded this morning into the Branson jail. So while the real jury continued to wrestle with the question of the murder of Belle Hardwick, the thirteen remaining shadow jurors who had gathered around the conference table in Warren's offices spent *their* morning in awed discussion of the spy recently in their midst.

Actual juries sometimes have to deliberate twice in Missouri, if it's a death-penalty crime. The first deliberation deals strictly with the question of guilt or innocence; if the jury decides the defendant is innocent, or is guilty of a lesser crime, that's it, they can go home. But if they decide the defendant is guilty as charged, they have to stick around for part two of the trial, in which prosecution and defense can both produce witnesses all over again, this time to discuss the punishment to be meted out; that is, whether the defendant should be gassed to death or should do jail time instead.

In this part two, the defense can bring forward witnesses it couldn't use before, people to testify to the defendant's miserable childhood or evil companions or weakened mental capacity or whatever else might sway the jury toward clemency. On the other hand, the prosecution is very likely to parade the most tearful of the victim's relatives on and off the stand, interspersed with the most grisly available photographs. At the end of all this, the jury goes back into solitude for its second set of deliberations, which are likely to be much more hair-raising and scarring than the first. They will at last produce a recommendation, death or something less, which the judge may, but probably will not, override. Then the whole jury can go into therapy.

Unfortunately for Ray Jones and his defense team, this scenario is never spelled out entirely to the jurors in advance, so most of them don't realize the personal consequences involved in bringing in a verdict of guilty. At this point, the jury's innocence becomes the defendant's worst enemy.

The Ray Jones defense team managed to keep hope alive until 10:30 that morning, when the jury sent out its first request to the judge. They asked for clarification of two terms: *manslaughter* and *depraved indifference*. In a court now cleared of everyone but herself and the jury, Judge Quigley discussed these terms until all jurors had claimed a satisfactory grasp of the concepts. Then she and they retired once again to their separate rooms.

When the word came across the street to Warren, seated in his office with Ray and Jolie and Cal and Jim Chancellor (the shadow jury being in possession of the conference room), he took it stoically. "Well, we did our best," he said.

Ray, who'd been sitting sulkily in the corner, failing to distract himself by writing lyrics to a new song, looked up. "What's that? They just wanted to know what some words meant, right?"

"Ray," Warren said, "they've decided you did it."

"Well shit. They're wrong, you know."

"You don't get to argue with a jury," Warren said. "They've decided you're the one killed Belle Hardwick, and now they're grappling with the question of just which crime it was."

"Littering," Ray said callously. "*If* I'd done it."

"You didn't say that," Warren advised him, and turned to Jim Chancellor. "Jim, time to put together our list of witnesses."

Ray said, "Warren?"

Warren's expression was neither warm nor comforting when he turned back to Ray. "Yes?"

"I want you to know," Ray said, "*I* know you did a hell of a job. You're worth every penny. I screwed it up all by myself."

"Yes, you did," Warren said.

"So we can at least agree on that."

"Yes," Warren said, and turned his back on Ray to continue his conversation with Jim Chancellor.

That was 10:30, or just a little after. At 10:55, the girl called Julie, the file clerk who doubled as Warren's press spokesperson, came into the office to say, "Excuse me. There's some sort of federal man named Caccatorro who wants to see Mr. Jones."

"Leon the Prick," Ray commented. "Trust him."

"I'll deal with him," Jolie said grimly, heaving herself to her feet.

"He wants me to sign a little something," Ray suggested.

"I know he does, the bastard," Jolie said. "I'll send him on his way."

"Nah, bring him in," Ray told her. "Let's get my whole life settled, in one day."

Jolie said, "Ray, you're in no condition to—"

"What are you talking about? I'm not drunk; I'm not running around raving. You want me to wait until *after* those twelve assholes over there decide how *much* I killed old Belle? Bring him in, and then neither of us ever has to gaze upon his face again."

"I love the way you take legal advice," Jolie said, and pounded out of the office, to pound back in again shortly afterward like a major low front, trailed by the measly little rain cloud of Leon Caccatorro, who held a manila envelope to his breast with both hands, like a girl carrying her schoolbooks home.

"Good morning, Mr. Jones," T P said, around the bulk of Jolie.

"Good morning, Mr. Caccatorro," Ray said. "I bet you got a little something for me to sign."

"As a matter of fact . . ."

There was a refectory table near where Ray was seated. Warren had already made it clear with a silent but deafening lowering of the eyebrows that the taxman would not be welcome to use any part of his own personal desk, so Caccatorro veered over to the refectory table and there shook out the contents of the manila envelope, being five copies of a four-page document.

"Have you a pen?" Caccatorro asked.

"Yeah, but I'd rather use yours," Ray told him.

"Of course." Smiling, Caccatorro produced his father's pen from inside his father's suit coat and extended it toward Ray.

Jolie said, "Ray, none of us have had a chance to read that."

"You'll have plenty of time to read it, Jolie," Ray said, looking for the signature space on the last page.

"I'll read it *now*," Jolie announced, yanking up one copy.

"Be my guest." Ray signed the first copy, then scanned its pages, nodded, and grinned at Caccatorro, saying, "Decided to go with the old stuff instead of the new, huh?"

Caccatorro smiled and spread his hands. "My superiors in D.C. . . ."

"Sure. A bird in the hand is worth two in the gas chamber."

Caccatorro's smile wrinkled. He turned away, blinking at Warren and Jim Chancellor as though he'd just awakened and had no idea how he'd come to be here. Then, regaining control over himself, he turned back and watched approvingly as Ray signed copies two and three and four.

By that time, Jolie had finished reading copy number five. Grudgingly, she said, "It seems all right."

Ray said, "It's the deal I offered them, right?"

"In essence."

"I knew we could cut through the bullshit," Ray said, and with a flourish, he signed copy number five.

Jolie said, "Will I do as the witness?"

"Of course," said Caccatorro.

Jolie preferred to use her own pen, so Ray returned Caccatorro's, who put it back in his father's suit. Then he put four of the signed and witnessed copies into his manila envelope and handed the fifth to Jolie, saying, "There will be further documents, details."

"By correspondence," Jolie said.

"Yes, of course." Caccatorro smiled around at them all. "I won't be needed here anymore," he said.

Jolie said, "I hate long good-byes."

Caccatorro left.

Lunchtime, and no verdict. "Maybe they're hung," Jim Chancellor said hopefully.

"Sooner them than me," Ray said.

The shadow jury was sent to a nearby restaurant for lunch, but Ray and his lawyers and his best friend Cal ate sandwiches, as usual, in Warren's office. There wasn't much conversation.

Ten minutes after three. The phone rang on Warren's desk. He picked it up, said, "Thurbridge," listened, said, "Thank you," hung up, said, "They're coming back."

State troopers escorted the Ray Jones group across the street and into the courthouse.

Sara Joslyn, girl reporter, was in her usual place in the courtroom, looking worried but excited. Ray winked at her and she gave him a smile that was probably supposed to be encouraging but was too frightened to do the job. Cal and Jolie took their seats, the courtroom filled around and behind them, and then Judge Quigley entered. All rose. She banged her gavel. All sat down. She told the bailiff to lead in the jury and he did. The jurors looked solemn and exhausted, and none of them glanced over toward Ray—another bad sign.

The ritual was remorseless and nerve-racking, but at last the foreman, who had been doubled in the shadow jury by Juggs, the retired postal worker, rose and read from a small sheet of paper in his trembling hand: "We the jury find the defendant, Raymond Jones, guilty of murder in the first degree."

"Poll the jury!" demanded Warren, over the sudden hubbub in court, because sometimes a juror, when forced to make the individual statement in public, face-to-face with the defendant, will back off from that most draconian of verdicts.

So they polled the jury, with Judge Quigley directing the jurors to look directly at the defendant when responding, and each and every one of them stared straight at Ray and announced, "Guilty of murder in the first degree."

Then Ray was led off by state troopers. There would be no bail from here on. The Ray Jones Country Theater was closed until further notice.

46

Jack was off masterminding *Trend*'s coverage of the court appearances of the *Weekly Galaxy* thirty-seven—not all the stringers and stray photographers had been gathered up in the dragnets of the law—so Sara did the packing for both of them. It would be a week or two before Ray Jones was sentenced, and she didn't have to be here for that, or anything else in the interim. She had her story, even though there was something about it, just something about it, that didn't satisfy.

Oh, she could *write* it; that wasn't the problem. She could find the social meaning, the undercurrents, the linkages with the great world of thee and me; she could do all that without even raising a sweat. No, it was just . . .

Well, she didn't know what it was just, except it was. Not entirely satisfying.

There was a little clock radio in the room and she had it tuned to a local country-music station while she packed, still drinking in local atmosphere. And she was glad she had, too, when she heard the announcer say, "Well, you probably know old Ray Jones went down today. Murder one. Sentencing in a week or two. Well, it just yet again goes to prove the old saying, Don't drink and drive. We're sorry about what happened to Ray, and we expect you are, too. Here's a tune of Ray's we haven't been playing of late, because it somehow seemed just a mite too rowdy, the way things were going."

Oh please, thought Sara, not "My Ideal."

Not to worry: "But it's one of my personal faves," the announcer went on, "and I happen to know it's a favorite of Ray's, too, so I think he won't mind if I play it now. It's the song he wrote some years back for his onetime wife. It's called 'L.A. Lady,' and I'm sure you remember it."

On came the familiar guitars, drums, stringed instruments of half a dozen kinds, and then here was the familiar Ray Jones rasp, in an ironic ballad, an antilove song:

> *L.A. Lady, stay in L.A.*
> *You knew you were right when you went away.*
> *Come back here, I'll only spoil your day.*
> *So L.A. Lady, stay in L.A.*
>
> *L.A. Lady, don't come back.*
> *The skies are gray, the hills are black.*
> *It's dank and dark inside this shack.*
> *So L.A. Lady, don't come back.*
>
> *L.A. Lady, stay right there.*
> *The views are fine, the skies are fair;*
> *There's soft contentment everywhere.*
> *So L.A. Lady, stay right there.*
>
> *L.A. Lady, fare you well.*
> *If you need me, give a yell.*

But stay right there; you're doin' swell.
L.A. Lady, go to hell.

Oh my God, Sara thought, he didn't do it!

The musical instruments did something mock-lush on their own for a while and then Ray sang the song through again. Sara listened closely, even more closely than before, and when it was over, she reached out and switched off the radio, then sat on the edge of the bed to think about it.

He didn't do it. Ray Jones was innocent of murder, just as he'd said all along. Sara knew that as well as she knew anything. But she also knew she had no evidence, no proof, nothing that would persuade—well, persuade Jack, for instance.

All right. Pretend you're explaining it to Jack. Marshal your arguments; gather your thoughts. Ready? Go.

Ray Jones had been married to Cherry. It was a difficult marriage and a nasty divorce, in which he also lost his daughters. What did he do? He wrote that song. He thumbed his nose at her.

Belle Hardwick got to him deeper than his ex-wife, Cherry? *Belle Hardwick*? There was nothing that woman could have done, nothing, to make Ray Jones do anything more than laugh her to scorn.

That's why Sara'd had that dissatisfied feeling, that sense that something was wrong somewhere, out of place somewhere. Because it was.

How had it happened? How had Ray Jones wound up in the dock for that crime and been found guilty, maybe even to be executed for a murder he couldn't possibly have committed?

Had somebody framed him? *Cal*? Was the best friend the actual murderer, working out years of silent envy and feelings of inferiority? In a mystery story, wouldn't Cal be the least-obvious suspect?

Well, he's still the least obvious, Sara thought. There's no way on earth that Cal would—

The phone rang. She could just reach it from where she sat on the bed. Expecting to hear Jack's voice, she picked it up and said, "Hello?"

"Sara?" It was Cal Denny.

"Cal!" Sara said. "I was just thinking about you!"

"Sara, I found something here." He sounded worried, maybe bewildered, like he was out of his depth all of a sudden. "I don't know what to do."

"About what? Where?"

"Over to Ray's place. He asked me to get him some stuff— you know, he's gotta stay over there now. Toothbrush, stuff. Sara, I found something here!"

"What?"

"I don't wanna— Listen, could you come over here?"

"To Ray's house?"

"I'll call the gate, tell them to let you through. You remember where the house is, don't you?"

"Sure, but—"

"What are you driving?"

"A Buick Skylark."

"What's the license?"

"I don't know; it's a rental."

"What color is it?"

"You know, that sort of brownish gray-blue. You know, it looks like a rental."

"Okay, I'll call the gate now. Could you come over, Sara? Is it okay?"

"Well— Isn't this something you should show Warren? Or Jolie?"

"They wouldn't like this, Sara," Cal said. "That Ray was holding out on them, like."

"I'll be right over," Sara said.

47

Cal was standing in the open doorway. Sara parked the rental Skylark behind Ray's Jag, then walked over to Cal, who looked as worried in person as he'd sounded on the phone. "I sure appreciate this, Sara," he said. "Come on in."

Sara entered, looking around, seeing the place unchanged, as Cal shut the door and said, "Lemme show you where I found it."

"Where you found *what*?"

"I'll show you," he said, and led the way through the house, Sara following, Cal saying, "I was in the bedroom. Socks, shirts, he needs everything. He ties his socks up in pairs— you know, he's always been neat, Ray—and I dropped a pair of socks on the floor and it rolled under the bureau."

They entered Ray's bedroom. Sara saw a crumpled piece of duct tape all mixed up with Saran Wrap on the carpeted floor. Pointing at the wide dresser opposite the bed, Cal said, "I went down on my knees, you know, and reached under, and I hit something."

"Something duct-taped there."

"Right. I couldn't figure it. So I *lay* down flat on the floor and looked, and it was a tape, a regular videotape in its box, stuck onto the bottom of the bureau."

"A tape," Sara echoed.

"I pulled it out," Cal said, miming the gesture, pulling hard on a package duct-taped to a hard-to-get surface. "It was the kind of tape Ray always uses," he said, "but it didn't have nothing written on it, no date or nothing."

"You put it in the machine."

"I surely did," Cal said, and started out of the bedroom again, saying over his shoulder, "Lemme show you."

"I can hardly wait," Sara said. She was very aware of her shoulder bag bouncing against her hip as she followed Cal back through the house.

"It's one of Ray's practice tapes all right," Cal said, walking ahead of her. "For about an hour, it's just him practicing the IRS song—you know that song."

"He sang it on the bus."

"Right."

They were back in the living room. The heavy Mexican doors were open to expose the VCR and monitor. Moving toward them, Cal said, "After about an hour, on the tape, there's something happens I want you to see."

"I want to see it, too."

Turning on the machines, Cal said, "I backed it up to just before that so you could see what was going on." He hit PLAY.

Neither of them sat down. Standing side by side, near the monitor, they watched the instant of snow, then the sudden appearance of Ray, with acoustic guitar, one leg up on the chair, in the middle of "Singin for the IRS": "—own these great-lookin' threads. I'm bein—"

Ray stopped and looked over his shoulder toward the door,

in the background of the picture. His voice hushed, Cal said, "I figure he heard the car pull up."

"This is that night, isn't it?"

"Yes, ma'am, it is."

The front door, at the rear of the TV picture, burst open and a man half-ran, half-stumbled into the room, crying out incoherently. He was dressed in what looked like the filthy remnants of a tuxedo, white shirt ripped down the front, jacket and trousers mud-stained. The man and his clothing were wet, his hair plastered to his head, torn shirt stuck to his heaving chest.

Sara had never seen him before in her life. "Who's that?"

"Bob Golker."

The other victim. The dead man pulled out of Lake Taney-como in his car, and Ray charged with his murder.

"Ray!" was the first understandable word shouted by Bob Golker as Ray slapped his guitar onto the chair and ran toward the man. "Ray, Jesus Christ, *help* me!"

"What the hell happened to *you*?" Ray went past Bob Golker to shut the door, then came toward the man again, who stood weaving no more than three steps into the room, still in the semidark back there. "Christ's sake, Bob, you're all wet."

"I killed her, Ray."

The hair stood up on the back of Sara's neck. Her throat was dry. This was not staged; this was real. She clutched her shoulder bag to her side like bagpipes.

On the screen, Ray came forward to Bob Golker's side, to stare in wonderment at the man's profile. "*What* did you do?"

"Oh, Jesus, Ray, I didn't, I shouldn'ta done it!"

Ray was clearly as agitated on screen as Sara was in person. "For fuck's sake, Bob," he yelled, "will you tell me what you *did*?"

Bob Golker staggered a few steps forward, as though wanting to sit in the chair Ray had been using as a footstool. But he didn't make it. His legs went out from under him and he fell into a lumpish sitting position on the floor, bent to the left, both hands splayed out on the floor on his left side to keep him from falling any farther. "Belle," he mumbled. "Belle."

Ray crossed to the chair, put the guitar on the floor, carried the chair to Bob Golker's side, and sat on it himself. Leaning down toward Bob, he said, "You're drunk again, Bob, you know that."

"Not anymore," Bob said. He lifted bleary eyes to Ray. In a shrill and ghastly whisper, he cried, *"I killed Belle!"*

"Oh bullshit," Ray said. "You had another fight, that's all."

"I killed her, Ray," Bob insisted. "Honest to God. I buried her in the lake."

Ray sat back, frowning, studying the man on the floor. "Are you shitting me?"

"They'll never find her, Ray," Bob said. "The fuckin' fish'll eat her."

Exasperated and astonished, Ray spread his hands. "What do you wanna go kill Belle Hardwick for?"

"She wouldn't come with me. Fuckin' bitch, she knew — She promised she'd come to California with me. She said—"

"Belle doesn't belong in California."

"She wouldn't come with me."

"Then she has more sense than I thought."

"What am I gonna do, Ray? Shit, I used your car; it's all fucked up—"

"Oh thanks," Ray said. "What'd you do to the car? You hit a tree with it?"

"I didn't hit *nothin'*. Except Belle. Oh, *Jesus*, Raaaayy! There's blood all over the car, Ray!"

"Blood?" Again Ray reared back, this time considering Bob with more concern. "Did you really and truly do it, you simple shit? You fuckin' *killed* Belle Hardwick?"

"I'm *sorry*, I didn't—I'm *sorry*!" Bob was weeping now, tears running down the face he held up toward Ray. Wailing, voice breaking, he cried, "What am I gonna *do*, Ray? I don't wanna fry!"

"You don't fry in this state," Ray told him, flat, still thinking.

"I know I shouldn'ta done it, but Jesus. Oh *shit*! What the fuck am I gonna do?"

"Turn yourself in."

"I don't *want* to! I don't want them to kill me, Ray. I don't want to spend the rest of my life in *jail*!"

"Shit," Ray said. He looked around, shook his head, said, "Then go to California."

Bob stared up at Ray, face wild with hope. He looked like a rabbit, Sara thought. He said, "Should I?"

"Turn yourself in or get outta town," Ray advised him. "Don't stick around *here*."

"They'll never find her, Ray," Bob said, his voice suddenly a confidential murmur, making the two of them conspirators together. "I wedged her down in there, in the roots—"

"I don't wanna hear about it," Ray said. "Do you mind? You're some kinda crazy drunk asshole *animal*, you know that, Bob?"

"I know. I know I know I know, oh, Jesus, Ray, I just got crazy out of my mind, I didn't want to go anywhere without—" He rolled back onto his haunches, getting his balance, putting his hands to his face. "Why did I do it?" he wailed. "Why did I do it?"

"Because you're a dumb shit," Ray told him, though with a heavy sympathy in his voice. "And so was Belle."

Bob lowered his hands from his face, rested them on his bent legs, palms up, fingers curled. He seemed calmer at last. "I can't stay here," he said.

"*That's* the truth."

"You always been a good friend to me, Ray."

"Better than you've been to me, Bob."

"Oh shit, I know I'm a fuckup. I've always been a—"

"Bob, it's late at night, you know? You wanna call the sheriff from here?"

Wide-eyed again, Bob yelled, "No! I'm gonna take off, I swear to God I am. I'm goin' to California."

"Fine," Ray said.

"Don't tell on me, will you, Ray?"

"I won't tell on you, Bob."

"Swear you won't. Swear it, Ray. Don't *ever* tell anybody."

Ray got off the chair, went down on one knee beside Bob Golker, put his hands on Bob's shoulders, stared him in the eye. "I swear," he said solemnly. "All right? I swear I will never say a word to anybody at all anywhere about you and Belle Hardwick, no matter what. I swear. All right?"

"God bless you, Ray, God bless—"

"Yeah, good. Now get up, Bob, get on your feet."

With Ray's considerable help, Bob struggled to his feet and stood there, swaying. Ray said, "Can you walk on out of here? Don't take my car anymore, Bob."

"No."

"Where's that heap of yours, out by Jjeepers!?"

"Yeah."

"Can you get there?"

"Yeah. I'm okay now, Ray. I'm okay."

"Sure you are. Bob? What you should do—"

"Yeah?"

"Go home tonight, get some sleep."

"I couldn't sleep, Ray! Jesus, not after—I couldn't *sleep*!"

"Well, lay down, then. Get some rest somehow. In the morning, decide what you want to do. The sheriff or California. Decide it then. All right?"

"Okay, Ray."

"You got a bottle in your car?"

"Sure. Yeah, sure."

"Don't drink it. You hear me? Don't drink it."

Solemn: "I won't, Ray."

"Good. Get some rest. Decide in the morning."

"Thank you, Ray. God bless you, Ray."

"Yeah, that's all right," Ray told him, steering him toward the door. "That's fine."

Bob kept mumbling his thanks and Ray kept consoling him with friendly words until they reached the door. Ray opened it, Bob stumbled into the darkness beyond, and Ray shut the door behind him.

Ray took a step or two away from the door, shaking his head. He put the heels of both hands to his temples as though struck by a severe headache. "What a fuckin' mess," he muttered. Then he looked up, looked directly at the camera, and seemed for the first time to remember it was still running. "Oh *shit*," he said, and came purposefully forward, hand reaching out.

Snow.

48

Cal ejected the tape without rewinding it, put it in its box, and turned to face Sara. "That's it," he said.

"Why didn't—" Sara was still stunned by the scene on the monitor. "Why didn't Ray *say* something?"

"He promised Bob; he swore to him—"

"Come *on*, Cal! When he's indicted for murder?"

"Ray never took it serious," Cal said. "I talked with him; I know that's true. Right up to when he went on the stand, he never took it serious. That's how he got himself in so deep, not being careful. *He* knew he didn't do it, didn't have any reason to do it; he couldn't believe anything really *bad* would happen to him."

"After they found Bob Golker's body," Sara said. "Why didn't he show everybody the tape then?"

"I don't *know*, Sara!" Cal said. "I didn't talk to him yet. I can't talk to him in where he is now; they got guards right there listening to every word you say. I didn't talk to anybody but you."

"Why me?"

"You're a smart lady," Cal said. "I know you and I like

you, and I figure you'll know what to do with this." He held up the tape, almost but not quite offering it to her.

"Give it to the authorities," Sara said. "Give it to Warren."

"I don't think so," Cal said slowly and carefully. "That's what I thought at first to do, but then I thought it over, and I don't think so."

"Why not?"

"They just got themselves a big murder conviction over there," Cal reminded her. "Now, after it's all over, Ray's best friend shows up with this tape, they'll say, 'It's a fake.' They'll say, 'Where's it been all this time?' They won't even look at it; they'll throw it away."

"Give it to Warren; let *him* give it to them."

"Same thing. Even if *Warren* believes me, so what? The smart-ass out-of-town high-priced lawyer, and this is his *latest* cute stunt, you know that's how they'll think."

"But they can't *ignore* this."

"Sure they can," Cal said. "Law people ignore stuff all the time if it don't fit what they want. Bigger evidence than this come around in cases sometimes, got ignored. That guy on death row on television? Years later, you see it on TV, how nobody paid any attention to this evidence, that evidence."

"Not if it's out in public," Sara said. "Like the Rodney King tape."

Cal looked hopeful. "So you think I oughta give it to a TV station?" Then he looked worried again. "They'll say the same thing. Best friend, can't trust him. Don't wanna get in trouble with the prosecutors."

Then Sara got it; all of it. "You want *me* to take the tape, don't you?"

Cal lit up. "Would you? What could you do with it? You're on a magazine, right?"

"But still, that's the idea," Sara said. "I should print something in *Trend* about this unknown tape, maybe get a copy of it to somebody at one of the networks. Then they'd *have* to pay attention to it, wouldn't they?"

"Gee, Sara," Cal said, blinking in all his redneck innocence. "Do you think you could do that?"

"I think I could," Sara said. "I'm not sure I will."

Cal's blinking now was suddenly more real. "What? Why not?"

"Socks don't roll on shag carpets," Sara said.

He went right on being innocent, good old shitkicker Cal. "I don't know whatcha mean," he said.

"What we saw on the tape there, that's real all right," Sara allowed. "Ray figured Golker really would run away, didn't plan on him drinking up that bottle in the car and kill himself."

"Or accident himself," Cal said. "That would be Bob, too."

"Either way. Ray believed him, there on the tape, that the body wouldn't ever be found. But the next day, when the police came around, looked in that car, started asking questions, Ray suddenly saw what an opportunity this was."

Cal said, "I don't getcha. Opportunity?"

"To solve his income-tax problem," Sara said.

Cal gawked. "You ain't serious!"

"It was golden, wasn't it, Cal?" Sara grinned at him, on solid land at last. "He could let the IRS think there wasn't gonna be much of Ray Jones to kick around anymore, and once he did it, he could pull the plug anytime with that tape."

"Naw, Sara."

"Yeah, Cal. Only Ray didn't realize at first, I bet, what a lot it would take to convince the IRS to cave in. But that was the idea all right, from the very beginning."

"Ray wouldn't *do* nothing like that!"

"Of course he would," Sara said. "To save himself millions of dollars? Millions! There was no way for Warren to get Ray off, not before a settlement with the IRS. Warren thought *he* was running things, but Ray was, from the get-go. Warren could pull every slick lawyer stunt he knew, but every single time Ray would make sure to screw up just enough to keep himself on the hook. And meanwhile, Jolie's supposed to get him a better deal from the tax people, because maybe he won't be an earner any more. His only problem was, he couldn't tell either of his lawyers what he was up to, because they wouldn't have let him do it. Nobody could know about it but *you*."

"Aw no, Sara."

"Aw *yeah*. And when the feds *still* wouldn't back off, he insisted on taking the witness stand, because he just *knew* Fred Heffner would give him a chance to accidentally blurt something out and buy that guilty verdict. Accidental! That 'cocksucker' line was deliberate. Ray's a showman—I should have remembered that—and the witness chair was a stage, and Ray doesn't do *anything* accidental onstage."

"Sara," Cal said, more in sorrow than in anger, "you don't make any kind of sense at all."

"And *me*," Sara said, starting to get mad. "That was the other part of it, find a patsy—"

"Aw no, Sara, don't say that."

"Some dumb little girl reporter, somebody from the media who can carry the water for you on this when it's time to do the big reveal. 'Gee willikers, look what *we* just found!' That was my job, wasn't it? Handpicked."

"Aw, Sara."

"*That's* why I had the inside track. The whole goddamn thing was a scam."

"Sara," Cal said, "Ray's really and truly found guilty of murder. *That's* no scam. They mean to kill him."

"And the dumb little girl's supposed to save his wicked hide."

"Well, won't you?" Cal asked. "I mean, gosh, Sara, nothin' you said is what happened at *all,* but even if it was true, you wouldn't let Ray *die,* would you?"

"Why not?" Sara asked.

Cal just gaped at her. She reached into her shoulder bag, and he was still gaping when she Maced him, grabbed the tape out of his hands, and ran for it.

49

Monday in New York, four days after Sara had come back from deepest Missouri. The little apartment on West Eleventh Street was dusty but nice, the neighborhood still full of a variety of good restaurants, work at *Trend* still interesting—particularly with Jack's *Weekly Galaxy* story in this week's issue all over the newsstands, Jack himself booked onto a whole bunch of public-affairs TV talk shows, solemn discussions on the duties and privileges of the fourth estate. The Prrreessss, don'tcha know.

All day Friday, the *Trend* switchboard was flooded with calls from Cal, down in Branson, none of which Sara responded to but some of which attracted Jack's attention by Friday afternoon, when he came out of his office—*he* had an office—and over to her desk to say, "Cal Denny's calling you."

"I know."

"You aren't taking his calls."

"No, I'm not."

"You're up to something, Sara."

"Of course I am."

"What?"

Sara smiled at him. Exasperated, Jack said, "I'm your editor!"

"So what?"

"I'm your lover!"

"So what?"

Jack reared back. "Is nothing sacred to you, Sara?"

"One thing," Sara said.

Interested despite himself, Jack said, "What?"

"The first typewriter I ever had, back in high school. It was a Smith Corona."

After that, he left her alone.

On the weekend, they went away for a minivacation upstate in the Shawangunks, steep rocky hills beloved of weekend mountain climbers. Seated in luxurious comfort in rocking chairs on the wide wood porch of Mohonk Mountain House, high in the Gunks, glasses of lemonade within handy reach, they refreshed their souls by watching the laden climbers schlepp on up the road away from the sparkling lake.

Monday, back in the office, Sara threw away another stack of phone messages from Cal. She also noticed on the wire that the jury down in Branson was still listening to witnesses discuss what should be done about that rapscallion Ray Jones. Then, around four, she left for the day, alone, Jack being off for another television look at journalism. Sara cabbed down to the West Village, did a little shopping at D'Ag, and the phone was ringing when she unlocked her way into the apartment.

It was Cal. "I *gotta* talk to you, Sara."

"So now you've got my home number." She'd wondered how long that would take.

"I gotta *talk* to you."

"I'm not interested in talking to the dog," she said cruelly, "but I wouldn't mind hearing from his master."

"Aw, Sara."

She hung up and put away the groceries.

She was watching the six o'clock news, in fact a piece from Florida in which a lot of *Weekly Galaxy* executives who'd never before been exposed to sunlight stuttered and stammered and took the high road by announcing that every employee implicated in the Branson scandal was being summarily fired, when the phone rang again. "Nice guys," Sara commented at the TV, shot it dead with the remote, and picked up the phone.

It was Ray, sounding gruffer and rougher and raspier than ever. "Cal tells me I owe you an apology."

"Oh really? Why?"

" 'Cause you're smarter than we thought you were."

Sara couldn't help herself; she laughed. "You *are* a rascal, aren't you?"

"Part of my charm."

"I'd love to write your obit."

"Hey, wait a minute, now," he said, sounding honestly startled for once. "Fun's fun."

"Ray," she said, brisk and cold, "is there any other reason for this call?"

Hesitantly, he said, "Well, in a way, yeah."

"Go ahead."

"It'd be easier if you could talk to Cal."

"No way."

"Sara, you understand, we aren't alone on this telephone line."

"That's all right; *we* know what we're talking about."

He took a deep breath. She could almost hear him squeezing the phone. "What do you want, Sara?" he asked. "You want to mention a number?"

"Two," she said.

Bewildered silence. "Two? Two what?"

"Two things, Ray. Did you know I went to see you at that fund-raiser for the hospital there?"

"Oh yeah?" He wasn't very interested. "You went to that?"

"What's that hospital called again?"

"Skaggs Community."

"Have you ever actually given them any *money*, Ray?"

His voice more guarded, Ray said, "Not actual cash money, no. Just my time and efforts and celebrity and like that."

"You can do better, Ray," she told him.

"Jesus," he said, breathing his disbelief and disgust down the phone line. "*That's* your favorite charity?"

"No, it's yours."

He thought about that. "How much do I love them?"

"You tell me."

"Ten grand."

"Cheapskate."

"Fifty?"

"Piker."

"Listen, Sara, fifty thousand's a lot of money."

"Not for you," she told him. "If you get out from under this little trouble of yours—"

"Hah!"

"—you'll have a lot more money to spend than you had, say, a couple weeks ago. They might even name a wing of the hospital after you."

Really alarmed, he said, "I can't afford any wing!"

"What *can* you afford, Ray?"

Another little pause while he calculated. Then he said, "You said two before. How about two?"

"Two what?"

"Hundred grand."

She nodded, though of course he couldn't see that, being in a room in a jail in Missouri, a thousand miles away. She said, "Publicly announced?"

"First thing tomorrow morning," he offered, "if that's what you want."

"Thank you, Ray."

His voice more insinuating, he said, "Nothing for *you*, personal?"

"Well," she admitted, "that was the other thing."

"Uh-huh."

"What if it should happen," she asked him, "you should beat this rap?"

"That would be nice," he said.

"A whole lot of press would want to interview you, wouldn't they?" she asked. "*People* magazine and Barbara Walters and all kinds of press."

Startled, getting it, he said, "You want an exclusive!"

"A thirty-day exclusive."

"Jesus, Sara, the rest of them, they'll tear me to shreds!"

"Well, Ray, *somebody's* going to anyway, isn't that true?"

A longer pause this time, before he finally said, in a smaller voice than before, "All right."

"By the way, Ray," she said, "I think you ought to know, just in case the jail's phone-tap system breaks down, I do record all my calls."

Sullen now, he said, "I won't try to renege."

"Of course not." Having gotten what she wanted, Sara said, "Ray, would you tell Cal for me that I'm coming back to

Branson tomorrow, right after your charitable announce-ment?"

"Call him; he'll meet your plane. You have his number, don't you?" he asked without a trace of irony.

"Around here somewhere," she admitted.

"Nice talking to you," he said, with an edge to it.

"Come on, Ray," she said, "don't be bitter. You're getting what you want. The original scenario and all."

With surprise in his voice, he said, "I guess I am, at that." Then he chuckled, back in a good mood at last, and said, "Okay, Sara. And you're getting what you want, too, huh?"

"No losers, Ray," Sara said, pleased with herself. And why not? "Everybody wins."

She hung up, then sat a while, smiling.

An hour and a half later, Jack came home, in a bad mood, sour and exhausted from having spent a lot of time listening to pundits. "Hi, baby!" Sara cried, and kissed him a good one.

He pulled away, snarling. "What are *you* so happy about?"

"Good news," she said, and laughed.